The Scroll of Kanavar:

LEGEND OF THE TWELVE STONES

BY: A. K. MAGE

ISBN: 0-615-81434-4
ISBN-13: 978-0-615-81434-6
Library of Congress Control Number: 2013909290
Abraham Kassin

Dedication

To my family and friends
for giving me the inspiration
and strength to move forward

Table of Contents

Introduction

I t was finally over. I sat waiting, playing my Game Boy. My dad was still a little nervous, but the tension was gone. Airports always did that to him. But we always make it to the gate in one piece, so I don't really get it.

"Boarding for gate D-nine."

Uh-oh. I knew what that meant. I stuffed my Game Boy into my bag and watched as my dad did the same with his book. He had always loved to read. I caught a glimpse of the cover, *The Centaur's Stone*. I don't know what he saw in books. I think Game Boys are much more productive. He took my hand and we followed the crowd of people onto the plane.

The next day we waited outside the airport in Israel, trying to catch a cab. I saw all different types of people were coming to Israel. Tourists from countries all around the world were walking back and forth, trying to find their tour buses. There were also Israelis coming back home. A lot of women wore kerchiefs on their heads. I heard people shouting in Hebrew, Arabic, and other languages. It was pretty cool. I've only ever lived in places that spoke English. We had to move a lot because of my dad's business, but we were never in a place as amazing as this. A cab stopped in front of us, and my dad told me to get in the backseat while he put the luggage in the trunk.

A strange aroma of different spices reached my nose, but that didn't bother me. I was too busy looking out the window and taking in all the views of Israel. Wherever I looked was a beautiful view. There hadn't been any mountains in the other cities I'd been to. Here I saw entire villages and cities made of stone sitting on the mountains. The altitude changed every few minutes. I hadn't known that my ears could pop in a car! I started to get nervous as we neared Akko.

This city, like many others, was made of stone. There was the new city that was residential, and there was an ancient city that was from biblical times, a few thousand years old. Akko was a port city, and my dad had said it was "strategically positioned" on the Mediterranean. That meant it had pretty much everything it needed, and when Napoleon had tried to conquer it, even he couldn't destroy its magnificent walls, which were built strong because they're constantly hit by the waves. My dad was telling me all these boring facts while we drove. Although an ancient city did sound kind of cool.

Before I knew it, we'd arrived. Dad gave the driver money, and we got out of the car. I looked around. It was a beautiful neighborhood. Children from neighboring houses were playing soccer in the street. I loved soccer. They looked so happy even though I noticed some of them wore patched clothing that would really stand out in my old school. It didn't look like any of them had a

Game Boy, but they were happy enough without it. I wondered if I could be happy without one.

My mouth dropped when I saw the house. "Dad! What *is* this?"

"Son…"

"Why didn't you tell me?"

"I didn't want to worry you. I know it's hard for you moving all the time, and I don't want to make it worse for you. But don't worry—we are going to give it an extreme makeover, and it'll look just as good as all the other houses here. Or even better."

The frown didn't leave my face. The windows were cracked, and the front door hung on one hinge. I could see green mold growing on the walls outside, and there was a half caved-in roof. All it needed were dark clouds and lightning, and it would look like the house from the movie *The Witch's Mansion* I had seen last week.

The inside was even worse. I ran into a spiderweb at every turn. Whenever I brushed one sticky web off of me, another took its place. Rodents and insects roamed the floors. The cockroaches reminded me of my school lunchroom where one came by and scared every girl into standing on the benches. This place had a lot more than one, though. I jumped as a rat scurried past my foot. I coughed and realized that the dust in the air was suffocating me. And even though I was tired from the long day, there was nowhere to sit because there wasn't a piece of furniture that wasn't torn or broken. The couches had no stuffing, and the chairs had no legs. Every step I took made a creaking sound, and it felt like the floor would give way beneath me. Worse, there seemed to be a green glow coming from the walls—more mold?

I couldn't even go upstairs to see how my room was—probably a rundown dungeon. One step on the rotten old wooden stairs, and they would collapse under me. The termite damage was evident.

We walked out of the house and I looked up at my father unable to say a word.

"It'll all be fine. I've already contacted a construction team. It'll be done before you know it. The only problem is—"

"Is everything all right?" A woman with a pleasant face came up to us. There were a few black strands of hair sticking out of her kerchief. Her brown skirt matched her eyes. Her skin tone was a bit darker than ours. I tuned out while my dad introduced us and started talking to her. Adult conversations were usually boring.

But then one sentence grabbed my attention. "You are welcome to stay in my house until yours is ready," the woman generously offered. "We have a guest room."

"I will pay you back someday," Dad told her.

"Don't worry about it," she said.

Dad thanked her over and over again as we walked into her house. I didn't even want to compare her house with ours. Everything in her home was perfect, while mine was, well, not so perfect. Her furniture was intact, and she even had carpeting in some rooms. It was comfortable.

We walked into the dining room. Three kids were sitting around the table, waiting for dinner. They looked like nice kids, my age or younger. My dad again thanked the lady as we sat down to a dinner of roast, potatoes, and Israeli salad, which was basically cucumbers and tomatoes, not lettuce like our salads. I had really been craving falafel and schnitzel ever since I had smelled it at the Tel Aviv airport, but this dinner was good too. Fried food would have to wait until another day.

Dad finally realized that he didn't even know the lady's name. He asked and she laughed and said "Fortune." By the end of dinner, I had made friends with Fortune's children: Albert, Barbara, and Meyer. I was able to make them laugh, which I've always been able to do to other kids. It was good I got them as neighbors and not some creepy old man like last time. We would be able to hang out and play together. Albert turned out to be my age, eleven. Barbara was one year younger. And Meyer was the youngest at eight.

After dinner we said goodnight, and Fortune showed us to the guest room with two beds. It had been a tiring day, and I was jet-lagged from the flight. I think we both were because Dad conked out right away.

The next few months flew by. I got to hang out with my new friends every day while Dad handled the house construction. We both got a lot done. I was making new friends so the new school year that was approaching wouldn't be horrible. And he was getting to know Fortune a lot better. I think he liked her. I got to play a lot of soccer, and he got to make a lot of house plans.

"I see you are happy tonight," Fortune commented one night at dinner.

"I am almost done with the house," Dad replied.

"Aww, that means you guys have to leave soon," Albert complained. The others agreed. Albert was now my best friend. We were like brothers, and I liked the others also. It was a lot of fun living with them. But we would still be next door.

"We'll be right next door." Dad echoed my thoughts with a laugh. "I'll tell you what: tomorrow, after the painters arrive, I'll take all of you to the beach in Netanya."

"Yay!" was the response. Dad laughed again, and this time Fortune joined him. Albert and I exchanged looks.

The beach was awesome. We played Frisbee and jumped the waves. I hadn't had that much fun in a while. I tackled Albert in the sand and we started to wrestle. Meyer tried to join in, but couldn't get between us. Barbara just watched from the side.

Later in the week I went to the market with Dad. It was my first time there since I had arrived in Israel, and it was amazing. There were crowds of people walking back and forth, browsing the outside shops and stalls. Fruits, vegetables, beans, spices, and nuts on display added color to the scene. I took a deep breath every time I passed a bakery. I couldn't resist any longer. I think Dad had the same feeling, because he bought some of the baked goods for both of us. He also bought some nice couches, chairs, tables, and beds for our house to be delivered later.

The house was ready, and everything looked new. There was only one thing left to do: the wallpaper in the dining room was hideous. It was an ugly shade of yellowish red—my least favorite color. Personally, I thought there was still a green glow coming from that wall—not good. Dad said he wanted to take down the wallpaper and put up a new one. He said we would do it ourselves to make the finishing touches on our new home.

I began to tear down the wallpaper on one side while Dad did the other. I reached the window when I was halfway done. This area seemed to be the origin of the strange green light. Behind the wallpaper near the window, I found a strange box hidden in a hole in the wall. Of course, I pulled it out. The dust that I blew off it caused me to sneeze. Dad looked over his shoulder, but I said I was fine. I didn't want to show him what I had found just yet. He went back to his job, and I examined the box. It was made of pure silver—at least what seemed like silver to me—and appeared to be old. There were green designs on each side of the box. There was also what looked like some sort of ancient writing. I didn't recognize it as any language I'd seen, and I'd seen a bunch of new ones recently. It was a thrilling feeling to find this box in the wall of an old house. A mystery! As I opened it, I wondered, *Why would this be hidden here, and better yet, what could possibly be inside?*

An ancient scroll was what I found. It seemed as if the box was somehow preserving the scroll, because I knew paper is usually fragile. My heart was beating fast. *Why would a scroll be hidden here? What was on it?* I began to unravel the thick scroll. It said:

The scroll of Kanavar

What was Kanavar? I'd never heard that word before. I was a little nervous, but I decided to read the rest. As I started what seemed to be the beginning of the story, I forgot that it was strange I could understand what was written. I felt overwhelmed by excitement, especially as a green light shimmered off the scroll. My eyes went wide, and my mouth gaped. It felt like the light pulled me into the scroll itself. Instead of reading the story, I felt like I was seeing it happen before me...

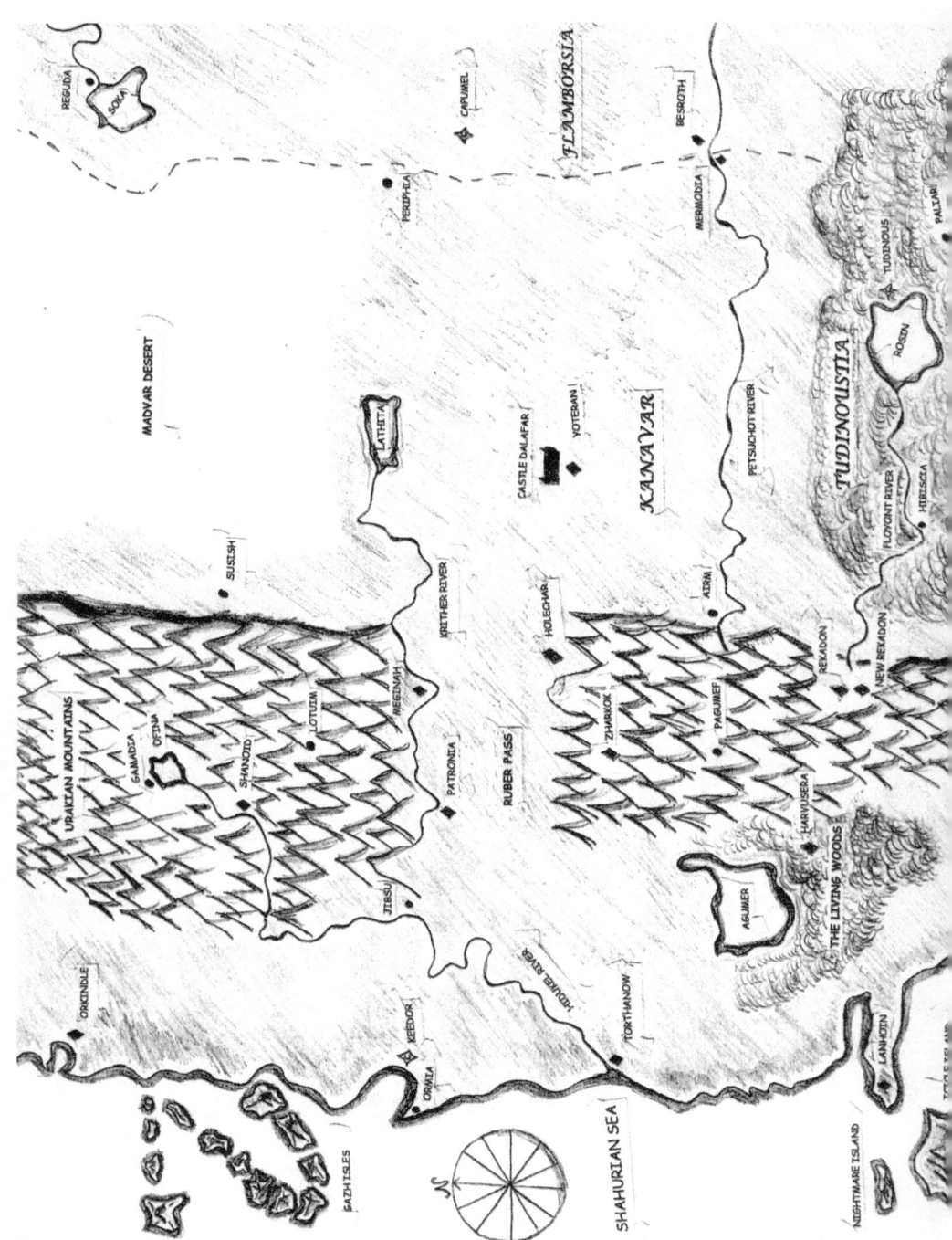

Beginning

K anavar was one of the five countries on the planet of
Charldena. Settlement started in Kanavar in a forest
that was later called the Living Woods. The first king of
Kanavar was King Brin. The people selected him to rule. He and
his descendants ruled for many years. His dynasty was fair to the
people. The people loved the kings, and there was never much
conflict in the nation.

It lasted until King Lucent. Unfortunately, he had no relatives
to take after him. He died at a party before he was able to name an
heir to his throne. After his death many rose and tried to become
the ruler of the land. One of them was Dalafar, a fuman, a large,
hairy, muscular form of a man who had been conceived by a giant
and a dwarf. Lord Dalafar and his trusted advisor, Hanfei Zi,
stopped at nothing to gain the throne.

Periphia

Periphia was a small village that no one really cared about. It was located on the outskirts of Kanavar, not near any other civilized area. There weren't any special attractions or monuments in Periphia to draw in any outsiders. There wasn't even much rain to moisten the arid air that came from the bordering desert. The only plant life in the village was some cacti on the side of the dirt roads and the few gardens of the villagers who managed to save enough water from the occasional rainfall. Nevertheless, to its inhabitants, Periphia was their life. They lived peacefully in the village and did not care that no outsiders ever came. No outsiders just meant that no trouble ever came their way, and they enjoyed the isolation. They did their work and lived their simple lives. No city folk would be able to handle the simple and quiet life in Periphia, but the villagers loved it. Most of the villagers always wore a smile.

Unfortunately, when Dalafar became ruler, their peace was disturbed. The whole country was affected by Dalafar's takeover, and that included every little village like Periphia. Every month, avengers, creatures like humans with hawk-like features, stormed the village to collect the taxes for Dalafar. These new taxes forced outsiders to come to their village. It confirmed their dislike of outsiders. The avengers were never polite or kind. But that was all the trouble that came to them. Only the avengers ever came to their village. No one else cared to bother them. Dalafar didn't even send a small group of troops to watch the village. They were fine if the only intruders in their simple lives were the avengers.

One beautiful morning when the sky was a bright blue and the sun shone down on the village, a few men and women walked down the road to the market or to shops to start the day of work. Mrs. Lormin was up early, tending her garden. She loved her flowers and took good care of them. She was admiring a rose when her next-door neighbor, Margot, came out of her house. Mrs. Lormin had always thought of Margot as a beautiful woman. She didn't know why Margot had never remarried when she moved to the village, a pregnant lady with two children, twelve years ago. There were many bachelors eligible for her.

Margot had long, straight black hair. Her brown eyes were sparkling this morning. She had a slender figure. It was a shame. Mrs. Lormin hoped that Margot would find the right one someday. Beauty like that shouldn't be wasted. Mrs. Lormin was sure that having a grown man and father in the house wouldn't hurt the family either. It would be a good influence on the kids and add income.

"How are you doing today?" Mrs. Lormin greeted her with a smile.

"The same as always," Margot replied in a polite voice. Mrs. Lormin felt bad for the woman. She and her family were not doing too well. They had come with no money and were hardly getting by. They had little food and even less money. Not to say that anyone in the village had a lot of money. Most of the people there were poor, mostly from those taxes. She knew that Margot never really paid the full tax. Mrs. Lormin thought that soon the avengers wouldn't allow it any longer.

After another few minutes, Margot's children came out. What blessed children they were. The older boy, Michael, was young and handsome. He didn't look much like the other two. He had straight blond hair that matched his fair skin. His hair reached the back of his neck. She could always see that same twinkle in his glowing green eyes. He was about eighteen; at least that was what Margot claimed. But she knew he had to be older. He was too tall for eighteen. His muscular body and his height made him look like he was in his twenties. But Margot was never one to lie. Then again, she never told the full truth either. She never told anyone where she came from, why she had come there, who her husband was, and what had happened to him. Her previous life was a mystery.

But Mrs. Lormin knew why she had come here. Periphia was a place where nobody cared about the answers to those questions. Margot had moved here hoping to forget about her past, and so far that had been successful, so Mrs. Lormin never brought up the subject.

Then there was the young girl, Julie. She was much like her mother, with long black hair, brown eyes, and a slight tan. She was as beautiful as her mother too. Mrs. Lormin hoped she would find a handsome man one day. That day could be soon. She was already fifteen. Julie was a pretty girl, and she could see the boys pass the house and sneak looks at her. She always waved back at them. She was kind. Any boy would be lucky to have her. There was one boy in particular who Mrs. Lormin thought really liked Julie. This was Michael's friend, Marki. They would make a good match.

The cute thirteen-year-old, Steven, joined them. His silky black hair waved in the wind. He had fair skin like his brother, but that was the only resemblance they shared. His eyes were brown like his sister's. Mrs. Lormin knew that he wasn't that little boy she once knew twelve years back. He had grown up. He was starting to get strong and muscular like his brother. She remembered carrying him as a baby. He was chubby back then, and Mrs. Lormin had loved to pinch his cheeks. She thought that she had permanently scared Steven. He was still cautious of her and guarded his cheeks whenever she was close by.

The day was beginning. Mr. Lormin came outside. He gave Mrs. Lormin a kiss on the cheek and greeted Margot and her children before heading to work. Mrs. Lormin watched him go. They were an old couple and had never been able to conceive children. She thought of Margot's children as her own. She remembered the times before Michael was old enough to work and Margot had her job in the clothing shop. Dear old Mrs. Lormin was always called over to babysit the children. Margot was caring for her garden with Julie. Michael went next door to the wine shop to work as he always did. The money he made, which wasn't much at all, and the vegetables in the garden were how the family had been surviving these past years. She didn't know if it would last much longer, but she hoped it would.

Steven went inside to do the everyday chores. By now Mrs. Lormin knew her neighbor's daily routine as well as she knew her husband's. But she had a feeling that their routine would soon have to change.

A man came into the village one day. There was murmuring among the villagers. Nobody ever came to the village since Margot and her children had come. There was tension in the air. Michael was in the cellar, carrying a barrel of wine to bring it upstairs to this mystery man. His boss said that the man wanted to buy the whole barrel. That was strange. Wine was expensive, and nobody in Periphia could afford a barrel of wine. Most people would only buy small bottles.

Michael came up with the barrel and saw the strange man talking to his boss. Michael wasn't too fond of his boss. He looked like a nasty guy. His ragged and unshaven beard was the only hair he had on his dirty-looking head. His tattered clothes looked even worse now as he stood next to the strange, fancy-looking man. The man was definitely different from anyone in the village. His clothes looked foreign. They looked too expensive for anyone who lived in the village. He looked like one of those rich aristocrats. His short, neatly combed black hair and the evil grin on his face made him look suspicious. Michael thought that it must be because he was a man of high class. Most men of high class during the days of the reign of Dalafar were evil and wicked. They picked on the poor and helpless for their own selfish desires. Michael hated these types of people. He knew he shouldn't judge this man at first glance, but he couldn't help but dislike him.

The man was frowning. Michael knew that it was because he didn't approve of the wine shop. It was a small wooden shop with not many choices. It consisted of two shelves on both sidewalls, which held a few bottles of wine. There was a desk against the back wall, where Michael's boss usually stayed. The stairs to go down were behind the desk.

The man wore gloves, but he still tried to avoid touching Michael as he took the barrel from him. Michael was disgusted.

All the higher-class people thought of anyone less than them on the social scale as garbage. Michael thought that the higher class was the real garbage. The man hauled the barrel onto his carriage. The two white horses and the black carriage with a driver proved that he was indeed of high class.

The man turned back to the wine shop to pay Michael's boss. Michael shuddered when the man looked at him. It felt as if the man were looking right through him and seeing exactly who he was. He didn't like the feeling and turned away. The man turned to the door and looked around before heading to the doorway. He dusted off his jacket before leaving the wine shop.

Michael watched the carriage pull away from the wine shop. *And don't come back*, Michael thought. The man continued down the road to take a look at the village. He rode in the direction of the market. Michael assumed that he was going there. The market was the nicest area in the village. Most of the shops were outdoors. There were always people there, doing their errands. It was crowded, but it was where you went if you wanted to find someone.

Michael saw the man pass the wine shop a few more times during the day. He rode down a few different roads, including residential ones. The residential areas of the village were all identical wooden houses with occasional gardens. After the man finished his route, he went on his way, back to where he had come from. Michael didn't know what he was doing here. The peaceful village wanted nothing to do with the upper classes. They already starved the villagers with their taxes, and the villagers didn't want one of them there. Everyone settled down when the man left, and things returned to normal. But there was still an eerie mood in the village. Some were worried about why the man had come.

Night fell on the village. The sky above was black, filled with the white lights of stars and the bright moon. There weren't any lights to illuminate the roads as the last of the villagers returned to their homes. The village fell into darkness in the night. There were only some lamps outside of a few houses, like the Lormins' house. But no lights were needed outside. Nobody went out at night. Everyone was home eating supper.

Michael said good-bye to his boss, and his boss just grunted back. Michael left the store and headed home. He spotted Mr. Lormin a few houses down, covering himself with a cloak to protect himself from the wind. It was a chilly night. It was not so unusual for Mr. Lormin to be out this late. He had been getting home later and later every day. Michael guessed that his fruit business wasn't doing too well and he needed to make some extra money with a second job.

Michael walked inside his house and saw his brother and sister waiting at the table to eat supper. Steven licked his lips. Their mother came in with the food.

"Hello, Michael. How was your day?" His mother always greeted him the same way.

"You know, the same as usual," was his usual response. But then he remembered the man. "Actually, today was a bit different."

Margot looked up from putting the clay plate of potatoes on the wooden table. She shivered and moved closer to the fireplace in the wall. The fire crackled.

"What do you mean?" she asked.

"This man came to the village. He looked upper-class. He bought a whole barrel of wine—"

"Slow down," Margot said.

"A whole barrel! That's insane!" Julie was surprised anyone could afford to drink that much. She stopped when she saw that Michael was serious. She knew that serious face all too well.

"Let him finish, honey." Margot calmed her daughter with a hand on her shoulder.

"The man wore fancy clothes and had a fancy carriage with a driver," Michael continued. "He put the barrel in his carriage and took a look around the village. He left when he was done before it got dark out."

"That's odd," Margot said. There was worry in her voice. Michael didn't know why. It was just a wealthy man who had probably needed supplies. Then again, what would he be doing all the way up here? There was nowhere else around that he could have been traveling to. He must have come here deliberately. But why? There was nothing here of interest to anyone.

The smile came back to her face. "Let's not worry about these things. Let's eat." They took one potato each. They didn't eat so much. They couldn't afford a decent amount of food. They just ate what they needed to get by. They survived. That was all they wanted to do in these hard times.

Then Michael felt it. He didn't know why, but he knew they were coming. The gut feeling in the pit of his stomach told him they were here. He shivered. He looked up to see Margot looking at him with worry. They locked eyes, and she understood what he felt. Then she heard it, and her face froze. She knew it too. They were coming.

The avengers.

The door suddenly flew open. An avenger, a man with hawk feathers, claws, wings, and a beak, stood tall in the doorway. His expression was grim. He eyes were asking for blood. He had a sword at each side. He let out a noise that sounded like the cry of a hawk before killing its prey.

Margot pulled her cloak tighter around herself as she stood to face the avenger. She would be strong. She had to be for her children's sake. She couldn't let them see the emotions that she felt when an agent of Dalafar showed up. If she were to worry and fear, then her children would do the same. She returned the avenger's cold look.

"King Dalafar has raised the taxes to once a week," the avenger said in a harsh, loud voice. He let out another cry.

Margot sighed expectantly. Margot remembered the amount of money that she used to pay when the taxes were only once a year. Then Dalafar had changed the system to collecting that same amount every month. That was bad enough and hard for the people to keep up with, but they did their best. Now it was once every week. That would be impossible. Dalafar was worse than a tyrant. Dalafar was heartless and cold for doing such a thing.

Margot took out her little pouch of money that she kept for the taxes. Her face paled. There was hardly enough to pay half of the tax. She only had a few silver coins and about a dozen copper ones. The avenger reached out his long feathery arm and grabbed the pouch from her. He pocketed the silver coins and tossed the pouch along with the copper ones in the fire.

"Those are dools," the avenger spat in Margot's face.

She flinched. The avenger's breath was bad enough, but his spit was even worse. Michael had to restrain himself from jumping up to protect his mother.

"You know Dalafar changed the currency to bacs," the avenger said.

"I know," she replied quietly in fear. She lost it. She couldn't hold her courage, not even in front of her children. "This is all I have." Those were her last silver bacs. The family was now officially broke. The last of their money was gone.

"Next time I won't be so nice. You should thank me for my generosity and kindness." He went over to the table and took two potatoes. He stuffed them in his mouth as he went back to the door.

He turned one last time and made a face that Michael thought looked like a grin. He let out another cry before flying out the door into the dark sky to find more victims to haunt.

There was an awkward silence. Steven shifted his feet and played with his fingers. Supper took a long time that night as they ate in silence. There was usually something to talk about at the table.

When they were done eating, Margot cleared the table. She took the plates inside. They sat at the table without uttering a sound and waited for her to return.

"To the sitting room now," she said in a harsh tone when she came back. She only used that tone on the occasions when she meant business. It meant they were to listen to what she said without argument or complaints. They followed her into the sitting room. It was small but comfortable. The three children sat down on the sofa, and Margot stood in front of them.

"These are hard times," she started calmly. "If we all stick together, we can make it. Michael, I think it's about time you get a better job that will pay you more than that filthy wine shop owner." Michael let out a smile. "Tomorrow morning go to the blacksmith, Mr. Mim, and ask him for a job. You can keep half the money you make. The rest will go toward food and taxes. Julie, you continue helping me in the kitchen and garden, but you'll have more chores around the house now because Steven can take Michael's job in the wine shop."

The children just nodded. The awkward silence came back. When Margot saw that none of them had anything to say, she told them to get to bed because they would have to wake up early tomorrow to start their new way of life.

The next morning Michael woke up first. He looked in the bed next to him and saw Steven sleeping. His mouth opened to let out a yawn as he sat up. He stretched his arms. Margot's room was in the back of the house, and Julie's room was right next to it. Michael knew that they were lucky with their house. When they had first moved here, this house was empty, and they had been able to take it for free. That was his earliest memory. His mother never spoke of anything that had happened before the day that they arrived in the village, and Michael was too young to remember any of it. The only thing he could remember was running in large open gardens. Steven was born the first month that they were in Periphia.

Michael got out of bed and went into the tiny kitchen. There were only a small brick oven and a few cabinets to keep some clay dishes. There was a back door that led to their well, which supplied the water for drinking, bathing, and washing the clothes and dishes. Michael went over to the well and pulled up the bucket of water. He undressed, washed himself, and redressed in his finest clothes. They didn't even match up to the clothes that the upper-class man had worn, but they were the best clothes that they could afford to buy. It was only a shirt and trousers, but it was the only pair of clothing he had that wasn't ripped. He usually wore these clothes for any holidays. But today he needed to impress Mr. Mim.

When he was done getting ready, he went back to the room to wake Steven. Steven also had to wake up early and wash up because he had to impress the wine shop owner, but Michael didn't think that would be hard. The wine shop owner was the filthiest person he knew. Steven groaned before getting out of bed.

Michael went to the front room where they ate and waited for Steven to come. He knew they had no time to eat this morning. He didn't mind. He didn't get too hungry often. Steven, on the other hand…

Steven came in, and his stomach growled. He had a dour expression. He didn't like wearing his nicest clothes, and he especially didn't like skipping breakfast. Michael didn't understand why Steven was still skinny as a stick even though he was always hungry and ate a lot. Michael remembered the day when one of the cafes had had a grand opening and an all-you-can-eat dinner to promote their food. Steven was the first one there and the last to leave. Michael knew that the only weight Steven gained was from when Steven worked out to try to get as strong as Michael. Steven went running every few days and did a few exercises. Michael was naturally muscular. Steven was working hard to match Michael's strength.

Michael went outside, and Steven followed. The sun was beginning to rise. There were a few others walking along the road, starting their workdays. Steven plucked an orange from a tree in their garden as they were walking. He quickly peeled it and stuffed it into his mouth. Michael sighed. Steven just couldn't miss breakfast.

They walked next door to the wine shop. The shop owner was dusting off the counter. He was sweating. He wasn't sweating from his work, but rather because the fat on his body made him have to strain with everything he did. Michael could not remember a time when the fat old man was not sweating. He wore an apron with wine stains on it that that were a testimony of his years of work. Michael had to admit that no matter how much he disliked this man, his boss did work hard every day.

The wine shop owner heard them come in and took a cloth to wipe his forehead, but he didn't look up from his work.

"Hey Michael," he grunted. He looked up and saw Steven. "Why is he here?" He turned and looked out the window. "And why are you here so early? Is something wrong?"

"I have to quit," Michael started to explain. The wine shop owner's face turned white. He needed a helper. He couldn't do it alone. There was no way he would be able to carry wine from the cellar. He was speechless. He hadn't expected Michael to quit. How would he find a replacement?

Michael saw that his former boss was mad. "This is my brother, Steven," Michael introduced. He whispered something to his little brother and left the shop.

Steven wasn't too happy about what Michael had told him. His brother had left to go talk to Mr. Mim while he was stuck here to explain the situation to the devastated shop owner.

"My brother quit," Steven started after he saw that the wine shop owner was just standing there in shock. "But I will be able to fill his place if you're willing to hire me." Steven was nervous that the man would only want Michael as his worker. Michael was always better at everything than Steven. Steven always tried to measure up to Michael, but he could never do it. He always looked up to Michael and tried to be like him.

"Yes, please," the shop owner said desperately as he wiped his forehead with the cloth again. The shop owner examined Steven. He had enough muscles to take Michael's place. This boy would be good enough. Steven let out a sigh of relief.

Michael felt sorry for Steven. He regretted leaving Steven by himself with that filthy shop owner. But he had no choice. He needed to get to Mr. Mim early. He really wanted a job with the blacksmith, but Mr. Mim wasn't the friendliest guy in town. Michael knew that it would be hard to talk to him. The man had no social life. Michael remembered the first time he had seen Mr. Mim, back when he was a little kid, when he had said hi to everyone he saw. He had waved to Mr. Mim but had only gotten a cold look in return.

Michael was walking quickly down the dirt road. He saw fewer houses and more shops as he neared the center of the village where the market was. Mr. Mim's shop was outside of the market. He greeted some of his friends as he passed them.

He clasped hands with his best friend, Marki, before Marki headed to his job at the tailor. He always hung out with Marki when there was no work. There weren't many fun things to do in the village, but they always found a way to entertain themselves. They used to explore the desert. They never found anything except for one time when they had found some feathers near a formation of large boulders. But before they had a chance to explore the area, a fierce sandstorm started to form and forced them to head back. He stopped in front of the *Blacksmith* sign.

He straightened up, took a deep breath, and opened the door. It made a loud creaking sound as it opened. He stepped inside. He was standing in a room that was completely empty except for a desk with some papers on it. He walked into the second room. It was where Mr. Mim did all his work. It had all different types of metal, tools, weapons, and molds on shelves that lined the walls. There was a brick oven in the back corner. Mr. Mim was sitting on a chair, banging a piece of metal with another tool. It was a loud noise, and he probably didn't hear Michael walk in.

"I came to request a job," Michael said loudly and nervously. His voice was trembling. Mr. Mim didn't look up from his work. Michael repeated his request even louder. Maybe Mr. Mim didn't want to talk to him. He knew Mr. Mim was a loner and some sort of a hermit. Michael decided to say it one more time.

"I heard you the first time," Mr. Mim said, still not looking up from his work. Michael waited for him to say more, but nothing came. The man stayed silent. Was that a no? Did he want Michael to leave? Michael stood there, not knowing what to do or what to say. He hesitated for a moment, watching the sparks fly from the metal that Mr. Mim was working on, before turning around. He put his head down. Michael started to walk to the door. What would he do now? Maybe he should go ask someone else in the market for a job. He was already at the door when he felt a strong hand press down on his shoulder. He turned his head, and it was Mr. Mim. The old man was stronger than he looked.

"I thought you said you want a job, boy. Leaving won't really help you get one." Mr. Mim smiled. Michael thought that it was the first time the man ever smiled. "What's the matter? Don't you speak?"

"Ahh…"

"Well, then, come inside. If you are going to work than you must first learn how. Blacksmithing is an art. Come. I'll teach you." Michael just nodded. He followed Mr. Mim back into his workshop. "I'll take you on as my apprentice. I've been looking for an apprentice for some time now. I will teach you to be an expert blacksmith and more. You will also be my assistant. Therefore, I will pay you at the end of each week."

Michael smiled. There was less tension in the air, and he gained back some of his courage. "Thanks," he said. "I will do whatever you ask, no matter what it is. I will learn everything I can from you."

"You will regret those words. Anyone that ever said those words regretted them. You will see that you will not wish to do everything that I will ask of you, but you must do it anyway because it will help you. During your time with me, you will wish you never said those words, but in the end, you will be happy that you did." Mr. Mim sat back down in his chair. He used his foot to hook the leg of another chair and drag it near him. "Sit." Michael did as he was told.

"Let's begin your first lesson, shall we?" Mr. Mim said. "The first lesson will be the basics on how to make a weapon. I want to teach you how to make one. I will teach you details later, but first I will tell you the major steps. But don't think just because on the first day I went straight into the lesson of how to make a weapon that in the next few days you'll be making weapons. There are many more things I have planned for you before you will even start to think of making a weapon. So don't get your hopes up."

Well, thanks a lot for the encouragement, Michael thought sarcastically. *Leave it to a guy like Mr. Mim to give the truth straight to you.*

"The first thing is getting the right stone for the weapon that you want to create," Mr. Mim started. "Then you must extract the metal from the stone. The stone and metal you choose depend on what the customer wants. You can even use combinations of different metals." Mr. Mim pointed to the stones out back in the yard. "Those are some stones that I have found. Every now and then I must go searching for more. The desert has some places where stones like these can be found.

"You need to make a mold for the type of weapon that you are creating," he went on. "I already have most of the molds made. I make a new one occasionally when I have a request for a weapon that I have never made before. Many times customers ask me to make knives or other metal objects that are not weapons, and I may need a new mold for those as well. The mold is made from clay. You shape the clay and leave a shape of the object you are making in the middle of the clay. This is where you will place the metal. Then you place the clay in the oven to heat it so it will harden and be a solid mold."

Mr. Mim got up and went in front of a barrel near the back wall. He gestured to Michael to come see. Michael looked in the barrel and saw it was full of clay. There were two others just like it.

Mr. Mim went back to his chair, and Michael followed. "Now for the real making of the weapon," Mr. Mim continued. "The metal chosen must first be melted in a pot in the oven. Once it's a liquid, you pour it into the mold to shape it. Any part of the metal that is left over is put aside for another time. No amount of metal should be wasted. Metal is very rare in these parts of the country." Mr. Mim indicated a pot near the oven with a few drops of iron in it. "Even one drop will never be wasted.

"You let the metal stay in the mold for some time, however long it takes, in order for it to harden into a malleable state. When it's at this state, you can use the tools to sharpen the blade's edge and fix it by smoothing it. Then you stick the weapon in the fire again to harden it. When it's hard again, you have completed the weapon. And trust me. It may sound easy, but it's far more difficult than you think. It takes a lot of practice."

He gave Michael a few minutes to take it all in and understand it. Michael was a little overwhelmed by the process. A lot of things were involved in creating one weapon. He just hoped that he would be able to do it.

"Now for your first task as my apprentice," Mt. Mim said. "Take this hammer." Michael took the hammer from Mr. Mim's hand. He started to get excited when he thought that Mr. Mim was going to let him use the hammer to make something. "I want you to find a log outside and use the hammer to hit the log for the next hour."

Michael was confused. What was the point of that?

"Make sure that you hit the same spot every time. I will examine your work later. For every mark that is off target, you will receive another hour of this work. So be careful." Mr. Mim chuckled.

Did he think this was some sort of joke?

"Not to be rude, but—"

"Ah." Mr. Mim stopped him. "You said you would do whatever I asked. And this is what I am telling you to do, so now you must do it. I will come to examine your work in an hour."

Michael left the room with a sigh of disappointment. He knew he wouldn't make a weapon right away, but this was ridiculous. What would he gain out of hitting a log? Mr. Mim said that there were reasons for everything he would make Michael do and that Michael would regret it at first but later see how it helped him. Michael hoped this was true.

The Raid

The upper-class man, as the village of Periphia called him, returned at last to Castle Dalafar. It was good to be back. He sighed. There was yet more work to be done. There would always be more work to be done as long as Dalafar had the throne. But as long as he got his money and respect, it was fine with him. As long as Dalafar needed his assistance, he would get money and respect. When Dalafar had no more use for him…well, he would take care of that when the time came.

He stood in front of the large gates that led to the gardens of Yoteran and Castle Dalafar. A massive stone wall surrounded the city and castle. There was a metal gate that was always left open. Dalafar wanted to act like he accepted everyone into his city, but everyone knew that wasn't true. There were guards at the ready to kill anyone who Dalafar didn't like. He walked inside the gate. The gardens were grander than any gardens he had ever seen. There were many different exotic flowers and trees growing in the grass around the paved pathway leading to Yoteran. Some of the plants there were only found in Tudanosti Forest. The slaves and gardeners swarmed the garden, making sure it was always perfect. One slave bowed to him as he passed. He grinned. He had to admit to himself that he loved the bowing. There were citizens taking walks on the pathways that went through the gardens.

The gardens were a good place for a walk. Walking in the gardens would always calm him down and get him ready for his next mission. It relaxed him. The gardens were the most beautiful sight in Kanavar, in his opinion. There was nothing like it. Many would agree with him. There was nothing that could replace the magnificent gardens. He took a deep breath of the clean and fresh air.

The garden surrounded the whole city. There was a moat between the garden and the city. A second stone wall surrounded the city. Castle Dalafar was in the middle of Yoteran. There was only one way in and one way out. A giant oak drawbridge was lowered as he neared the moat. Guards stood at the entrance and bowed to him as he walked in. Even though the gates to the gardens were always open, the drawbridge would only be opened for someone who had the right papers. Sometimes citizens waited in the gardens for days until their papers were found.

Yoteran was a great city. It was not as large as Keedor, but it had a similar setup. The city was made up of mostly shops, restaurants, and bars. There were some inns and apartment buildings as well. Yoteran consisted of all the creatures that followed Dalafar. That included Minotaur, trolls, goblins, avengers, timen, dwarves, humans, and the giants that lived outside of the city. All of Dalafar's ministers, generals, and servants also lived in Yoteran.

The man continued on. He passed many paupers sticking their dirty hands in his face, begging for some spare change. They disgusted him. He ignored them and looked away. They were used to that. Nobody paid them much attention. He heard the laughter of the drunk fellows at the bar who were sitting around a table, gambling. They were almost as bad as the paupers. He had to hold his breath whenever he passed one of them to try and protect himself from their alcohol-smelling bodies. The only ones who weren't wastes of lives were the merchants and craftsmen doing their jobs, making a living. He even liked them better than the aristocrats that he exchanged greetings with when he passed them. No aristocrat liked another. They were all jealous of each other.

The cobblestone pathway turned into a smooth pavement when the shops and buildings disappeared from beside him. He was walking on an open pathway that led to the innermost wall that surrounded Castle Dalafar. This wall was smaller than the others but much better guarded. Battalions of soldiers walked back and forth in the empty areas around the wall. Archers were crouched on top of the wall, ready to shoot anyone who dared come too close. The iron gates were shut.

As he neared the walls, he bent on his knees. It was an act that Dalafar made anyone who wished to enter the castle do in order to show his or her allegiance. The man knew there was a deeper meaning. Dalafar wanted to make sure that nobody thought they were powerful. Dalafar made sure that all their honor and dignity were removed before they entered the castle. The man hated doing it. He felt embarrassed as he waited on his knees.

The guards posted at the gates had to examine whoever bowed and wished to enter. When they looked over the person's papers, they would either let them in or escort them away. The gates opened shortly after, as the man knew they would. The guards knew who he was, and he was always allowed to enter the castle. He walked past the small garden that led to the large golden doors with strange carvings inscribed in them. The guards by the doors opened them for him. He stepped into the large hall.

It was a large room. The floor and walls were made of marble. The golden chandelier that hung from the ceiling illuminated the room. Staircases lined the right and left walls. The castle was tall, with towers all around. The staircases led to different hallways that had many rooms and more staircases. Servants and guards ran this way and that. He wasn't headed to any of these staircases. He walked straight ahead to the silver staircase that led to an archway with the same strange carving as the outside door. He walked through the archway and to another room.

Guards crowded this room like sardines. No one was allowed past this point unless they had direct permission from Dalafar. The man walked into the center of the room and stood on the insignia of Dalafar, a red D with a red dragon in it. He put his chin up and cleared his throat. The guards looked up. They recognized him and made room for him to pass. He walked to the large doors that were opened for him when he reached them.

"You are back," Dalafar said in his familiar strong, malicious voice as he walked in and the doors shut behind him. He went flat down on the ground with his hands outstretched. If he didn't do that, he would be killed on the spot.

"My liege," he said as he came up, a response to Dalafar's gesture. He couldn't really see Dalafar. The throne room was always dark. Dalafar enjoyed sitting in the dark. From the strange rocks that let out a dim light, he was only able to see Dalafar's large, strong figure and a staircase in the back of the room that led to Dalafar's quarters. The rest of the room was in darkness. He was sure that there were guards around, but he could not hear or see any. "I have good news. Your predictions were true. They truly are there. I found them."

"You have done well, my spy. Now go to your quarters and await your next mission."

The monthly feast preparation began in the village of Periphia. On the first night of every month, the villagers would each hold a small feast in their homes to give thanks for surviving another month. It was not a major holiday or festival, but the villagers held true to their customs. The villagers were either in the market shopping or at home cooking and cleaning. Many of the villagers were heading home earlier than usual.

Michael sighed. It was time for him to go home. He'd rather stay and work for Mr. Mim than go home and help prepare. Mr. Mim became Michael's good friend and master. Not only did Mr. Mim teach Michael how to make weapons, but he also taught Michael how to be an expert swordsman. Mr. Mim was surprisingly swift and strong. His skills were like nobody's Michael had ever seen. Michael wondered where Mr. Mim had learned how to fight like that. Mr. Mim also taught Michael war tactics and strategies. Michael thought that Mr. Mim would make an excellent general. In a few weeks, Michael built a strong bond with Mr. Mim. Mr. Mim was like a father to him.

"See ya next week," Michael said to Mr. Mim. Mr. Mim handed Michael the sack of money and held out his hand.

"Good-bye, my boy. I'll see ya next week." Michael shook his hand. With a wave he left the house. He walked down the road that led back to his house. He saw all of his neighbors running about, preparing for the feast. Mrs. Lormin was picking flowers from her lawn. She waved as he approached his house.

Julie was in the garden picking some vegetables. He walked inside and saw Steven setting the table. Steven got home earlier than him every day. Steven didn't like his job, and Michael knew why. Michael remembered his days in the wine shop. They weren't the best days of his life. On the other hand, Michael loved his job now and what Mr. Mim was teaching him. He liked to stay there as long as he could. He walked into the kitchen and saw his mother cooking. She smiled at him. That's when he realized that the worst job was left to him: cleaning.

The three children, their mother, and the Lormins sat around a small wooden table for their feast. If any outsider had seen what they were eating, they would have hardly called it a feast. The food on their table included potatoes, bread, a small piece of meat, and corn. There were also flowers from Mrs. Lormin's garden in the vase at the center of the table.

"Thank you for being so kind as to have us over," Mrs. Lormin said.

"It's no trouble at all," Margot answered. "Now we may start our feast."

They began to make plates. Michael picked up his plate but dropped it as soon as he had the feeling.

"Michael?" Margot looked at him. Michael didn't answer. He was standing there, frozen in place. It was the feeling before the avengers came, but this time it was on a much larger scale. His whole stomach felt like it had overturned. Everyone was looking at Michael.

They stopped staring at him when the sound of trampling hooves filled the village. There were screams and shouts of both villagers and soldiers. Explosions were heard in the distance. They could feel the heat of the fires. Death scourged through the village. The screaming never stopped. The clattering of armor got closer to their door.

They were all staring at the door when it burst open. About ten soldiers stood in the doorway. The sign of Dalafar stuck out on their armor. They yelled out to their comrades in the streets as they drew their swords. Nobody said a word as they watched the soldiers.

They barged in. Margot jumped up and stood in front of her children. The soldiers rushed into the house.

"Run!" Margot screamed to the children. They didn't move. They couldn't move. Michael's muscles wouldn't respond. "Run!" she repeated. "Get out from here! Please!" she pleaded. She had tears in her eyes. She gave them a little shove.

Michael met her eyes. He realized that she wanted nothing more in the world than for them to get out of there. He gathered his courage, grabbed his brother's and sister's arms, and dragged them out the back door toward Madvar Desert. He let them go when they got outside. They were coughing from the smoke that was in the air. They ran into the desert and took refuge behind a sand dune.

Screams from the villagers pierced the night sky. Murder swept the village of its inhabitants. Michael, Julie, and Steven sat in silence as they hid behind the dune. They had nothing to say. Dalafar was taking their life away. The moon was already in the center of the sky when all traces of life left the village with the soldiers singing as they headed back from where they had come.

They still didn't move. Whether it was from shock or from the fear that it was not over, none of them knew, but they stayed behind the dune.

It wasn't until rain started to pour down on their heads that Michael said in a solemn voice, "Come on; let's get back to the house." He almost choked from tears when he tried to talk. The pouring rain tuned out any sound of the soldiers, who were some way off. It was very unusual for it to rain this hard near the desert. They ran back to their house. Mud stuck onto their worn-out shoes as they ran.

They stood at the edge of the village, staring at the catastrophe before them. Most of the houses and shops were burned down or destroyed. Dead bodies were thrown around in piles. They couldn't recognize most of the bodies, but the ones that they did recognize caused tears to swell in their eyes. Everyone they had ever known was now dead. The sound of laughter from children and the sight of villagers hustling by were all gone.

Their house was still mostly intact. The Lormins' house next door looked as if it were untouched. The back entrance to their house was blocked off by large pieces of wood. They went around to the front. The garden was trampled over and destroyed. The door was off its hinges. The floor was covered with blood. Mr. and Mrs. Lormin were both dead on the floor. They recoiled. This was the first death that they had seen up close. Their bodies were covered in blood. The sight struck them to their hearts. Their faces paled. Seeing death created a vision that would never leave their minds.

If it was possible, their faces got even paler at the next sight. Lying on the floor, sprawled over a large piece of wood that was blocking the back door, was their mother, choking blood. It looked like she was protecting the door. Her chest was heaving up and down. She was struggling to breathe. They rushed to the floor. Michael picked her head up in his arms. She slowly opened her eyes. Her mouth opened as if to speak. "Don't talk," Michael sobbed. "Please save your strength. Don't worry. It'll be all right. We'll find help." It was an empty assurance. There was no one around to help. He was trying to assure himself more than his mother.

She shook her head. "Children…my children…" She coughed up some blood. Her voice was hoarse. She was using her last bit of energy to talk.

"Please don't speak," Michael urged.

"You must…go…Master Wizard…"

"What do you mean?" Steven let out a sob. "You'll be all right. We don't need to leave you."

"Just always…remember…I love you." Those were the last words she said. Her head fell limp in Michael's arms. He turned to Julie and Steven. Tears were streaming down their faces. Michael tasted salty water in his mouth.

Michael laid his head on his mother's stomach and cried. His pride didn't stop him. He could hear Julie and Steven crying in the background. The only things that mattered in the world now were his tears. He thought of nothing else. He felt each drop fall off his face onto his mother. They were crying for what felt like hours. They had never thought it would end this way. Their whole village was destroyed, and most if not all of the villagers were probably dead. Their neighbors and friends were dead. Their home was destroyed. And worst of all, their mother was dead. Their lives had been simple and peaceful until now. In one night, their whole world had turned upside down. This one moment would change their lives forever.

The clouds still loomed over the village and blocked the sun. It was hard to tell what time of day it was and how much time had passed. Michael finally stood and wiped the tears from his eyes. There were none left to shed. He felt dehydrated. He tried to let one more tear fall but couldn't. He took Julie by the arm and helped her up. Then he did the same to Steven. They wiped their tears off. Michael put his arms around their shoulders. They stood looking down at their mother, taking a moment of silence. Her death was and always would be their saddest moment in their lives. All they had left was each other.

Michael bent down and picked up his mother in his arms. "Come on," he said to the others. "Let's give her a proper burial."

They followed him out the front door. The rain was still coming down hard. The floor was doused from the rain, so it was easy to dig a hole in the yard. Michael placed their mother in the grave and filled up the hole. He took a stone he found lying around and placed it at the head of the grave. He picked up a bloody knife from the floor. It had probably been dropped by a soldier. He hated himself for having to use a weapon that belonged to those brutal soldiers, but there was nothing else around and he needed to do this. He carved into the tombstone:

HERE LIES MARGOT
A GREAT MOTHER

A tear rolled down his cheek when he finished carving. The other two stood next to him quietly. The rain started to slow down. After they stood there for a few minutes in silence, Michael composed himself. Now he had to take charge. There was nothing for them in the village. They had to go.

"We have to fulfill our mother's dying wish," Michael said. "We have to go to the Master Wizard in Keedor. We don't know why, but that's what she wanted, so that's what we'll do."

Julie nodded, and Steven mumbled his agreement. None of them were in a good mood, but they would never disobey their mother.

"I have to go check something out first before we get going. Wait for me at the western end of the village." He started to run off.

"But wait. Where are you going?" Julie called out, but he was already out of earshot. He ran down the muddy road that led him to his destination. His eyes couldn't take any more of what he saw. Everything and everyone was destroyed. He saw children and elderly dead on the ground. It was horrible. Only monsters could perform such a task. He didn't want to think about what he would see when he walked into Mr. Mim's house.

It wasn't burned, but it was mostly broken-down. The door was gone. The inside was a mess. A few soldiers lay dead on the floor. Michael smiled. Maybe Mr. Mim had fought them off and gotten away.

Large pieces of the collapsed wooden ceiling were all over the floor. Mr. Mim was under one of them with a sword in his hand. At least he had put up a fight. It was more than could be said for any of the other villagers. Most of them were weak and had no fighting experience. Michael didn't know where Mr. Mim got his skills.

Mr. Mim was struggling to breathe. The plank of wood on top of him was crushing his lungs. Michael rushed to his side. He used all his strength to try to get the plank off of Mr. Mim, but his efforts were futile. He tried again and again. He didn't want to give up. Mr. Mim picked up his hand that was holding the sword. He was using all the strength he had left to raise his arm. "Take it." It sounded as if it was an urgent task. Michael thought it was more important to help Mr. Mim. "Please, take it," he was whispering. He wasn't able to talk any louder. "It's my most prized possession. It's the sword I made for the late king."

Michael started to get excited. He couldn't believe Mr. Mim made swords for kings. "You mean to say that you made this sword for King Lucent!?"

"That's it, my boy. Now get that scabbard over there." He pointed to a scabbard on the floor a few feet away. Michael picked it up and held it out to Mr. Mim. Mr. Mim sheathed the sword and handed it to Michael. "I want you to have it."

Michael took it with a grin. His smile instantaneously turned to a frown when he saw tears in Mr. Mim's eyes. He had almost forgotten where he was and what was happening.

"I won't leave you," Michael said firmly as tears started to roll down his cheek.

"Yes, you will," Mr. Mim said, even more firmly. "You have to get out of here and get to the Master Wizard. It's the only chance Kanavar has." Mr. Mim took his last breath before joining in Margot's fate. Michael had wanted to ask how he knew that they were going to the Master Wizard and why that was Kanavar's last chance, but that didn't seem important now. Tears were again running down his cheeks. He grieved for his mother, he grieved for Mr. Mim, and he grieved for the village and its villagers. Soon the amount of tears he could shed ran out again.

It was time to get going. He strapped the scabbard with the sword in it on the left side of his waist. He went out of the house and headed down the road to where his sister and brother awaited him.

Blending In

After Michael had left them, Steven and Julie headed outside the village to wait for him. They didn't know what he was doing, but they trusted that it was important. They knew he wouldn't do anything stupid at a time like this. They were all still shaken up and devastated from what happened. It felt like they were stuck in a dream, or rather a nightmare.

The sky started to clear up. There were still some dark clouds, but they started to leave and head west. There was only a light drizzle now.

They walked up a grassy hill and looked in the direction of their new journey. Their bodies went cold and their faces white. The army that had raided the village was about fifty yards away. They saw the red tents aligned in rows. The army should've been gone by now. They would never be able to go anywhere without getting caught.

Julie took Steven's arm and pulled him back down the hill. They hid behind a tree. Julie hoped that the army wouldn't hear their heavy breathing as they waited for Michael.

They saw Michael walking toward them cautiously. It looked like he knew there was something wrong. In fact, Michael did have a bad feeling in his gut. The feeling was trying to tell him that there was danger, but he kept walking. He saw Julie and Steven standing behind a tree, like they were trying to hide from something. He was about to call out to them when Julie raised a finger to her nose to quiet him. He ran toward them, wanting to know what the problem was.

When he reached them, he opened his mouth to ask what was going on, But Julie covered his mouth and took him up the hill. He gaped. There was nothing but empty land between them and the army. The soldiers would be able to spot them from a mile away. How would they get to Keedor now? It would take too much time for them to wait for the army to get far enough away before they could start traveling. Traveling to Keedor in itself was a long journey. It would take twice as long now.

"We better get a closer look," he suggested to the others.

"We might get caught," Julie protested. "Then they'll just kill us. We can't go down there." The worry in her voice was evident. Michael didn't blame her. These were the soldiers who had just destroyed their village and killed all of their loved ones. She didn't want to get near those wretched soldiers. There was also a fear that the soldiers would get them too. They were the only survivors, and she was scared that if they got too close, they would be killed just like all the others.

But Michael knew this was not the time to argue. They had to see what they were up against. They couldn't wait behind. It would get them nowhere.

"We have no choice. We have to see how many troops there are and how we can get past them. I'm going to have a look. You can either stay here or follow me." Michael started walking.

Steven, trying to be brave like his older brother, followed him. He always looked up to Michael as his role model. Michael tried to act like a role model for his younger brother, but sometimes, like this time, he felt like he wasn't being responsible for his brother. He was putting all their lives in danger. But they had no choice.

Julie hesitated for a moment before striding to catch up to them. She knew this wasn't a good idea.

"What's that?" Julie asked when she noticed the sword hanging from Michael's waist.

"It's a sword," Michael answered flatly. He didn't want to talk about it now. It only brought back sad memories.

"I can see that, but where did you get it from?"

"Mr. Mim."

Julie realized why Michael didn't want to talk about it. She knew that Michael must have gone to Mr. Mim earlier. Mr. Mim had probably given it to Michael before his death. It probably meant a lot to Michael. She kept quiet, even though she thought of it as a dangerous weapon. Swords had been used to kill their mother.

The children snuck behind one of the tents. The small squad of soldiers hadn't bothered putting out any scouts. They had no fear of anyone attacking them. Dalafar's soldiers were never challenged. There weren't any soldiers outside. They were probably all still sleeping in their tents, tired from the raid the night before. It infuriated Michael that the soldiers were peacefully sleeping while everyone in the village was permanently sleeping because of them.

Michael surveyed the area. There weren't a lot of tents. There were probably only about a hundred soldiers. That was all that was needed to destroy a small village. The soldiers were not all human. There were some dwarves, trolls, and goblins among them. Michael knew that they had to be heartless creatures. To destroy a whole village without a second thought and be able to sleep right after could only be done by heartless creatures. They had no regret.

Julie was about to say that they should get out of there when Michael gestured for her to be quiet.

"That's the plan." A grumpy voice came from inside the tent. "I'll take a few men that I think are necessary and report back to Lord Dalafar. And you, Captain, will take the legion back to the capital city, Keedor, to the army base."

"That's right," replied a deep voice. "Now be off with you."

Michael saw a man scurry out of the tent. Now it was time for them to get out of there. Julie and Steven followed him back up the hill.

"We only have a few choices," he started once they had put themselves a good distance from the army. "One, we can stay far behind the army at the risk of being seen and follow them to Keedor. Two, we can try and find another longer route around the army to get to Keedor in which we completely avoid them—"

"We have to do that," Julie interrupted. "We can't risk everything our mother died for just to get to the Master Wizard faster. So what if it takes us a little longer? We have to travel safely."

Steven shushed her. "He wasn't done yet. There is a third choice."

"That's right," Michael continued with a glare at Julie. "The third choice is to travel with the army."

"That's crazy talk, Michael," Julie said, a little too loudly. Michael turned toward the army to remind her to be quiet. "Why don't you just kill us now," she continued in a whisper, "with that sword of yours."

Michael flinched. Julie realized that she had hit a weak spot. She hadn't meant to mention the sword, but it had been the heat of the moment.

Michael frowned. "We have no other choice. We will blend in with them, Julie." "It won't be that hard. There are plenty of positions in any legion of soldiers that will be fit for us to blend in where nobody will notice us. We will disguise ourselves as part of the army and travel with them to Keedor. It's the best way."

Julie reluctantly agreed, not wanting to hurt Michael's feelings any more than she already had. Steven nodded. Anyway, she was outnumbered.

"Hurry up, Jerri," Fredrick called out. "We better get going before we're late and they lash at us again." Fredrick shivered at the memory.

Jerri came running out. He wiped his forehead. He wasn't late. His twin brother, Fredrick, waited next to the legion.

"Come on," Frederick said. "We're heading northeast. We got to get a few horses, one for the captain and a few others for the head officials."

Jerri rushed back in to the stables to get the horses. Fredrick started setting up the mobile stable that they always used when they traveled with the army.

Both of the twins hated their jobs. They didn't know how they had ended up being stable boys for the army at Castle Dalafar. Ever since they could remember they had been at Castle Dalafar working for Dalafar in any way possible. Now they were stuck being stable boys. They had to always travel with the army. The soldiers always treated them like garbage and would punish them harshly for their mistakes. Fredrick hated the soldiers more than he hated Dalafar himself.

Fredrick knew they were going to raid another village. They had been doing that a lot lately, but he didn't know why. They were traveling to small villages, destroying them and killing everyone in them. Perhaps Dalafar was looking for something or someone. It didn't matter to Fredrick. He just had to do his job, no matter where it took him. If he didn't do his job, he would probably be killed. Even though it was unpaid, it gave them food, water, and shelter.

His twin brother came out of the stables with the horses. Whenever he looked at his brother, it was like looking in a mirror. They shared the same features and both had beautiful blond hair. They both had light skin and were too tall and muscular for sixteen. They almost looked twenty. The only difference between them was their eyes. Fredrick's eyes were sparkling green, while Jerri's eyes were a dark brownish-orange that was almost red.

"I got the horses," Jerri said.

"All right then," Fredrick replied. "Let's get to the army and be on our way."

They started their journey with the army. It was a long and tiring journey like always. They passed no towns on the way to their destination. It was a deserted area. Fredrick felt the air getting drier as they neared their destination. The weather got hotter, and no rain fell until the day that they arrived.

The two stable boys always hated being with the army on a journey. Fredrick would get flogged for any tiny thing that he did wrong, or sometimes even for no reason. He could feel the chill of the beer breath on the back of his neck during the flogging. The soldiers were disgusting. They had no hygiene whatsoever. The soldiers had no minds of their own. None of them had any mercy. The stable boys were always getting pushed around. Other workers were also treated as badly. The soldiers had no respect for other living beings. Fredrick guessed that was the reason they were the soldiers for Dalafar. Only beings like them would be able to destroy whole villages.

A few weeks had passed before Fredrick could finally spot a small village. Fredrick was grooming his favorite black steed, Flash, when a soldier came in. It was early in the night.

"We arrived at the village," the soldier said. "You two scum stay here while we do our job. Don't do anything wrong or else." He left with that warning.

Fredrick sighed. He knew what would happen if they were to do anything wrong. He didn't want a taste of that cruelty ever again, not to mention the blood in his mouth.

He knew that this was just another raid like they'd been doing for months now. His brain told him it was the same, but the bad feeling in his gut told him otherwise. He felt like this time things would change. He didn't believe the feeling, but deep in his heart he hoped it was true. Anything would be better than his life now. He always hoped things would change.

The soldiers returned after midnight. Fredrick could see the smoke over the hilltops from the burning village. It looked like most of the village had been set ablaze. He was sure that there were no survivors. The soldiers were cheering at their success in battle. Fredrick knew what was coming next. There would be a bonfire, drinking, and dancing. He hated the after-war effects. He knew that Jerri hated them too. The parties that the soldiers had were terrible. They were pushed around and beaten by the drunken soldiers. He was dreading what was to come, and every one of his waking seconds during the night he hoped that morning would come.

The next morning finally came. Fredrick awoke after hardly sleeping, except for the last hour, when all the soldiers finally got a taste of the hangover. The soldiers were all sleeping now. It would be a quiet morning. That was one positive thing that had come out of all this.

Jerri was already outside, working his shift. Fredrick went to groom Flash. He usually spent more time with Flash than the other horses. Flash neighed when Fredrick gave him some food. He moved on to the other horses.

It was about an hour when it was time to switch their jobs. Fredrick called out to his brother. "Coming now, Jerri."

When he got outside to Jerri, he realized that it wasn't Jerri. It wasn't like looking in the mirror with different eyes like it usually was. Instead it was like looking in a real mirror. The guy that looked back at him could have been mistaken for his real twin. Before he could say or do anything, the green-eyed boy picked up a large branch and knocked Fredrick on the head. Frederick blacked out.

Michael and Steven placed the two boys behind a bush. "Like we planned." Michael nodded his satisfaction. "Now let's go through with the rest." Steven nodded and walked into the army camp. Michael went back to Julie, who was waiting behind the bushes with the two unconscious boys.

"Michael, these two kids have an uncanny resemblance to you."

Michael shrugged the comment away. But he did feel some remorse for doing this to these boys. He was sure they would be able to survive, but it still didn't feel right. But that was not important now. He had to sneak Julie in the camp, where Steven would be waiting with the kitchen staff outfit.

They stealthily moved from the back of one tent to another as they made their way to the larger kitchen tent. None of the soldiers were out yet, so it wasn't too hard to sneak around. Steven was waiting behind the tent with the outfit. "I put the body in a tree nearby," he said. Michael nodded. Julie slipped into the white outfit.

"We'll meet up with you when we can," Michael said.

The two boys left and headed for the stables as Juie made her way to the kitchen. They met with each other about twice a week after midnight, when all the soldiers finally went to sleep. Julie was trembling every time they met. Michael wouldn't admit full bravery on his part either. The thought of getting caught and killed at any second was terrifying no matter how brave you were. But the soldiers never noticed that they were any different.

During the traveling, they saw what brutes the soldiers really were. The soldiers got drunk most nights. They acted worse than animals. Michael was horrified and disgusted. He had nightmares of the soldiers for weeks after he saw what they were like. The soldiers were very nasty to the other staff among the camp. They looked down on everyone else and demanded things in harsh tones. They didn't care about anyone but themselves. No wonder they had been able to destroy and kill everyone in Periphia. They had no feelings. They were the worst of the worst.

The only peaceful time they had was late at night when all the soldiers were sleeping. Michael would look up the star-filled sky, and hope for a better future. He didn't know what the future would bring him, but he had trusted his mother. She had always wanted the best for them, so this must be what was best. The Master Wizard would give them a new and better life.

They had already traveled with the army for two months when they reached a river. If Michael remembered correctly from the maps he used to look at with Mr. Mim, it was the Hidukel River. He realized that now they were close enough to Keedor to ditch the army. They could get ahead of the army and make it on their own.

Steven was grooming a black steed when Michael came to talk to him about their plans of escape. "It's time for us to get out of here," he told Steven. "I'll go and tell Julie while you get three horses ready for us to take. Make sure you don't get caught." They were so close to reaching Keedor and being free of the army. There was no way they could get caught now. It would ruin everything.

They had to sneak away with three horses to ride to Keedor before the army realized they were gone.

"OK," Steven agreed.

Michael left to go to the kitchen tent. He walked past soldiers who grunted their dissatisfaction at him. He had never even heard of half the curses that they said under their breath. He had learned to ignore them. He wouldn't give them the satisfaction of tormenting him.

He reached the kitchen tent and peered inside. It was full of both male and female cooks. Michael knew that it must take a lot of food to feed those animals outside. He spotted Julie, who was kneading a piece of dough.

The cooks all stared at him as he walked in. He knew he needed an excuse. He didn't think a stable boy ever walked into the kitchen tent. "The captain said he wants a personal cook and told me to come here and pick one," Michael said quickly.

The one seeming to be the head chef walked over to him. "What are you guys looking at?" he growled at his workers. "Get back to work." The rest of the cooks went back to their cooking. "So you say the captain sent you."

"Yes, and if you don't want to make him angry enough to come down here himself, then you better let me pick one fast," Michael answered in a loud, deep voice, trying to sound intimidating. He knew that the kitchen staff were probably also scared of the soldiers, and he tried to use that to his advantage.

"Oh, yes, of course," the chef said with a little terror in his voice. Michael smiled. The chef actually believed him. The threat was too great for the chef to bother to check if it was true. Because if it was and he didn't do it right away, he would be in a lot of trouble.

Michael walked around as if to inspect the work of the cooks to see if they were good enough. Each cook was cooking something that was part of the big meal that would serve the army. Michael thought about how the food was wasted on the soldiers instead of going to the poor citizens in Kanavar.

Michael asked some of the cooks a few questions about their cooking experience. He wanted them to think that his excuse was real. He also took a few tastes of the food. He was becoming thinner every day. He needed more food than he was getting. The soldiers gave them only scraps to eat after they were done eating, and there was never much left. The soldiers devoured everything. Hopefully they would get better meals in Keedor. He still had some money left from Mr. Mim, and they would be able to use that to buy some food.

He went to Julie and started asking questions about her cooking in a loud voice. He lowered his voice and continued talking. "We're getting out of here today," he said, almost in a whisper.

"Finally," she answered, a little too loud. Everyone turned to her. "Finally the captain is realizing my talent as a great cook." They all turned back to their work. *That was a little too close,* Michael thought. The last thing he wanted now was to look suspicious.

"Be more careful," Michael warned. "Pack some food and other supplies for us if you can, and meet Steven and me by the stables in an hour." He left without waiting for her to protest his plan. He hated when she did that. But she probably wouldn't even have argued this time. He knew how much she wanted to get away from this army.

Fredrick felt himself being pushed back and forth. He opened his eyes. Jerri was kneeling over him. Fredrick put his hand to his head. His head was hurting. He thought back to what had happened. The last thing he remembered was being hit by a boy who looked more like him than Jerri did. He looked around. He was lying on the hard ground in the middle of nowhere. Jerri stood up and surveyed their surroundings. The army was nowhere to be seen.

"They're gone," Jerri told him in a depressed voice. Fredrick actually smiled. He hated working for the army. The beatings, harassment, and insults were all gone. It was a miracle. They could start a better life. He sat up and looked at the sky.

Jerri was frowning. Jerri enjoyed working for Dalafar at the castle and in the army. Fredrick didn't know why. They used to both hate it. Then in the recent months, Jerri had started to like working for the tyrant of Kanavar. They had been drifting further apart ever since.

"We better look for new jobs," Fredrick suggested. Jerri grunted his agreement. "We can head to Keedor and find jobs there." Jerri didn't answer.

Keedor was a place for new beginnings. There was plenty of opportunity there to start a new life. It would be great for them. Jerri didn't seem to agree.

Fredrick stood up and started to walk west. He knew the way to Keedor. They had traveled there so many times before with the army. Jerri reluctantly followed, like Fredrick had known he would. It would take a long time to get there. They were far from Keedor, but at least it would be quicker than traveling with a whole army.

They walked every day and camped at night. Fredrick knew many plants and was able to point out the edible ones. Jerri spat it out the first few times, but eventually his hunger overcame his taste buds and he ate whatever Fredrick would give him. They traveled for weeks. They were far from any civilization. Jerri was getting restless. Fredrick didn't mind the quiet. He wished they could just live alone forever and have no trouble come their way, but even he was getting sick of the plants for food and hard ground as a bed.

Finally they reached the city of Holechar. Jerri was thrilled to see other people. They got to eat normal food and sleep in an inn by using the small amount of money they had accumulated over the years.

Jerri wanted to stay there longer, but Fredrick urged him on again after two days, explaining that they had no more money. As soon as the innkeeper heard that, he chased them out.

Jerri sighed when they started to travel again. They went on for another month, living on plant food. After another month they reached the Hidukel River. By this time Fredrick was also getting tired of the traveling. They both wanted nothing more than to reach Keedor.

"We're almost there." Fredrick tried to cheer them both up.

As they were crossing the bridge of the Hidukel River, the clear blue sky turned black for a split second before turning back to a bright blue. Both kids stared up at the sky, not knowing what had just happened.

Master Wizard

Walking as fast as a 120-year-old man could walk, a bald old man with a white beard down to his belly button, wearing a green cloak, was walking down the road. If he were in any other city, he would've looked strange, but since it was Keedor, nobody recognized him or paid any attention to him. Everyone looked strange in Keedor.

He hurried past the salesmen and bystanders. They were all going about their daily business. That day was definitely not a regular day for the old man. He could feel his magic energy fading and leaving him. His end was near. There was only one chance left for the world, and he had to put it into place before he left the world. He couldn't let everyone down. He couldn't let Margot and her children down. There was no time to waste.

Dalafar loved his new pet. The man bowing in front of him would prove very useful in the future.

"Do you swear complete loyalty to your new master?" Dalafar asked the formal question.

"I do, Master Dalafar," replied the man. "I swear my complete loyalty to you and will never fail you. To my death I take this oath. I will never forsake it. Please accept it, Lord Dalafar."

"Put out your hand," Dalafar commanded. The man obeyed. Dalafar took out his knife that was infused with the sacred oath magic. He cut the man's left pinky off. Dalafar took the blood and smeared it against his own left pinky. It was done. He had this man in his grip. This man would play a powerful role in the future. He would be of great help.

The old man headed to what looked like a small shack. But he knew better and knew what was really inside. He looked sadly at the large tower across the street of Tower Lane. It used to be his old home. Once Dalafar came along, he'd had to move to the shack to hide. Dalafar had searched for him but was never able to find him. He'd chosen the perfect place to hide.

The old man walked inside the shack. It was a wonder to walk inside a small shack and see a grand room with many twisting staircases and hallways leading to all sorts of doors. It was like a maze. Actually, it was worse than a maze. A normal man could wander in here his whole life if he got lost. The old man knew the place as well as any other person knew his or her house. He knew exactly where everything was.

A voice spoke, "The usual, Master Wizard?"

"No…" he answered in a sour voice. "I need to…six hundred and twelve…" Before he spoke any more, the floor under him turned into a moving platform. It rushed him to a door that said:

612
Apprentice to Master Wizard

The door detected him coming and opened. The man sitting on his chair in front of his desk stood up as he saw his master walk in the room. The room was an elegant room. His apprentice always had a taste for fancy furniture. The Master Wizard dropped to the floor. He no longer had strength to hold up his body. His apprentice rushed down to his side. The Master Wizard didn't have time for anything else but his task. He held out a hand that had two pieces of parchment in it.

As the apprentice took the first, the Master Wizard whispered in his hoarse voice, "To…three children…" and as the apprentice picked up the second, "to…two boys…" It was finished. He had started the wheels of fate. It was no longer in his hands. He'd done what he had to, and he was pleased. It was at this time, he decided, that he was able to die.

The Master Wizard's hand fell to the floor. He took his last breath before leaving the world. The necklace around the Master Wizard's neck dimmed. The sky turned pitch-black for a split second, as the apprentice knew it would. The apprentice excitedly took the necklace from his previous master's neck and placed it around his own. The sky returned to normal. There was a new Master Wizard.

He left the room after he watched the body disappear as its particles joined with nature. He didn't need the moving platform and ignored the magic voice that questioned him as he went to the door on the right that said:

613
Master Wizard

It had always been his dream to enter this room. He also had a desire for the power. Now he had the power; more power than even his master. Before he could get to work in his new position, he had to fulfill his master's dying wish. He had to get these two papers to the people his former master had mentioned. It was the only way he would be able to be the real Master Wizard. Until then he was nothing. That rule was his worst enemy at the moment. But the apprentice oath he took when joining the wizards prevented him from doing anything else.

He looked around the room. Everything was green. The bed, carpets, ceiling, and walls were all green. The wooden desk and chair were painted green. The door of the magic cupboard was green. *Uch!* He hated green. It was his least favorite color. With a flick of his hand, he turned it all to red. That was more like it. The red room appealed to his nature. He sat on the chair and waited. He knew the children wouldn't take long to show up. After all, his master had told him that they were on their way.

The children stopped their horses as they watched the sky go black for a split second. Michael patted the head of his black steed.

"What was that?" Julie asked the question that was running through all their heads. The sky returned to normal.

"Let's get going before it gets dark." Michael shrugged it off. He had a bad feeling about what had just happened, but he didn't want to put down the others' moods. They were all cheery now that they were safely in front of the massive walls of Keedor. They had left the army a few days ago and finished all of their food already. Once they got to the other side of the walls, they would be away from the army forever. The soldiers wouldn't be able to track them in Keedor. It was a large city.

They were all staring at the hundreds-of-feet-tall wall of the capital city of Kanavar. Not only was it tall, it was also at least twenty feet wide. A few wagons were able to fit along the width of the top of the wall. Dozens of soldiers were atop the wall, bows in hand. More soldiers were able to fit up there, but Michael didn't think they were needed. Dalafar had probably moved them to his castle. There were four gates in the wall, each in another direction. The west wall's gate led to a large harbor that consisted of many docks. Each dock had many ships docked, and even more ships were out to sea, trading. The west gate was almost always open during the day, letting the merchants travel in and out of the city.

They rode their horses to the eastern gate. Ten guards were stationed by the entrance, five on each side. The guards didn't move.

"What is your business here?" A guard on the left spoke first. "The gates are closed. Night is upon us."

"It's not yet night, and they may still enter." Another guard intervened. "State your business."

Michael spoke up for them. "We are cousins," Michael explained as they had rehearsed it, "who have come to work for our uncle. He's a tradesman and asked our mother if we could help him out with his job and work for him. Business isn't doing so well, if you know what I mean."

"Another merchant," the guard on the left mumbled as he opened the gate.

They rode their horses through the gate. Once in, they stopped and looked up in awe. The buildings in the city were amazing. It was nothing like their village. They had never seen anything like it. The setting sun reflected off the white and gray stones of the buildings. There were small stores and houses between the large buildings. Michael guessed that the buildings were castles where the lords, ladies, nobles, and government officials lived. He expected that the upper-class people had much better lives here than the lower class. It didn't look like there was much of a middle class. There were all types of people and creatures walking in the streets. Many were wearing ripped and tattered clothes. Michael knew they would fit right in. There were also carriages like the one that the strange man who had come to Periphia had. These must belong to the upper class of the city. The larger buildings were more toward the center of the city, while the smaller ones were closer to the walls.

Small booths ran on the sides of the roads. Each person was trying to sell something else to make a living. Most people were selling food and clothes. The others were mostly selling junk.

A beautiful woman who reminded Michael of their mother called out to them. "Come here children," she said in her sweet voice. She had long black hair that matched her black eyes. She wore a long green cloak and circular gold earrings. "I will help you in your quest."

Michael was drawn to her. He dismounted and walked to her booth. The other two followed.

"I will tell your future," she said. The three children stood before her in a trance. Her booth had a curtain blocking the draft coming from outside. There was a table and three chairs in the booth. "Please sit down." They took their seats opposite hers.

Michael knew they had to get going, but he couldn't get up. He couldn't get away from the woman. His legs felt like they were tied to the chair.

"You wish to see the Master Wizard," she started. As soon as she said "Master Wizard" the children got their senses back. How could she know about that?

"What—" Michael was cut off.

"Ah, yes, the new Master Wizard. I see. He dwells on Tower Lane. You must go see him. It is of the utmost importance. The fate of all of Charldena is at stake." She finished with a few snorts and gasps for air.

"Who are you?" Michael stood up from his seat. He sat down again as she glared at him.

"I am a fortune-teller," she replied, "here to tell your fortune." There was a pause.

Michael realized that she was only giving direct answers. "How do you know us and where we need to go?" He didn't believe in fortune-tellers. Who was this lady?

"I already told you. I am a fortune-teller, here to tell your fortune," she repeated.

Michael let out a sigh of frustration. "Is there anything else that you need to tell us?"

She shook her head. "That is all for now, but we will meet again in the future." Michael sure hoped that they wouldn't. This woman was creepy. It could be that she said the same thing to everyone who walked by.

Michael was still a little confused. He still had a few questions. "You said there is a new Master Wizard. What happened to the old one?"

"The old one," she answered, "died a few hours back. I'm sure you saw the sky go black. It happens every time a Master Wizard leaves this world. The Master Wizard's young apprentice became the new Master Wizard. However, he must first fulfill the old Master Wizard's final request before becoming the real Master Wizard."

"And how do you know all this?"

"I am a sorcerer," she explained. "Sorcerers have special types of magic."

"Thank you," Michael concluded. "We have to get going now." He motioned to the others to get up and go. Julie, followed by

Steven, left the booth. They were anxious to get out. Michael took one last look at the woman before following them.

None of them spoke of the fortune-teller. They didn't know what to make of it. All they knew was that they had to get to the Master Wizard, and now they knew where he was. They had to find Tower Lane.

They were soon lost in the maze of roads that made up Keedor. Finding Tower Lane was harder than they'd thought. They didn't even know how to get back to where they had come from. Michael didn't understand how anyone could find anything in this city. Julie kept nudging him about stopping and asking for directions, but he refused and said that he would find the place. But he knew that he would never find it.

"What is it with you and asking for directions?" Julie said as she trotted over to a man selling fruits. "Excuse me, sir—"

"You have come to buy my fruit, young child?" he asked happily. A smile brightened his face. Half his teeth were missing, and the other half were yellow. His body smelled worse than his ragged clothes.

"Actually," Julie continued, "I was wondering if you were able to tell me where I could find Tower Lane."

"Oh," he said, disappointed. "Tower Lane. Yes, I know the place. I've sold my fruits on that busy street before." He started talking lower when he was explaining to Julie the way to go. Julie felt sorry to leave the man without buying something, but they had to save their money for when they really needed it

"Follow me," Julie said when she came back to them. Michael sighed as he followed her. Julie let out a giggle. They followed her as she led them down different streets, turning right or left every so often. Michael tried to remember the way, but it was no use. Steven was just looking around, fascinated by his surroundings. The city was bigger than anything he had ever seen. Michael felt like he had once been in a place with large buildings, but that couldn't be true. Then his memory of running around in large gardens came back. He pushed that aside.

In the distance Michael could see the ruins of King Lucent's castle. It was almost as big as the whole city. There were soldiers guarding the area and other men digging up the ruins, looking for something interesting to give to Dalafar.

They reached Tower Lane after another few minutes. Like the man had said, it was a busy street. It went as far in both ways as Michael could see. They were near the center of the city. They turned on Tower Lane and kept riding.

"How do we know where the Master Wizard is?" Julie asked. Any of the buildings on Tower Lane could belong to the Master Wizard. It would be impossible to check all of them. Michael had no answer for her. Instead, he went on.

They stopped in front of a large tower. The tower was probably the biggest building in the city from what Michael could tell. It looked as if the top scraped the sky. The only thing that was probably bigger than it was King Lucent's castle, but that was in ruins. But there was one strange thing about the tower: it was deserted. Dust covered the outside walls. No lights or movements could be seen from any of the windows. Nobody gave the tower a second glance as they passed.

Something in his mind caused Michael to turn his head. Across the road from the tower was a very small shack. Julie and Steven were still looking at the tower, assuming that was the place that they needed to go. All three of them dismounted. Michael pulled Julie and Steven back by their shirts as they were walking toward the tower. "Don't go in there. It looks dangerous."

They turned to where he was looking. "And you think the Master Wizard lives in that shack and not this tower?" Julie asked suspiciously.

"I…I have a feeling," Michael stammered. Without hearing their consent, he walked to the door of the shack. It was his instinct that was drawing him to it. His instinct had never failed him before. Mr. Mim had taught him to always trust his instinct. He heard Julie and Steven's footsteps trailing behind him in the distance of his mind. When he reached the door, he regained his senses. He reached for the doorknob and opened the door without knocking. He stood there awestruck. Julie was pushing him to the side to get in. When she saw what waited inside, she froze.

After Steven followed them in, he was the first to speak. "This wasn't really what I expected to be inside a small shack." They were in a large room with twisted hallways and staircases that led off to all directions. Doors lined the walls. It was hard to take it all in.

"Well," Michael commented, "this must be the place." There was no doubt about it. Steven and Julie agreed. The only explanation for this place was magic. The Master Wizard was definitely here. The question was where to start looking.

Just as she was about to ask, a voice called out, "Where do you wish to go, sire?" The children all jumped with a fright. "Sire?" the voice repeated. They looked around, not knowing who the voice was talking to or where it was coming from.

"Say something, Michael," Julie urged.

"Why me? It's clearly not talking to any of us."

"Do you want to get to the Master Wizard or not?"

"But—"

"Michael," Steven interrupted, "it doesn't matter whether it's talking to us or not. We have to get to the Master Wizard, so just say it."

"The Master Wizard," Michael said in a loud and commanding voice.

"I will take you, sire." The floor under them started moving. It became a flying platform. The platform flew so fast that they couldn't see which way they were going. Before they knew it, the platform stopped and turned back into the floor in front of a room.

613

Master Wizard

"This is it," Michael said. The door opened by itself as he reached for it.

A voice that seemed to come from the door said, "Royal visitors," as they entered the room. The red color of it hit them when they walked in. It was like a bloodbath had happened there. The bed, carpets, walls, ceiling, closet, desk, and chair were all red. A young man sat in the chair, working on paperwork on the desk.

He was a handsome man. He had wavy black hair and beautiful brown eyes that would get all the girls in Keedor to trail him. He had a tan. His black cloak matched his hair. He turned and smiled at them. His teeth were perfect.

"I was beginning to wonder when you three would show up," the Master Wizard said. "Come. Please sit down. I was expecting you."

Three chairs appeared across from his chair, which was now turned away from the desk. He gestured for them to sit. They sat.

"You were expecting us?" Michael asked. Had his mother arranged this?

"Of course," the Master Wizard replied as he reached into his pocket. "My former master gave me this to give to the three children that come to me." He took his hand out of his pocket. He was holding a piece of parchment. He handed it to Michael. Something was written on it.

> *To the children of Margot*

His assumptions were true. His mother did know the Master Wizard. But what was their connection and how did they know each other?

He opened the parchment. It was a simple map of Kanavar. A line was drawn from Keedor to the center of The Living Woods. A mark was placed there. From the woods the line continued to an area of the Urakian Mountains where the mountains met the beginning of the woods. Another mark was placed there.

He exchanged looks of confusion with Julie and Steven.

"I know nothing of it," the Master Wizard said, seeing their obvious uncertainty. "That is all. You may be on your way." The door swung open for them to leave. Michael got the hint. The Master Wizard wanted them out of here. Michael guessed that he probably had a lot of work to do. Being the Master Wizard must be a busy job.

Michael turned to the others. They seemed to get the hint, so he signaled them to leave. He followed them out the door.

"Anywhere else, sire?" the voice asked.

Michael still wasn't sure why the voice called him "sire," but he thought that it must be because it called everyone in the shack that name out of respect.

"No thanks," Michael said to the air. "We just want to leave now."

"Very well, sire." The floor under them once again started to fly, and before they knew it, they were at the large golden doors that led outside.

It wasn't long before they reached Keedor, but it was nighttime when they finally reached the gates. They had to camp outside and go into the city the next morning. Jerri complained to the guards, but they didn't change their minds. Fredrick assured Jerri that this would be their last night without dinner and without a bed to sleep on. Jerri just mumbled back.

Sheri had been doing well ever since she left her home. She remembered the day that she left her father behind. She needed to get out of the small village that she lived in. Nobody in the village really knew that she even existed. Her father wasn't much of a talker. She had decided to leave and head to the big city. She missed her father, but it was the best decision that she had ever made. Her new business was doing pretty good. When she first came to Keedor, she had found a deserted inn on Tower Lane. Tower Lane was one of the busiest streets in Keedor, and she was very lucky to find an inn there. She had renovated the inn with the little money that she had taken from home and started a business. Most travelers who came to Keedor came to Tower Lane to look for a place of lodging. So she never had a dull night.

Although she was sixteen, she had never had a real crush, but now she was blushing beet red in front of the handsome young man standing before her. His sparkling green eyes made her forget that he had two other companions with him. Now she knew what they meant when they talked about love at first sight.

"Do you have a room for us to stay the night?" the boy asked. The sound of his sweet voice broke her daze.

"Yes, I do," she replied. She hid her trembling hands behind her desk. She blushed. She wished that she were wearing nicer clothes at the moment when she met her true love. Instead of a beautiful dress, she wore a simple white blouse and blue skirt. Her long blonde hair was braided. There wasn't a strand of hair out of place. She took a quick look in the mirror on the opposite wall and smiled. At least she looked pretty decent. Her skin lit up when she smiled. She thought that her hazel eyes matched the boy's green eyes.

"Come, right this way. Let me show you the room."

They walked across the lobby. Well, she liked to call it a lobby. But it was really a small room with a few couches and chairs. To the right of her desk was the front door. She pointed out to her guests the dining area on her left. The inn was only two stories, and the stairs were on the other side of the lobby. She led them upstairs and down the hall.

"Here you are," she said as they reached the room. All the rooms in the inn were identical. They each had two beds with a nightstand, a couch, and a closet.

"This is fine," the boy said. He handed her some money with a smile. It was a little more than the price.

She smiled back and giggled a little when she left the room. It looked like he might like her. She hoped this would work out.

She went back downstairs and locked the front doors. They were her last customers for the night. She didn't like to take more guests late at night like some other innkeepers. She always got tired and liked to have some sleep. Maybe she just needed some help.

She would nap for a few hours and then open the doors again for some men to come in for a drink. She didn't like those men, but they brought in money. They always got drunk. She was scared to get near them, let alone chase them out. She always waited until they left to really go to bed.

Michael couldn't sleep. He was twisting and turning on the couch for hours. It wasn't because the couch was not comfortable. It was because of all of the thoughts running through his head: the memories of Periphia, Mr. Mim, his mother, the heartless soldiers, the strange fortune-teller, the Master Wizard, the map, and that beautiful girl downstairs. His mouth grew dry. He decided to go downstairs to get a drink.

The door creaked a little when he opened it. Julie and Steven didn't wake. It was the first time that they had slept in a bed since the night before the raid. They wouldn't wake up easily. Michael tiptoed out of the room and down the stairs to the lobby.

Michael heard the laughter of drunken men before he reached the dining area. There was a group of men sitting around a table with drinks in hand. They were loud. He was surprised that nobody from the inn had woken up and complained. Michael spotted the innkeeper cowering in the corner. Some of them men were whistling in her direction. These men reminded him of the soldiers in the army. Michael knew what he had to do. He walked up to the thugs.

"Hey! Leave her alone."

They just laughed. "And what are you going to do about it?" one asked. They kept laughing.

The largest one got up and stood in front of Michael. "Do you have a problem with us? If you do, you take it up with me. Otherwise just go back from where you came from, kid."

He had gotten himself into a jam this time. This wasn't like protecting his little brother from some bullies back home. There were always those groups of kids who liked to pick on Steven, but they went running when Michael came along. These guys were definitely not going to run anywhere. This was the real deal. He had to stand his ground. Mr. Mim had told him to always be courageous and never back down.

He pulled out his sword. "I said leave her alone."

"You better put that thing away before someone gets hurt," the large one said. The others stopped laughing. He and Michael stared each other down.

"Leave her alone," Michael repeated.

The large one just grunted. "You don't have the guts to use that." He pulled out a knife. "But I know that I do have the guts to use this. And I got experience to prove it." He raised the knife. With exceptional speed, Michael dodged the knife and ended up behind his opponent. The edge of his sword was resting on the back of the large one's bulging neck.

"I said leave her alone."

The others were already out of their chairs, headed toward the door. "You'll regret this," the large one said. He hurried out after his buddies.

The girl ran up to him and hugged him. "Thank you."

Michael felt her heart beating against his chest. She kissed him on the cheek, and Michael blushed.

"No problem," he replied. Michael kissed her back. "Well, have a good night."

"You too, and by the way, my name is Sheri."

"I'm Michael," Michael called back from the stairs.

Julie was in her bed when a noise came from outside. She turned to the window. It was dark outside. The window faced an alleyway, and the only lights in the city were in the streets. She reassured herself that it was nothing. Keedor was a large city, and it was probably someone working at night. It wasn't like Periphia.

People roamed the streets at night in Keedor. It could have just been a cat looking through the garbage for some food.

But then the noise came again. It was like someone was climbing the wall of the inn. She couldn't reassure herself any longer. They weren't used to noises like that at night. She was shaking under her blanket. Before she could get up and go over to wake the others, something came crashing through the window. She jumped out of bed.

The thing that had come through the window was a figure of a man. The shadowy figure dove down at Steven's bed, holding something sharp. Steven was already awake from the noise and jumped out of the bed in time. The man just missed stabbing Steven. His knife was embedded in Steven's bed. Steven stood next to Julie.

Julie searched around for the candle. She couldn't find it. It must've rolled under one of the beds.

The man turned from Steven's bed and lunged at her. Michael was up now and knocked him in the back with the hilt of his sword just in time. The man tripped over something and fell to the floor. Steven and Michael surrounded him. The man took out a second knife and started for Steven. Michael swung his sword. The man turned at the sound of the blade and rushed to the door. He broke through the door and made a run for it. Michael and Steven ran after him. Julie was too terrified to move. She stood in the dark, silent room by herself.

Then she realized that Steven had no weapon to protect himself. The man would have no trouble attacking him. Julie reached for her pack and searched it. She had taken a kitchen knife from their house before they left. She had known it would come in handy. She found the knife and rushed out the door.

Michael was fighting the man. It was too dark to tell who had the upper hand. Steven was standing in the background, trying to figure out how to join the fight.

"Steven," Julie called out to him. Steven turned. She held out the knife in his direction. Steven ran over and took the knife from her and joined the fight. The man realized that he was outnumbered and didn't stand a chance. He looked both ways before breaking through another door into the hallway. The man ran to the far side of the room and escaped out the window.

Michael, Julie, and Steven stood in the room, looking out the broken window where the assassin who had just tried to kill them had escaped. It was a good thing this room was empty so nobody else was involved.

"What just happened?" Julie exclaimed.

"Someone just tried to kill us," Steven answered.

"I know that," Julie said in an annoyed tone.

"The question is, why?" Michael said. They exchanged worried looks.

"You have failed," his employer said in a harsh tone.

"I am truly sorry-"

"There are no excuses."

"Give me another chance."

"No more chances."

"I'll get them the next time."

"There will never be a next time. Now you die." A flash of red light came from his employer's hand and shot straight at him. The last thing that came out of his mouth was a piercing cry that filled the night sky.

Sheri woke up sweating the next morning. She had had a terrible nightmare. And it turned out that there was a real nightmare waiting for her when she looked around the inn. Her three new guests were gone, including her love. And their room, the hallway, and another room were trashed and destroyed. Windows and doors were broken. She didn't know what to think. How would she pay for this? And what could have happened to her love? She wanted everything to work out between them, and after the kiss the night before, her hopes had risen. Now they were all gone. She just hoped that he was all right.

She decided to go out and eat breakfast at a café to clear her mind. She walked down the roads that she knew so well. After living in Keedor for years, she had learned all the streets. She thought about how a foreigner could easily get lost in this city. It reminded her of when she had first come to the city and had no idea where to go. She had gotten lost countless times. She was lucky that a nice lady had found her and told her where the deserted inn was located. The lady had claimed to be a fortune-teller, but she didn't believe that.

She passed a few cafés that she never actually went to. As she passed one, her heart fluttered. Sitting down and eating breakfast inside were her love and his two companions. It was a relief. He was all right. She turned her head away after she realized that she had been staring at him for a few minutes.

Michael saw her. He excused himself from his two companions and left the café. He started walking toward her. "I was wondering if you would like to join me for breakfast," he said.

She couldn't find her voice. He had just asked her on a date. It was what she had been waiting for.

"Of course," she finally managed. "I even know of a great place we can go." Her voice was failing her. She knew actions spoke louder than words, so she took his hand and led him down a few different streets to her favorite café. It was a romantic place and had excellent food. Some tables and chairs were set up outside. A sign that hung over the café said

He pulled out a chair for her. He was so polite. She knew that he was the one. Her father had always told her that everyone had one person in Charldena who was meant for them. They were meant for each other.

He called a waiter, and they ordered their breakfast. He ordered the same as her, explaining that he didn't recognize the food here and trusted her taste.

She finally remembered why she had been so worried. "What happened last night? When I woke up I saw the whole place trashed. I thought that maybe you were hurt."

"You shouldn't worry yourself. We were attacked, but we managed to chase the attacker away. We're all fine. I'll let you have our three horses to compensate for the damage. Sorry about that."

"It's fine, and thanks for the horses. I saw that you left them in front of the inn."

By the end of breakfast they were both laughing and having a good time. She had forgotten all about what had happened that morning. Nothing else mattered to her more than Michael. Her father had been right. Michael was made for her. He was the one, her true love.

"I had a great time," he said when they finished eating and paid the waiter.

"Me too." She was smiling. She had a beautiful smile. Michael complimented her on it.

"I have to get going now," he said. "My brother, sister, and I need to travel down south."

Her whole world turned dark. She was devastated. She couldn't believe it. They were just starting to get to know each other, and now he had to leave. She thought that they would be together forever. She knew that she would never find another boy like him. She was about to cry. He realized something was wrong and leaned in to kiss her. She leaned toward him. Their kiss was like soaring to heaven. It was better than heaven. She was engulfed in pleasure. She never wanted to let go. It was ecstasy. It was rapture. And then it ended. He hugged her, and she hugged him back.

"I hope I will get to see you again," was the last thing he said before he took off. Tears rolled down her cheeks as she watched him go. She needed more than hope. She needed to know that they would see each other again. She would never have true happiness or true love in her life unless he returned.

Morning came at last. Fredrick had a sore back from sleeping on the rocky ground. He went to wake Jerri, but Jerri was already up.

"Finally," Jerri said in a grumpy voice. He was still mad that they'd had to wait an extra night. Jerri ran ahead of Fredrick as they headed to the gates of Keedor.

Fredrick felt like he was losing his relationship with his brother. They had been so close when they were just kids. Now it seemed as if every day they drifted further apart. They weren't talking as much. It was like they weren't even brothers anymore. He felt this feeling often. He knew that it had started when Jerri had started to like Dalafar, but now it was getting worse. They never really agreed on anything. They had opposite personalities. When they were younger, they had planned to one day become the rulers of Kanavar. They played games, pretending to be the twin kings. Jerri wouldn't even acknowledge that they were twins anymore.

The guards recognized them from the night before and let them pass. They had been in Keedor many times before with the army. Its massive walls and buildings didn't impress them anymore. Even the thousands of beings that the city held didn't cause them to marvel at Keedor's splendor. They had been to the gardens of Yoteran and Castle Dalafar. Nothing really impressed them anymore.

It wouldn't be too hard to find a job in Keedor. Hundreds of beings came in every day, starting new businesses and looking for help. There were also hundreds leaving the city every day, giving way to job openings.

As they were walking, a beautiful woman called out to them. Her long dark hair and sweet black eyes appealed to Fredrick. She had a pleasant face. It was like a woman he'd seen in his dreams. It was how he pictured his own mother looking.

"Come, my children. I am a fortune-teller. Come. Let me tell you your fortune."

Jerri tried to pull Fredrick back as he walked to her booth, but Fredrick wouldn't comply. He very much liked this woman, and Jerri wouldn't stop him from hearing what she had to say. Jerri was forced to follow.

"You boys must hurry and see the Master Wizard if you want your future to be better than you foresee it as." She talked in riddles. She didn't say anything more. Her mouth was shut. Fredrick thought that she wanted money or something, but there was no indication of it.

Jerri nudged Fredrick as a sign to get going. Fredrick followed his brother out of the booth. He turned and looked back at the woman. Tears were streaming down her cheeks as they left. "Go my children," she blessed them. "You will have a good life if you choose the right path."

"I think we should listen to her," Fredrick said when they were far from the booth. He had a good feeling about that woman.

"Are you mad?" Jerri said. "She was a crazy woman, just another one of those freaks who wander around the streets of Keedor trying to make a living. You know the like. We've encountered 'em before. They're everywhere. Just look around. I can't believe you're falling into this trap." Jerri frowned.

"I know, but she seems different. She didn't even ask for any money. She must have been sincere. And besides, it can't hurt. The Master Wizard sounds like an important guy. I mean, wouldn't he have more money to pay us for a job than anyone else?" Fredrick knew how to persuade his brother. Even if they were drifting apart, they were still twins. Twins shared a closer bond than normal brothers. At the words "more money," Jerri's face brightened.

"Fine, we'll go. There's just one problem. We have no idea where to find this Master Wizard person. He can be anywhere in this massive city. We may know some areas, but you know how impossible it is to find anything in here."

Fredrick remembered all the times that he had been in Keedor. He retreated into these memories and thought of all the places he had seen. When he thought of the large tower that he had once seen on Tower Lane, he felt something flicker inside him. He couldn't ignore this feeling. "I think I know," Fredrick said before running off. Jerri ran after him.

"But how can—"

"Just follow me!" Fredrick called back. Jerri followed without asking more questions. He decided to no longer question his brother. Fredrick would always think of something smart to say to make Jerri agree with him.

Frederick found himself running on Tower Lane. He stopped in front of the tower. Nothing in Keedor had amazed him until now. The tower must have been the largest building in Keedor, but no one paid it any attention. It looked deserted.

Before either of them could speak, a man came running out of the shack behind them. "It is about time you two showed up. Here, take this. It is from the Master Wizard." The man rushed back inside. Fredrick held the piece of parchment in his hands.

"That was odd," Jerri said. Fredrick didn't answer. He unfolded the piece of parchment. It was a map of the city. A line was drawn from where they were to another spot on Tower Lane. It looked like an inn.

"It tells us where to find a job," Fredrick explained. He showed it to Fredrick.

You must work here until the time is right for you to embark on your journey to help those in need Never leave here to go to work anywhere else

"I don't know about this," Jerri warned. He knew what Fredrick was about to do. Fredrick didn't listen to him, and he ran off. Jerri ran after him. It was the only way that Fredrick could ever get Jerri to follow him. They were never apart and needed each other. Fredrick knew Jerri would follow whenever he ran off.

Following the Map

They finally found their way to the southern gate of Keedor. This time Michael was the one who asked for directions. The guards at the gates paid no attention to people who were leaving Keedor. They took one last look at the massive walls of Keedor before turning in the direction of their new journey.

Sure enough, just as Sheri had told him, there was a barn outside the southern wall. There was only one man tending to the horses. The wagons lay at the side of the barn. During his breakfast with Sheri, Michael had found out about this barn that took travelers to different parts of Kanavar. They didn't want to waste too much time traveling to the Living Woods, so they decided that they would take a wagon.

"Excuse me." Michael cleared his throat. The man turned his head. He was wearing overalls and a straw hat. He eyed the three children.

"May I help you?" he asked in his polite business voice.

"We need a ride to the Living Woods," Michael said.

"I will be able to take you there," the man scratched his beard, "in just a moment. I must wait for my partner to come back from the market so he can watch the barn while I'm gone."

"That's OK. We can wait a bit," Michael said. The three sat on a bench near the barn.

"How long is this guy going to take?" Steven complained after a few hours of waiting. "We've been sitting here forever." He got up and stretched his legs.

"You're always complaining," Julie reprimanded him. Steven looked down at the floor.

"Well, maybe if he would hurry up, I wouldn't have to complain," Steven shot back.

"Don't worry," the man said, overhearing their conversation. "My partner should be back soon. He only went to go fetch some horse food."

Steven groaned. "Yeah, well then why isn't he back yet?" He remembered when he had tended the horses back in the army. He'd hated it. He liked horses, but he hated being a stable boy. He hated the smell that got stuck to you for days. Working with horses wasn't the cleanest job either. He tapped his fingers against the bench impatiently.

Michael was engrossed in thoughts about the time he'd had with Sheri. He wondered if he would ever see her again. He hoped so. He knew that he loved her and thought that she loved him back. He wanted to run back to her and take her with him. But he didn't know where they were headed and what danger could be in their future. He didn't want to put her in any danger. The man from the other night had scared him. Why would someone want to kill three children? It only made him worry more about where they were headed.

He came out of his thoughts when a man, holding bags of horse food, came to the barn. He was talking with his partner. The man in the straw hat came to where they were sitting. "OK, guys, let's get going." He went in the barn and took out two horses and tied them to a wagon.

"Storms 'a coming," the man said. "We better get goin' before the storm hits. You guys can pay me when we get to the destination."

He was right. Michael could see gray clouds in the northeast heading their way. He didn't want to get stuck in the rain. It didn't rain much back in Periphia, and the thought of the last time it had rained didn't bring back good memories.

The man sat up in the front of the wagon, and the three took their seats in the back. The man scratched his beard again before they headed off.

Fredrick stood next to his brother in front of the inn. Fredrick looked at the map again.

"Yup," he said to Jerri. "This is the place."

Jerri looked at the small inn. It wasn't much, but it was on Tower Lane, so it probably got a lot of business.

"Well, let's go inside and see if we can get a job," Fredrick suggested. Jerri grunted his agreement. Fredrick opened the door and went inside. Jerri followed.

There was a young girl at the desk. Fredrick thought she looked somewhat attractive. But he was sure that she probably had a boyfriend.

"How may I help you two?" she asked. It sounded like she was a little depressed. It must not be a good day. She examined Fredrick closely with an almost hopeful face before returning to her depressed state.

"We need a job," Fredrick said confidently, "and we were wondering if perhaps we could work here." She looked exhausted. He was sure that she could use some help

"Well, I could use some help around here." She sounded desperate. "I guess I could afford to hire two workers. Yes, I will give you a job. When can you guys start?"

"Whenever you like," Fredrick answered. "The sooner, the better." They needed money now. They were both starving. They also needed a place to sleep. They would probably be allowed to sleep in the inn if they worked there.

"Great! You can begin right away and help me tend to the guests."

"What about the payment?" Jerri asked.

"Oh. Well, I guess I can let you live here in the inn. Also you can have free food from the dining area." She was giving them an offer like the army provided. No pay, but food and shelter. That was all they really needed, and that was all she could really afford at the time.

"We also need money," Jerri said flatly. He still wanted a better deal. If the army had paid them, he would have made sure that they found them. Money was the only thing keeping him from going back to working for Dalafar.

"Well, I have some horses that I can give you for the first payment. We'll worry about the rest afterward." She was sure that if she had more help, she would be able to take in more guests, especially at night, and get more money to pay them later. But right now all she had were the horses from Michael.

Jerri groaned. He hated horses. His stable boy work was the second thing keeping him away from the army. If they would give him any other job, he would do it.

Fredrick's face lit up. He remembered his favorite horse, Flash, and how he loved to take care of him. He and Flash had become great friends. That was the only thing he missed from the army. Maybe he could make a new friend. He loved horses, working and caring for them. It was sad to think that he might be a better friend with a horse than his twin.

"The horses are out back," she said as she led them past the dining and kitchen areas to the back of the inn. "Oh, and by the way, my name is Sheri."

"I'm Fredrick. And this is my brother, Jerri."

Behind the inn was a small area where they kept their garbage. It was dirty and smelly. The floor was sticky, and bugs flew in the air. Three horses were squished together with not much room to move. It was hardly the place where horses should be kept. Horses needed to be free to gallop.

Fredrick's eyes widened. "Flash!" he couldn't believe his old buddy Flash was standing right in front of him. He didn't care how he had gotten there, but he was there. He rubbed his eyes to make sure he wasn't seeing things. No, he knew Flash when he saw him. He rubbed the horse's back. Flash neighed excitedly.

"You know these horses?" Sheri asked, confused.

"Of course," Fredrick answered. "These horses used to be with Dalafar's army. We use to work there and—"

"Fredrick," Jerri warned as he nudged Fredrick in the side. He didn't want Fredrick to reveal too much about the army. That would be treason against Dalafar. And for some reason that Fredrick didn't understand, Jerri still liked Dalafar.

"Then you'll be happy to take them," Sheri said.

"You bet!" Fredrick said with a smile. Jerri sighed.

The man had been driving the horses hard to beat out the storm. The storm hadn't caught them in the past week and a half, but it was getting closer. Michael felt like the storm was following them. The Living Woods were now in sight. It was a good thing too. If they didn't reach the woods by tomorrow, the storm would surely catch them, and that would be a disaster. The horses wouldn't be able to travel in the storm, so they would have to travel on foot. It would take too long, and they would have no shelter from the storm until they reached the umbrella of trees. Michael expected that they would reach the woods by tomorrow.

He opened up a bag that was in the wagon. He took out three apples and handed two to Julie and Steven. The wagon ride came with free food. That was the first lucky thing that had come to them in the past few months. Michael didn't know if he had enough money left to buy some food. He hoped they would find some in the woods.

Soon night fell, and the three took their last sleep in the wagon. The next night they would probably be sleeping in the woods.

The galloping was heard throughout the woods in the night. The hooves came down hard on the ground. Animals scurried out of the way of the mighty creatures. They galloped to the edge of the woods. They noticed bodies lying in a clearing. They trotted closer. The two could see the three humans sleeping in the clearing.

One nodded to the other. The other nodded back and got the point. These two were beyond exchanging words to understand each other. They had been together for enough years to know each other's thoughts. They knew what they had to do. One of them put the older boy on his back, and the other took the other two humans. They galloped off the way from which they had come.

It was a prize that they had found the three here. They were just doing a scouting expedition to make sure they were safe when they had come across them. How lucky they were. One of them had been waiting for this all his life, and the time had finally come. Now he would put his plans into action. He grinned in the darkness as they galloped back to the center of the woods.

Steven woke up in a comfortable bed. He turned over on his side. He hadn't had such a good sleep since he was back at home in Periphia. He sat up, stretched his arms out, and let out a deep yawn. The three of them were in separate beds in a cozy room. They were in a wooden house. The only other thing in the room besides the beds was a fireplace that warmed up the room.

He got out of bed and walked around the room. He wondered why his mother hadn't come to wake them all up yet. Maybe it was a holiday or something. He decided to go back to bed.

He cleared his mind before going back to sleep. It was then that he realized that something was wrong. They didn't live in a house anymore. Where was he? He remembered that they had left Keedor in a wagon. They had paid the man and left him in front of the Living Woods. He then remembered that they had found a clearing and slept in it for the night. They were actually sleeping on the floor of the woods, not in cozy beds, no matter how much he wished that they were. The last thing that he remembered was hearing the sound of horses' hooves before he fell asleep.

Steven suddenly realized that he, his brother, and his sister were prisoners of the men who had been riding those horses last night.

He let out a gasp. This must be the house of his captors. But if they were prisoners, why would they be treated this way? As far as Steven knew, prisoners were usually sent to jail. And who would imprison three kids, anyway?

The door squeaked as someone's head peeked through a small opening. "You're up," the head whispered. "Good. Follow me, but don't wake the others yet."

Steven complied. He didn't want to anger his captor. That could only make things worse. He left the room. His jaw fell when he saw the creature before him. They hadn't been men riding horses at all. Standing in front of him was a centaur in all its glory.

Steven remembered when he was little and his mother use to tell him about all the creatures that lived in Kanavar. He had never seen any of them except the avengers. There were some in Dalafar's army and in Keedor, but there were no centaurs. Centaurs were marvelous creatures. They had the head and torso of a human and the body and legs of a horse. He could tell by the centaur in front of him that they were majestic creatures.

"I'm Ravanak," the centaur said. "I am the leader of the rebellion."

Steven just stood there gaping. The centaur was talking to him. It was like a dream. He was hardly paying attention to what the creature was saying. Then the words processed in his mind, and he was more in shock. The centaur was talking about being the leader of a rebellion. What was that supposed to mean?

"Surely you've heard of us." When Steven shook his head, the centaur went on. "I lead the rebellion against the evil tyrant, Dalafar. There are many others who have joined my cause in ending Dalafar's reign and bringing back peace to the land. I need your help. You and your siblings have something that can lead to our victory. I need you to join us so that we can defeat Dalafar and demolish his evil ways." Steven didn't know what to say. "I'm sorry if I threw everything on you so fast, but it's urgent, and I need an answer quickly."

Steven didn't answer for a while. The two of them stood there in silence. Ravanak stood patiently, waiting for an answer. Steven was still trying to understand everything Ravanak had said. This was too much for him. He wished that Michael and Julie were here. They would know what to do. They wouldn't be dumbstruck like he was. Then he reminded himself that he would never be like Michael unless he found his courage and dealt with this himself.

All right, he thought. He reviewed everything that had happened that morning. The centaur was the leader of a rebellion against Dalafar. That made sense. Being that Dalafar was evil, there was probably a group of people who wanted to stop him. This must be it. And Ravanak was the leader. That wasn't too hard to understand. The next part was that Ravanak was asking them to join the rebellion. Well, that wasn't Steven's decision. He had to talk about it with Michael and Julie. He knew Julie wouldn't trust the centaur, so he had to make that argument first.

"How do we know that you can be trusted?" Steven asked. Ravanak didn't answer at first. Instead he took Steven by the arm and pulled him away from the doorway. They were now in a room with one long wooden table with chairs around it. On the table was a piece of parchment.

It was the map.

Ravanak motioned for Steven to sit. Ravanak opened the map. He pointed to the first stop that the former Master Wizard had drawn for them to go to. "You are here now, in the center of the Living Woods. This is the city of Harvusera, where the rebellion lives. This is where you were supposed to go. You were meant to join us. You were coming here on your own anyway. I just hastened your journey. You would have asked me to join if I had never found you."

Now Steven knew Ravanak was telling the truth. It must be what their mother had wanted. She always used to tell them to fight for what was right and what they believed in. She had meant for them to ultimately reach the rebellion and make that their new home. Now the hard part would come. He had to convince Michael and even more so Julie.

"I believe you," Steven said.

"Good. Then will you join us?" Ravanak smiled.

"I will have to discuss this with my brother and sister first."

"I understand. Go and wake them. Let me know when you're done." The centaur spoke gently. He didn't seem like a captor.

"Join a rebellion!" Julie yelled out. Her face was turning red. "Are you mad?" Steven tried to quiet her down by gesturing to the door, indicating that the centaur was right outside. She turned to Michael. Michael was still pondering what Steven had told them. "You're actually thinking about this?" Julie was screaming at Michael now. She made an angry sigh. "How can you boys be so ignorant? We can't just believe this centaur, and even if what he says is one hundred percent true, we can't join a rebellion! That would be dangerous. We would probably get killed. What would Mom think of this?"

"Exactly," Michael interrupted. "What would Mom think of this? That's how you have to look at it. You're looking at this in the wrong way. Mom wanted us to go to the Master Wizard, who told us to come here. That means that Mom's ultimate desire was for us to join the rebellion."

Julie was speechless. There was no way to disprove Michael now. This is what their mother had wanted. They had to do it. It had been her last wish for them. They didn't know why, but they had to do it for her anyway.

"You're right," Julie finally admitted. "It's what Mom wanted all along. She must have known this would happen and had this all planned out for us to join the rebellion and help stop Dalafar."

They all knew it in their hearts to be true. There were always those hints of their mother telling them that Dalafar should be stopped and that everyone should fight for what was right.

"So should I tell Ravanak that we accept?" Steven asked.

"Yes," Michael replied. Steven smiled and left the room. Michael turned to Julie. "What you just said makes me wonder."

"Me too. It also makes me worry."

"It could be that she just had a backup plan. Let's not worry. Come on; we should go join Steven," Michael said to calm both of their nerves. But he knew better. He knew there was something more to it. He wished he knew what. Maybe if they continued with the rebellion, they'd find out the truth about what their mother's true intentions were and how she knew of the rebellion and the Master Wizard.

All this thinking of his mother's dying wish made Michael remember all the good times they had together and the love they shared. It put his mood down. He wished they could just go back to those times before the raid. Then Michael remembered the other love in his life. Sheri was a beautiful woman. He remembered their kiss. He would never be able to replace her in his heart. He promised himself that he would go back to her after this was all over. He only hoped that she felt the same way.

"We made our decision," Steven was saying. He was talking to the centaur. Michael looked up at the fascinating being before him. His horselike body was a radiant brown. He had strong muscles and broad shoulders. His long black hair swept down his horseback. He was a majestic creature. There were no other words to describe him. Michael guessed he was probably in his thirties, but it was hard to tell. He could've been seventy for all Michael knew. It could be that their life-span was different from humans. He definitely acted like a wise old man.

"What have you decided?" the centaur said in his strong, empowering voice. The centaur's eyes caused fear like arrows striking your heart, but they also held compassion.

Steven stepped back and let his older brother stand before the centaur to state their decision. Michael stepped before the centaur with courage he never knew was inside him. "My name is Michael from the humble village of Periphia." Michael wanted the introductions to be formal.

"I am Ravanak, leader of the rebellion against the evil tyrant, Dalafar. My people and I are here to bring peace back to the world and dispose of any tyranny that can harm the people of Kanavar. We ask you to join our rebellion in hope that it will lead to more humans joining us so that we can grow and be able to defeat Dalafar and thwart his evil plans. What is your answer?"

It was an inspiring speech. Even Julie couldn't say no now, especially with the tall centaur standing over her.

"We accept," the three said together.

A smile beamed on Ravanak's face. "It's good to hear it," he said, happy and excited. "We must get to work at once. There is no time for delays." The mood in the room changed. It went from formality to a warmer and friendlier atmosphere.

"So now what?" Michael asked.

Ravanak studied the three children. That was what was bothering him. They were only children. How could it be them? The evidence was inevitable. It had to be them. He remembered his meeting with the Master Wizard, almost twelve years ago, as if it were yesterday.

"It's your destiny, young centaur," the Master Wizard said.

"How will I accomplish such a difficult task?" Ravanak asked the old man standing before him. The Master Wizard had come to his home in Lanhoin to speak to him. He wanted Ravanak to go into hiding in the Living Woods and start a rebellion to one day fight against Dalafar. Ravanak didn't see how this was possible or how anybody would join. Why was he supposed to do it anyway? Why not someone else who was more suitable?

"For now just take centaurs and whoever else you are able to get, but there will be a time when you will need to grow as a rebellion to have a fighting chance."

"How?"

"One day three humans will be sent to you with a map. They will be the key to join all the creatures of Kanavar and perhaps even outside of Kanavar to fight against Dalafar. They will also help you obtain the necessary magic to be able to stop Dalafar." The Master Wizard strode out, and Ravanak never saw him again.

That was all the Master Wizard had to say. Since then Ravanak had gathered the centaurs and went to hide in the Living Woods. Together they had built the city of Harvusera. Later a clan of timen happened to stumble upon them, and when asked to join the rebellion, the timen immediately accepted the offer, explaining that they were just running away from Dalafar's wrath. When the time came that they were low on money and supplies, Ravanak took a trip to Lanhoin, where he recruited satyrs to join the rebellion. Now the three humans were here, and he knew what must be done.

"First we have to go to the other marked place on your map," Ravanak answered flatly, as if it were obvious.

How did you—" Ravanak pointed to a piece of parchment on the table. Michael walked over to get a closer look. He saw that it was the map.

"I have been looking for something for some time now. I know that Dalafar has been looking for it as well. My sources tell me that he knows of the location and is very close to it. Based on what I have found out, it's close to the location marked on your map. I believe the place marked on the map is the location we need to find." He didn't want to reveal too much to the humans.

"What exactly are you guys looking for?" Michael asked.

Ravanak lowered his voice. "It's a legendary cave that contains prophecies once said by the great wizards of old. Some consider them to be only legends, but others believe them to be true. No one has found the cave in centuries. There is one essential prophecy that Dalafar wants, and we need to see it in order to stop him."

"It's that important?" Julie asked. It was unbelievable that one little legend could be so important.

"Of course it is!" Ravanak continued. "It's an essential asset to the war. If we acquire the knowledge and power needed from this prophecy, we can win. If Dalafar acquires it, we will surely lose without a chance, and Dalafar will soon rule all of Charldena." Julie was silent. She still couldn't believe that a legend could decide the outcome of the world. "You know what? Let's go, and you'll see what I mean."

Ravanak motioned for them to follow him. He led them back to their bedroom. Against the back wall was a door. "Let's head out the back," Ravanak said. "I don't want the others to know about this until I'm sure about everything." He didn't want to tell the humans yet that there weren't many "others." It might turn them away. He needed them. Perhaps after they saw the legend, they would be more convinced and join regardless of how many members were in the rebellion.

"Wait here," Ravanak said when they were outside. All the children could see were trees and mountaintops in the far distance.

After a few minutes, Ravanak came back with three horses. Michael knew by now that Julie wasn't a fan of horses, but he and Steven had come to like them. After spending so much time with them as stable boys, there was no way that they couldn't like them. Julie hadn't gotten the hang of riding yet.

Steven mounted right away. Julie had a little trouble. Even though they had ridden horses before, when they went to Keedor, she still wasn't skilled with a horse like the other two. Michael mounted his horse.

"It's a few days' ride to the mountains," Ravanak said. "We can make it in two days if we ride fast."

The children agreed, but Julie wasn't so sure about riding fast. Michael gave her a "you'll do fine" look.

The forest was thick with trees. The horses that they had must have been trained to be able to ride in and out of the trees. Any normal horse wouldn't stand a chance. Michael could hear Julie gasping every time they almost hit a tree and the horses dodged it just in time. Ravanak kept reassuring her by explaining that the horses knew the way.

A deer ran in front of Julie. She screamed. The horse moved in time and missed the deer by inches. "This is crazy," Julie said. Steven laughed at her.

"I told you not to worry," Ravanak called back. He was riding even faster than the horses. "The horses know what they are doing.

They were trained well. They know the way." Julie wasn't so sure she could believe Ravanak about that. Steven laughed again.

They slowed their pace when it started to get dark. Ravanak urged them to keep going even though the sun was setting. "As long as the horses can see," he said, "we will be fine."

But when it finally got dark enough, they stopped and set up camp. "We are only one day away from the foot of the mountain," Ravanak said. "Our next stop will be there. From there it will take one day to climb. You will need your rest."

"I'm hungry," Steven groaned. Michael felt his stomach. It was empty. They hadn't eaten all day. Ravanak answered by taking out some fruits for them. Steven grinned and grabbed one first. The rest of them took them, and they all munched down on their food. When they were done, they took Ravanak's advice and went to sleep.

Dalafar smiled his evil grin. He knew that his puppet would pay off. "Are you sure?" He had to confirm that it was the truth. He would not waste his time. This would be a major step in his plans if it were true.

"Positive," his puppet answered. "I saw it myself. That was the marked spot. It must be what you're looking for."

"Excellent." Dalafar dismissed his puppet. His puppet proved to be very useful in a few different ways. Dalafar knew that there would be more use for him in the future. He would have to keep him alive for now.

Now he had to make arrangements for the trip. He had to get to the Urakian Mountains near the Living Woods. He had to get there before the pathetic rebellion. If he got the power he wanted, then he would surely take over not only Kanavar, but also all of Charldena.

He summoned his giants. He would take five giants and nothing else. It was all he needed. He had to travel quickly. There would be no time for an entourage on this trip. He would leave right away and get back before anyone knew that he left.

"*Maher*," Dalafar yelled out. He concentrated on his body as well as the five giants. The power surged through him. The magic flowed from him to the giants. He had performed this spell countless times before. It was a difficult and tricky spell that took a lot of power and strength, but he was a mighty magician. He was ready for the sudden speed that overcame him. He was running. The giants were running beside him. They raced out of the castle and turned west. They ran past Holechar and then down south. They were almost there.

It took only a few days for them to arrive at their destination. They didn't need to stop at all on their way. Dalafar loved that spell. It allowed him to attain a speed beyond imagination. But there was a side effect. Using that much power for such a long time left him immobile. He knew his giants would protect him as he lay there on the floor. He would be lying there for a few days before he could recover and regain his strength.

"I'm tired," Steven complained. The climb up the mountain was more difficult than anything they had done before. They'd had to leave the horses at the bottom. The mountain was very steep and narrow. Julie looked down and gulped. They were far up. Steven kicked a rock off the mountain. He couldn't see it hit the bottom.

"We'll take a rest stop," Ravanak suggested. As soon as he said that, they all plopped to the ground. It was hard and rocky, but they were too exhausted to care. Ravanak sat next to them. They only got to rest their legs for a few minutes before Ravanak urged them on again, explaining that they had to reach the top before nightfall or they would have to climb in the dark. That would be dangerous. The children agreed and followed him up.

They reached the top with the setting sun. None of them could go on any longer. Only Ravanak was still able to continue if he wanted. He was muscular and strong. He probably trained every day with the rebellion. "We'll spend the night here," Ravanak said when he saw their inability to continue. They didn't have the proper training yet like he did. But soon they would.

The children fell asleep without dinner. Ravanak stayed up for a few more hours. He studied the maze of caves that was in front of him. He frowned. It could take years to search the whole thing. And that was if he didn't get lost. He paced as he thought. He knew there must be a way to find the right path. He suspected that the children were the key to finding it, just as the Master Wizard had once told him. He finally lay down on the floor. With those thoughts, he drifted off to sleep.

The Cave of Legends

Ravanak was already up studying the map and the many caves in front of them. There were dozens of caves in the mountainside, and it was probable that there were dozens of caves within each cave.

Michael walked up to Ravanak. He stood beside him quietly. How would they be able to navigate through this maze?

"Do you have any ideas?" Ravanak said. Michael shook his head. He couldn't think of any way to find the right path. He wished the map from the Master Wizard was more specific.

Ravanak gave him the map. The map just had a marking on the area. It was not drawn to detail and didn't show all the caves. The map was useless for this. But it couldn't be. Why would the Master Wizard lead them only to a dead end and not take them all the way? Michael held the map tight and concentrated on his thoughts.

The map started to glow a yellowish color. Michael didn't know what was happening, but he couldn't let go. Ravanak was still staring at the caves.

"Aw, Ravanak…" Michael was getting nervous.

The map started to get hot. It was getting even hotter, to the point of burning. Ravanak turned to Michael and realized what was happening. He watched in silence.

Julie and Steven came over when they heard Michael scream from the pain of the heat. He could bear it no longer.

"Drop it!" Julie cried.

"I can't," he said. Steven ran back to where he'd left his pack and grabbed his water skin, made from the skin of a bull. By that time Michael was finally free and had dropped the map, but it continued to glow. It was bouncing up and down. Ravanak was watching the map. Michael looked at his hands. They were red with burns.

"These are only first-degree burns," Julie said, relieved. "They will heal. Just put some water on them."

Michael took the water from Steven and poured it on his hands. His face relaxed. "That feels better," Michael said. His hands were still a little numb, but he could tell that they would be back to normal soon. The map stopped bouncing and started jumping forward toward the caves.

"Let's follow it before it gets away," Ravanak said. Michael abandoned his concern for his hands when they started to run after the map. The map was moving fast. It went into one of the caves.

"Shouldn't we think it over?" Julie protested. "I mean, following a piece of parchment doesn't seem like a good idea. What if it gets us lost in these caves?" She tried to be reasonable, but Ravanak and the boys were already running after the map and ignoring her. They didn't have time to think about it. The map was moving without waiting for them, so they had no choice but to follow it.

The map headed down the cave. The cave was damp and dark. The only light came from the glowing map. They followed the light. They came to a fork, and the map went down the path on the right. There were many more forks and many more turns that the map made. If the map left them where it took them, there would be no way back.

Ravanak lost track of their turns. It would be impossible to get back if they got lost. Michael just hoped Julie wasn't right about following a piece of parchment.

They were getting tired. They couldn't stop and rest because the map kept on going. Steven slipped and almost fell, but Julie caught him from behind.

"Thanks," Steven said. "That was close."

As soon as they couldn't run any longer and were about to fall on their faces from exhaustion from following the map for hours, the map came to an abrupt halt before massive iron doors. The children all went down to the floor, panting. Ravanak was the only one who was composed enough to walk up to the iron doors. He tried to push the doors open, but they wouldn't budge.

"You can't open those doors," Julie said between breaths. "The combined strength of all of us can't open that. Look at the size of them."

Ravanak stopped trying to push. He pondered a moment. "You're right. These doors are too heavy. But perhaps Michael can do it. Just like the map started glowing in his hands. Maybe he can open the door."

Michael decided it was worth a shot. The Master Wizard had obviously caused the map to lead them here but only when Michael held it. The Master Wizard must have known that they would reach these doors and have given them a way to open it. He went to the doors and pushed with all his might. Nothing happened. He sighed. "No use."

The map stopped glowing and returned to its original form. Darkness filled the cave. If they couldn't get through the doors, there would be no way out. Michael felt around on the floor for the map. He found it and picked it up. A bright green light shone from the map, and it hit the doors. The doors shattered into millions of pieces that flew at them. One piece just missed scraping Julie's arm. This time the map's magic hadn't surprised them. But Julie was a little angry that the shattered door had almost hit her.

All of them, including Ravanak, took a few steps back. Light shone from the room inside. There was no source of the light. It felt like they were outside again, but the room was completely closed in. They shielded their eyes as they walked inside. They had to adjust to the new light. It was a large circular room. In fact the room seemed too large to fit in a cave. The room was filled with large boulders situated in circular patterns. There were carvings on each boulder. Most of the carvings were in a language that Michael didn't recognize, but there were some in their native tongue, Kanvric.

Ravanak kept on walking toward the middle of the cavern, passing many boulders on the way. He didn't pay attention or even turn his head to the boulders. Michael and Julie followed without question. Steven was behind them and was a little more curious than them. He glanced at some of the boulders that he could understand.

THE DYNASTY OF KING BRIN
WILL NEVER BE VANQUISHED

THERE IS AN UNDERWATER
COUNTRY BEYOND THE
BARRIER IN THE SEA

IF YOU ARE WISE
YOU WOULD HEED
ALL OF THESE LEGENDS

THERE IS GREAT POWER WITHIN THE DYNASTY OF KING BRIN

They stopped in the center of the cavern. There was a boulder in the center of all the others. It was a bit larger than most of the rest. Ravanak was studying it. Michael could tell that it was the one they were looking for. That was what the Master Wizard had wanted them to see. And their mother had wanted to them to see the Master Wizard, so this was indirectly what their mother wanted. He leaned forward to read it.

> THERE ONCE WAS A MOST POWERFUL
> SORCERER WHO WAS SO POWERFUL THAT
> HIS POWER WAS OVERWHELMING HIM
> UPON HIS DEATH HE TRANSFERRED
> ALL HIS POWER INTO TWELVE STONES
> THEN THE STONES SCATTERED THROUGHOUT
> THE CONTINENT IN HIDDEN PLACES AND
> THERE WAS A GUARDIAN CURSED BY THE
> SORCERER TO GUARD EACH STONE
> WHOEVER POSSESSES ALL TWELVE STONES
> WILL BRING CHAOS UPON THE WORLD
> AND WILL BECOME THE MOST POWERFUL RULER
> HOWEVER EVEN ONE STONE ALONE IS VERY POWERFUL
> FOR EACH STONE POSSESSES ITS OWN POWER

Michael, Julie, and Steven exchanged expressions of confusion. Ravanak didn't seem surprised. He must have known all this already or at least predicted it to be true. The children didn't know what to make of it.

"Just as I feared," Ravanak explained. "Dalafar is after the stones. He wants to gain the power to rule Charldena mercilessly. He will dominate everyone and everything. Once he gets all the stones, there will be no stopping him. That's what I need you guys for. I need you to help me find the stones before Dalafar does. We need to collect each one."

"What do you need us for?" Michael asked. He still didn't know the reason that they were involved in all this. Now he understood the importance of the stones, but the rest was still a mystery.

"You'll see," was all Ravanak answered.

Michael didn't know what joining a rebellion would be like, but he had somewhat of an idea. They would probably train and gather more allies and troops, eventually to have a war to defeat Dalafar and place a new ruler of Kanavar who would be just. He agreed with those ideas and wouldn't mind joining the rebellion to fight Dalafar, whose troops killed his mother, and their mother sent them here, so she wanted them to join the rebellion. But he never expected that a rebellion would have to travel to find some magical stones.

"Let's head back." Ravanak broke his train of thought. Julie agreed. To her this place was somewhat creepy. Michael knew that Steven would want to look around at the other boulders, but there was a countless amount of them. They couldn't stay here for hours. Then, suddenly, a loud rumbling sound came from one of the walls of the cave. Large rocks started to fall from the ceiling and the wall. The wall started to collapse.

Dalafar was awake. The aching was gone. He had made a full recovery, and he had only been asleep for two days. But he hated the long sleep and the feeling of powerlessness after he used that kind of magic. He vowed to himself never to make a trip like that again. Magicians always kept their vows. Like his pet had kept his vow.

His surroundings were blurry. His eyes had been closed for two days. Now the bright sun blinded him. His eyes needed to adjust. They adjusted quickly. The giants were standing in a circle surrounding him, just as they should be. His subjects obeyed him even when he was powerless, and they would have been able to kill him in an instant. He smiled his evil grin. It was one of his trademarks. He had learned to perfect it. It struck fear into the hearts of his enemies and his allies. That was why they all obeyed him. Except for that filthy rebellion, but he would soon take care of them. Once he collected the power he needed, no one would dare to question him.

There was emptiness in his stomach. He hadn't eaten in a week. His body was trained to handle that, but he wouldn't be able to climb the mountain without food. He turned to the giants. "Fetch me food and water," he ordered.

The giants were startled. They hadn't realized he had gotten up. One of the giants ran off into the forest to fetch fruits and water. Dalafar sat there waiting. He went into his meditating stance and began to fall into a deep trance. He always did this to calm his nerves. Anytime before a big event, he would meditate. It focused his power. Time didn't matter in mediation. It could've been a few hours or a few days when he opened his eyes and saw the giant standing in front of him, holding a handful of fruit and a jug of water.

Dalafar took a piece of fruit and ate it. He took the jug and gulped down half of it. He finished the fruit and then the water. He was satisfied for the time being. It was time to find what he was looking for. He remembered when he'd first found out about the legend of the twelve stones. It was about twenty years ago. That was when he'd put his plan into action. All of his research had paid off. He'd found it. Now was the end of one plan, but the beginning of something new. He would have to find all the stones.

He started to climb. The giants came after him. Just a few more years of using his resources, as he liked to call them, to find the stones, and he would soon rule the world.

There was no time to search all the caves. With a nod of his head, the giants took their giant metal spiked clubs and started to smash the walls of the caves. They kept on smashing. Dalafar knew they would only stop at his command. He was searching every cave that came crashing down for the cave of legends. He knew he would be able to tell when he found it. It would be different from all the rest.

The giants hit a wall. It didn't break at first contact. It had to be the one. It was a stronger wall than in the rest of the caves. They hit again. The wall started to crumble down. They kept going. Rocks were falling from above. The wall finally broke. The giants were blocking the way, so Dalafar couldn't see what was inside.

"Move, you big oafs," he growled. The giants made room for him to walk between them. They were terrified of him. That was just the way he liked it.

Dalafar walked past the giants. It was here. He had finally found the cave of legends. It was magnificent. There were thousands of prophecies in there. Dalafar thought most of them to be nonsense. But there was one that he knew to be true: the one he was looking for. He strode past all the other boulders to the one in the middle, the one that really mattered. The legend of the twelve stones was finally found. He read it a few times. The words sank into his mind. He memorized it. He had found what he was looking for, and it was time to go.

He turned around, and his glance passed over to the other side of the room. The ones who were hiding there weren't sure if he saw them. When he walked away, they assumed he hadn't seen them. But he saw all. He smiled as he walked out of the cave, the giants following.

It was time to go home and make preparations for the next step of his plan.

"That was as close as it gets," Julie said as they got up from their cramped hiding positions. As they went on in their journey, they got into more and more dangerous situations where the risk of getting caught and killed grew.

Ravanak was frowning. "Dalafar has seen the prophecy now also. We have to move fast to gather the stones before him." Ravanak was on a fast pace. He never wanted to waste time. Michael liked that characteristic. It was just like Mr. Mim.

The hand on her shoulder stopped Julie from walking. "We can't leave yet," Ravanak said. "Dalafar just left. We don't want to run into him. Let's wait a little, and then we'll go out using the same exit as he did. That way we won't get lost by going back into the maze of caves."

Julie couldn't just sit still. She started to walk around, looking at the boulders. Most of them were in some ancient language. She found one that was in their language.

THE CONTINENT WILL ONCE AGAIN
BE AS IT WAS IN THE DAYS
OF KING BRIN

Why were these legends always in riddles? Julie wondered. *How was the continent different in the time of King Brin?* Before she could finish her thoughts, Ravanak called her. It was time to go. They left the way that Dalafar had.

The Rebellion

It was another few days until they got back to Ravanak's house. Michael was getting excited. He wanted to see what the rebellion was made of. There were probably tons of other creatures that he would be able to see.

"Welcome to the city of Harvusera," Ravanak said when they walked out the front door of his house. Michel frowned. It was way below his expectations. It was a large city. Nobody would believe that such a city could exist inside a forest, but it was mostly unpopulated. He saw houses that were identical to Ravanak's, and centaurs were walking around and training.

Ravanak saw them frowning. "I didn't tell you the whole truth," he admitted. "Let me explain. As you can tell, the dominant species in the rebellion are centaurs. When I first started the rebellion, the centaurs willingly joined me. They knew who I was and knew I was trustworthy. All the centaurs are against Dalafar. Many of them came here to live in Harvusera and train for battle when necessary. The others still live in Airm. They will join us when we need them.

"Most other creatures don't want to join. The elves don't want to get involved. They want to stay isolated in their forest. Their leader is arrogant and wants no part in our world. He believes his people to be better than us and believes he does not need to get involved in our inferior affairs. The elves of old are gone. They are no longer graceful as they used to be.

"Some of the dwarves are on Dalafar's side. The others don't want to fight against their brethren clans, so they choose to stay neutral. The malicious creatures like trolls, Minotaur, and goblins that live in the northern Urakian Mountains are with Dalafar.

"The avengers and giants all work for Dalafar, as you probably know. They all live in the city right outside Castle Dalafar, Yoteran. There are also timen in Yoteran. Most of them are with Dalafar. We do, however, have one clan of them with us here in Harvusera who are opposed to Dalafar. Come and I'll introduce them."

The centaurs turned to the humans in surprise when they saw them, but they didn't refrain from their work. Michael thought about how cool it was that he was now in the middle of a bunch of centaurs. They were amazing creatures.

"Nice to see that you are back, Ravanak." A centaur with long brown hair trotted over to them. He was almost as strong as Ravanak.

"This is my right-hand man, Kojmeer." Ravanak introduced the centaur.

"Greetings," Kojmeer said. "We are happy to have you join us. I will see you around, but right now I have work to do." He left them just as fast as he had come.

"Let's move on," Ravanak said. Michael was anxious about going to see timen. He had heard about the little people but never seen one. He had never even dreamed of seeing such rare creatures.

Ravanak led them past all the houses. They were now in an open grass area. There was nothing here. Michael couldn't see any timen anywhere. He squinted to try and see if he could glimpse any of them in the grass. Ravanak kept walking, so they followed. He stopped a few feet from the center of the grassland.

A tiny speck jumped out of the small mound in the middle of the grassland. The speck came running toward them. As it got closer, Michael could see that "it" was a she. A female timen was soon standing in front of them. She only reached about Michael's ankle. Her beautiful red hair almost reached the floor.

"Hi, I'm—"

"I'm Rumin." A male timen interrupted her. He had sleek black hair. The timen's hair was the only feature that Michael could really see. It stuck out. The rest of his body was too small to see clearly. "I lead the clan of timen here. I will be the first of the timen to welcome you to the rebellion. I look forward to working with you. This is my secondary, Barki."

"Hello," Barki said. "It's a pleasure to meet you. We can use all the help we can get." She gave a warm smile that reminded Michael of his mother. Just like every other time he thought about his lost mother, he thought about his lost love, Sheri. He again promised himself to return to her.

"Come, Barki," Rumin said. "We have important work to do. We can't waste too much time."

Barki followed him back into the ground. Everyone seemed busy. Being in a rebellion must be busy work. Michael knew that their time would come to be busy as well. They would soon have to train and work like everyone else.

"Why do they live underground?" Julie asked.

"Timen have always lived underground to protect themselves from the outside world," Ravanak answered. "I asked them to build small houses above ground to live in since there is no danger here. Rumin told me that his people are used to living underground and don't want to change their ways. They keep to their customs."

"That's all that are in the rebellion?" Michael asked. There had to be more. Otherwise it was hardly a rebellion. All they had seen so far were centaurs. And timen didn't account for much. Michael thought them to be too small to do anything.

"There are also the satyrs. Most of the satyrs are on our side. Some of them have come to live here. Many of them still live in Lanhoin. The satyrs are merchants. They help us with supplies and weapons. They send them to us from Lanhoin. The satyrs that do not wish to risk their businesses by joining us remain neutral. Although I do believe that when the time comes for the final battle, they will help. Let me show you the ones we have here."

They walked past the grassland. Instead of cabins like the centaurs lived in, the satyrs had huts. The half-man, half-goat creatures walking around were almost as amazing as the centaurs.

As the day went on, Michael saw more creatures than he had ever seen in his life. He had no doubt that their future adventures would bring more. The satyrs looked very busy. They were working harder than any of the others that they saw before.

One satyr came up to them. "How are you faring these days, Ravanak?" the satyr asked. The satyr's brown hair brought out his brown eyes.

"Better than most, my friend," Ravanak answered. "I'd like to introduce our newest members and creatures of the rebellion."

"How good to meet you young fellows," the satyr said. "I'm Avram. I was chosen to lead the satyrs here in Harvusera. I will see you later then. I must be getting back to work." He rushed off.

"The satyrs are always working. They are busy folk," Ravanak said. "Avram's family is in Lanhoin. They are our largest supplier. Without them we would be nothing."

"There are no humans in the rebellion?" Michael asked.

"Now there are three," Ravanak answered. "Humans are very hard to convince. They don't like much of the other creatures. They don't want to join in with them. They also do not want to get involved. Some may want to put up a fight but don't have the courage to. I hope that one day the humans will join because I know they despise Dalafar as much as anyone. Hopefully with you starting the movement, more humans will come to join us.

"I believe we all had a long day. A lot was just thrust upon you three. You must have a lot to think about. We should be getting back to the house. You need to sleep. Tomorrow is going to be a busy day. You will start your training."

He turned around to go back. Before he started walking, he turned back to them. "I almost forgot something very important. Follow me. You must see this before we end the day."

They hurried after him. He was trotting now. The three jogged to keep up. Past all the huts was another grassland. This one was not empty like the other one. The three children froze as Ravanak rode on to what lay in the center. The ferocious beast had dark green scales. It had two sharp horns on its head and talons running along its back from its head to the end of its tail. Its white claws were sharp enough to slice a large animal with one swipe.

The dragon turned its head in their direction. When it saw them, it got up. Michael saw its light green belly. It opened its mouth and let out a loud growl. The three children jumped in fear of the mighty creature. Its large teeth frightened them further. It was the most breathtaking thing that they had ever seen in their lives.

"Darkon," Ravanak said in a warning voice.

The dragon let out a small growl that sounded like a laugh. "I was just playing with the humans." The dragon had a deep voice that suited his looks. He laughed again.

"This is Darkon." Ravanak introduced the dragon. "The dragons are all neutral except two of them. One is this one. Back in the time of King Brin, one dragon pledged his life and the lives of his descendants to serve Brin and his descendants. Darkon is from that family. He keeps his pledge till this day. The other one who took a side is Darkon's father. Darkon's farther used to serve King Lucent. When Dalafar took over, he changed sides to serve Dalafar."

"I will slay the traitor," Darkon said in a furious voice. A blast of green fire shot out from his mouth into the sky. He roared. The children took a few steps back. Ravanak held his ground. It must have been hard for him. His father had betrayed him, and now they must fight each other.

Michael's eyes were wide open. He couldn't take his eyes off the dragon to see that Julie and Steven were also staring. Ravanak tried to talk to them. Michael wasn't paying attention to what he was saying. Finally he tuned back in to the world.

"Well," Ravanak was saying, "we better get going. You three need your sleep for tomorrow. We have a lot of work ahead of us."

Michael's blade hit the ground. He thought he had some sword skills, but the centaur he was training with had showed him otherwise. He would be no use in a battle. He realized that Mr. Mim had taught only the techniques for a beginner; he had a lot to learn. He had been training for hours with the centaur. It was getting tiring, but he wouldn't give up. He knew he could do it.

He charged at the centaur again. The centaur quickly moved out of the way, and again Michael's sword hit the ground. "You must anticipate your opponent's moves if you are ever to make contact with him," the centaur repeated.

Michael was about to charge again when he saw Kojmeer walking toward him. He sheathed his sword.

"It is time for a break from physical combat," Kojmeer said. Michael smiled. "There is also an element of mental training for a battle. I must talk with you and your siblings before you do anything else." That didn't sound good.

He followed Kojmeer to his house. Julie and Steven were already sitting around the table. By the looks on their faces, he could tell that their training hadn't gone too well either.

Julie was training with a bow and arrow, not wanting to get directly involved in any battle. Ravanak had given her a golden bow. He said that the bow had belonged to his mother. It had been carved by elves who had given it to Ravanak's mother for performing a great deed for them. He said that she had never told him what the great deed was.

As always, Steven was the opposite of Julie. As soon as he had seen a mace, he'd wanted to use it. Michael remembered the smile on Steven's face when Ravanak had handed him the mace. Ravanak had told Steven that it would take a lot of training to master the mace, but Steven was determined. Michael guessed it hadn't gone so well. Michael thought it would take Steven time just to learn how to hold the large weapon.

"Now that you are all here," Kojmeer started, "let's begin your lesson. You may not like what you are going to hear, but it is necessary that you hear it now before you actually have to fight." Michael didn't know what he was talking about. "Ravanak told me the story of what happened to you in the past. I know you have seen people killed. Obviously you were devastated by the sight. Now listen to this. It's very important. However, now that you are part of the rebellion, I am sure you know that you will have to take part in a battle and fight the enemy whenever needed. I know that this comes as an obvious statement, but I don't think you realize the magnitude of this idea. You will have to kill. You will have to perform the act that you deemed to be monstrous. You must become those monsters. If you ever hesitate, then you will be killed. There will be no time to think of this matter during battle. The time is now.

"Decide whether you have what it takes or not to take a life because, trust me, you will have to if you stay with the rebellion. Before you start any training, you must figure this out first. If it helps, you can think of something you are fighting for that will be more important than the enemy's life. That can help to take the life away if you must to reach that goal. That's all that I can tell you. I just want you to take the rest of the day to think about this. If you think you are ready, then tomorrow you can resume your training."

Kojmeer left. The children sat in silence as they thought about what he had just told them. They would have to become the murderers that they hated. But it wouldn't be murder anymore. It couldn't be because otherwise they wouldn't do it.

Michael tried to think of everything that he was fighting for. He was fighting for Kanavar, freedom, his mother, Sheri, Julie, and Steven. The latter three were the reasons that he would be able to take a life. He looked at Julie and Steven. They looked back at him. The bond between them had grown even stronger in the past few months. They were closer than ever. He knew that he would be able to cut down anyone who was in his way if it meant saving them. They felt the same way as him. He could see it in their eyes.

That was what they would be fighting. That would be the reason that they would be able to kill: for each other.

The sound of an alarm woke the three up. Loud horns could be heard throughout the city. They jumped out of bed, startled.

The three children were barely dressed when Kojmeer came into their room. "Hurry. We are being ambushed. Grab your weapons and be at the ready."

Michael grabbed his sword and ran outside. The others followed. It had already been a few weeks since they joined the rebellion. Ravanak was coming up at dead end after dead end trying to find the whereabouts of the stones. In the meantime, they had been training. Each of them was a lot better than when they had first started. They were now skilled enough in both the mind and the body to be in an actual battle.

They were surprised what they saw when they came out the door. Satyrs, centaurs, and timen were all ready for battle. Michael wondered what timen could possibly do in a battle.

The rebellion was very organized. Everybody was ready at any moment for battle. They were all walking to strategic positions or standing in place silently. Michael, Julie, and Steven stood next to Kojmeer. He was ready with his bow drawn and arrow strung. Julie did the same. Michael unsheathed his sword. The gleaming green blade sparkled as it sliced through the air. The golden hilt shone like the sun's rays. Michael took a glance at the scabbard on his side. It was as green as the blade itself. Steven got his mace in position to attack.

"You three are eager," Kojmeer joked. "A dwarf clan has surrounded us. We don't know why they sent their army to attack us.

Until now they were neutral and we even believed that they would join us. Only time will tell what they are doing here, but we must prepare for the worst." He looked straight ahead, eyes focused on what was to come. Michael followed Kojmeer's gaze. He could see the courage in Kojmeer's eyes. Watching the mighty centaur gave Michael a newfound courage. He was ready for the battle.

Michael tried to focus. He tuned out the noise around him: the shouts, preparations, and other battle sounds. It was only him and whatever lay ahead. He didn't turn to see what Julie and Steven were doing. He assumed they were doing the same as he was. He was ready. He tightened his grip.

They saw two figures running. The figures were getting closer. Michael thought this meant that the battle had begun. These must be the first of the dwarves running at them. Michael got ready to charge.

"Don't attack!" Ravanak screamed as he galloped toward them. "Stop! They mean no harm." Michael lowered his sword, but there was still tension in the air.

Michael could see a dwarf running behind Ravanak, trying to keep up with him. The dwarf barely reached Ravanak's waist. It looked like the dwarf was almost tripping on his long red beard. Michael could see that the dwarf wasn't wearing any armor and his battle-ax was safely behind his back. He wasn't prepared for battle. But he did have a muscular chest and would be able to pull the ax out at any given moment.

"I am calling an emergency meeting," Ravanak announced when he and the dwarf reached Kojmeer. "Everyone lower your weapons and let the dwarves enter the city, but be cautious until I give the final orders."

Michael watched the members of the rebellion put their weapons away and escort the dwarves into one of the unpopulated areas of the city.

"You three come with us," Ravanak told them. Michael, Julie, and Steven followed Ravanak, Kojmeer, the dwarf, Avram, Rumin, and Barki into Ravanak's house.

Ravanak took his place at the head of the table. The dwarf went to his left. Ravanak motioned to the three of them to take a place on his right. Kojmeer went next to the dwarf. Avram stood next to Kojmeer. Rumin and Barki climbed up and stood on the table.

"The meeting is now in session," Ravanak said in a serious voice. "I have called this meeting for a great importance. This dwarf standing next to me, Jabertormitch, came from the city of Rekadon. He will tell his story."

Jabertormitch cleared his throat. "I am General Jabertormitch from Rekadon. My dwarves and I are from the clan Ish Ketanim. Our chief, Katensthiv, remains in the city with the rest of our clan. We and the other dwarf clans had made a pact that we wouldn't take sides in this war. We decided that we wouldn't fight each other. But just a few weeks ago, our brethren came with their army and threatened us that we must join Dalafar. They caught us off guard. We thought they may be supporters of Dalafar, but we never thought they would go this far.

"Our clan was the only dwarf clan who knew where the rebellion was located, being that my chief is on good terms with Ravanak. They threatened us and said that we must come and attack you to prove our loyalty to Dalafar and they would leave us alone. As soon as the army and I were sent to come here, the other dwarf clans left our city alone.

"My chief had a private meeting with me before we left to come here. He said that he always believed in what the rebellion stood for, but he didn't want to cause wars with the other clans, so he didn't take a side. Now that they were willing to fight us, he has decided to support the rebellion. He sent the army as Dalafar wished, though it wasn't to fight the rebellion. He sent us to help you. We wish to join you."

Rumin laughed out loud. Everyone turned to him. "You expect us to believe that sob story. You come here with a whole dwarf army claiming to want to help us. You could just be waiting for reinforcements. How do we know that you are telling the truth? Dalafar is half dwarf. I would think that all the dwarves wish to be on his side." He let out a loud grunt.

"I for one happen to believe them," Ravanak said. "I talked with the chief of Ish Ketanim back when I was first starting the rebellion. I do believe he is sincere when he says he wants to join. It always sounded like he wanted to join. I knew he wouldn't do it because he would never go against his brethren."

"Exactly," Rumin said. "They would never go against their brethren, even if it means joining Dalafar and fighting us."

Michael could tell that this argument could go on forever. They would both keep arguing their points. There was no real way for the dwarves to prove their loyalty yet. Trust only came with time. For now they would have to decide whether to let the dwarves stay and hope that they chose correctly. The truth would only be revealed later.

Ravanak was about to answer when Avram spoke up. "Jabertormitch is not lying. He is telling the truth. Being trained since a mere child as a businessman and merchant, I was trained to be able to tell when someone is lying and bluffing or telling the truth. I could tell that he's telling the complete truth."

"And we are going to trust our lives on your hunch?" Rumin was unconvinced.

Ravanak was going to answer again when Michael answered for him. "Yes." It was as simple as that. "We can keep arguing or we can trust him. Let him help us and get on with our plans. How did

Ravanak first come to trust you? Obviously trust has to be earned, but you have to start somewhere. Otherwise you would trust no one and the rebellion would never take off."

"Such wise words from such a young mouth," Avram said.

"Michael's right," Ravanak said. "We have to trust him. We need more creatures for the rebellion, and we can't just sit here and keep arguing. We have to work on getting the stones. There is no more time to waste. This is of absolute importance. If Dalafar gets the stones, then we are all doomed. It's time to act."

"Yes. That is our first priority," Kojmeer added.

"What's all this about stones?" Jabertormitch asked.

The Three Questions

I t was another week before all the dwarves settled in. They built stone houses near the satyrs' huts. They wanted to remind themselves of their home in the mountains, so they used stones and rocks for their houses. Dwarves had a special bond with the earth. They always liked to be as close to it as possible.

Michael continued his training during that week. He realized that there were always improvements that could be made to his fighting techniques.

Ravanak knew it was time for another meeting. He would gather all the leaders of the rebellion and brainstorm to see if anyone had any ideas about the stones. Dalafar was probably getting closer to them every day while they were doing nothing. Time was running out. He knew the children would be able to help. It was just like the Master Wizard had told him. They had already helped with the growth of the rebellion. In the short time that they had been in the rebellion, a whole dwarf clan had joined. The children were definitely something special. The only thing left was to figure out how they could help regarding the stones.

The meeting consisted of the same members as the last time. He was proud of his choice of the leaders for the rebellion. They were strong in heart, mind, and body. The only one that he wasn't so sure about was Rumin, but he had been the clan leader of the timen when they first arrived, and Ravanak was not about to take that away, so he appointed Barki as his assistant.

Ravanak took his place at the head of the table. They were chatting among themselves. He always had to ask for quiet before a meeting started. The noise didn't bother him. The fact that different creatures were talking to each other actually made him excited. They needed to get along in order to fight Dalafar. Ravanak's dream was to unite all the creatures. This was just a small step. He let them talk for a few minutes.

"The meeting is now in session," he finally said. Everyone stopped talking and turned to him. "As you all know, our first priority now is to find the stones. We need a place to start looking for them. Any clue at all would help. It could be anything to do with ancient magic. Anyone have any ideas?"

No one said a word. He didn't really expect anyone to think of an idea. The stones could be anywhere in Charldena. He only hoped that Dalafar was having just as much trouble. The legend didn't indicate where to start the stone hunt. They needed a clue from another source. He was hoping that one of the creatures would have something or know of something that might help.

Ravanak glanced around the room. Kojmeer was deep in thought. He was rubbing his chin. Ravanak could hardly make out the small beard of a few hairs that hung from Kojmeer's face. Jabertormitch seemed to be thinking, but Ravanak couldn't be sure what he was thinking about. He didn't think that Jabertormitch believed in magic that much, but it was possible. Ravanak always suspected that dwarves had some magic in them, even though they would never admit it.

Rumin's blank expression never left his face. Barki's usual smile had turned into a frown. Avram looked confused. He was staring at the ceiling. Julie wasn't even giving it much thought. She sat there idly swinging her feet back and forth. Ravanak knew that the children probably never came across anything that had to do with magic. But he trusted the Master Wizard and knew they would help somehow. He just hoped it was sooner rather than later.

Ravanak turned to the little boy. Steven was looking around the room. His face lit up whenever they mentioned magic. Ravanak didn't know how he was still so amazed by all the different creatures. The children had already been in the rebellion for weeks.

Michael was continuously flipping over the map from the Master Wizard. Ravanak had looked at the map and hadn't seen any clues on it. He was hoping that the Master Wizard had left some indication of where to start, but there was none. He wished that he could go to the Master Wizard now and ask for help, but he saw the sky go black. He knew the Master Wizard was dead. Ravanak didn't know if he could trust the new one. Even if he could be trusted, he might not know anything about the stones. It was too risky and time consuming to go to the Master Wizard. Although there was still the possibility that the old Master Wizard had given his apprentice a clue before he died. If that was the case, then they had to go. Maybe that should be their next move.

Michael stopped flipping over the map. He was staring at the back of the map. Ravanak saw Michael's forehead wrinkle up. He was concentrating on something. Ravanak walked over and stood behind Michael but saw nothing on the map.

"Roe et chabe!" Michael suddenly said in a loud, clear, and slow voice that sounded like he was chanting a spell. Everyone turned to him. He looked just as confused as the rest of them, if not more.

Ravanak pointed to the map. "Look," he said. Words started to form on the parchment.

"Umm…what just happened?" Michael asked.

"We should be asking you the same thing," Rumin said.

Michael turned his head to Ravanak, who was still standing behind him. Ravanak looked over Michael's shoulder at the map. Three sentences were forming. Ravanak knew what Michael had done. He had only heard those types of words a few times before. But there was no mistaking them. The question was how had Michael done it? He saw Michael's confused face.

"You performed a magic spell." Jabertormitch grunted. Rumin was glaring at Michael.

"But I don't know magic. I don't even know why I said that. I don't know what I was doing. It couldn't possibly have been magic, could it?" Michael sounded like a confused child.

"I'm afraid it was, my boy," Ravanak answered. "I know magic when I hear it." Julie and Steven were looking at Michael, surprised. "I will try to explain as best as I can. Magic is usually inherent, as far as I know. But the elves know the most about magic. Perhaps one day we will find out the truth, but for now the only way I can explain is that your father must have been able to do magic."

"Cool," Steven exclaimed.

Ravanak smiled. "Let's leave that alone for now." Michael's face was still confused. He frowned but let it go. Ravanak thought Steven would speak up, or maybe even Julie, but they both stayed quiet. They seemed to have a silent communication with Michael. They knew he didn't want them to say anything. "Let's take a look at the map." The words stopped. There were three questions on the back of the map.

WHERE IS THE PLACE THAT IS ISOLATED?
WHERE IS THE PLACE THAT IS THE BOTTOM OF THE TALL?
WHERE IS THE PLACE THAT IS NOW LIKE SABERIMA?

"Very interesting," Ravanak said. "Perhaps this is the clue we've been looking for." Ravanak was getting excited. The children were the key. He silently thanked the Master Wizard. "Here. Pass it around. Everyone have a look."

Michael passed the map to Julie. Ravanak kept talking as the map was passed around. "We have to answer the questions. Hopefully the answers will give us a clue to where the stones are."

Ravanak thought about the first question. *An isolated place.* He tried to think of all the places that he thought to be isolated from the rest of the world. He watched as everyone returned to his or her thinking pose. But Barki didn't return to her frown. She rarely did.

Ravanak gave everyone a few minutes to think about the first question. "Let's see what we got," he said when most of them seemed ready.

"Well, certainly all the cities and villages in the Urakian Mountains are isolated from the rest of the world," Jabertormitch said.

"The islands that include the Gazh Isles and Icicle Island are isolated by water," Avram said.

"Also, the elves are isolated in Tudanosti Forest," Kojmeer added.

"I think that's all of the isolated places," Ravanak said, looking at the map. They pinpointed each place. They needed to narrow down the choices. Maybe each question was a follow-up to the one before. Now they were ready for the second question.

"Where is the place that is the bottom of the tall? Let's think of it this way," Ravanak said. "The mountains on the islands and in the Urakian Mountains and the trees in the forest are the tall. Now we have to figure out what the bottom means."

Ravanak passed around the map for everyone to see. He knew that one of them would have an idea. He had chosen the brightest of creatures to be the leaders, and he knew the humans would be of great help.

"How about the bottom of the map?" Steven suggested.

"That could work," Kojmeer said. "It would mean the most southern cities."

"That would include," Avram said, "Icicle Island, Rekadon, and whatever city is the most south of Tudanosti Forest."

Michael looked at the map. "It's Paliar."

"Excuse me?" Rumin said.

"I said Paliar is the city in the most south of Tudanosti Forest."

"How would you know? Nobody knows the location of the elves' cities. They are hidden."

"It's on the map."

"It's not on any map."

Instead of arguing further, Michael passed the map to Rumin. The location of all the elf cities were named and placed.

"How can this be?" Rumin said, studying the map as if he were memorizing it.

"They got the map form the Master Wizard," Barki said. "Obviously he knows where the cities are and placed them on the map."

"That's important," Ravanak said. "We can't let this fall into the wrong hands. Otherwise things won't turn out so well for the elves or for us. Let's move on. The next question should reveal the place." He was rushing them. This meeting wasn't for talking about magic or elf cities. Their most essential mission now was to find the stones before Dalafar. That was what they had to focus on. They couldn't be sidetracked. "Where is the place that is now like Saberima? What could that mean, it's now like Saberima?"

"Julie?" Michael inclined his head toward her. Michael knew that their mother used to teach Julie the history of each of the countries. She focused a lot on Saberima. Michael had never thought it would come in handy.

"How would she know?" Rumin asked curiously. Rumin was very skeptical about the children and the stones. Ravanak didn't like his attitude, but he was entitled to his questions. At least his questions always brought out the truth.

"My mother used to teach her the history of all the countries, especially Saberima," Michael answered. "Julie, how is Saberima different from anywhere else?"

Julie looked nervous when everyone turned to her. "The only thing I can think of," she said, "is that Saberima once had a civil war and was split to North Saberima and South Saberima. They each have their own views. The north is run by women, while the south is run by men. The north has a monotheistic religion, while the south is polytheistic. There was constant fighting over these views until the split finally happened. That's all I got."

"That should be enough information," Kojmeer said. "However, there is still one question that remains. Why does it say 'now?' This place was not always like Saberima? The question must mean that only recently this place has the characteristics of Saberima."

"I think I understand," Jabertormitch said. "The only place out of the three that has a type of civil war is Rekadon. Like I told you last week. We just recently started to fight, and now we will soon split when they learn the truth about why we were sent here. There will be more fighting in Rekadon about whose side the dwarves should follow, and eventually we will separate. It has to be Reka-don."

"That makes sense," Ravanak said. "I say we give it a shot. It's the only lead we got." He smiled. It was the first lead he'd had since the children arrived and they went to the cave of legends.

"I don't really think there are any magic stones in Rekadon," Jabertormitch said, "but I'd love to get back home. I'd be happy to lead you there. When do you wish to go?"

"As soon as possible. How about tomorrow? We can get our things ready today, and we will all head to Rekadon tomorrow morning." Ravanak was still rushing them. Now that they knew where to begin their search for the stone, they had to get going right away. Dalafar might have found out about Rekadon. He had followers there. There could be trouble. The sooner they did this, the better.

"Sounds good to me," Jabertormitch said.

"Kojmeer," Ravanak said.

"Yes," Kojmeer answered.

"I will need you to stay here to lead the rebellion while the others and I are gone. It might be years. We might end up searching for all twelve stones before we come back. I know you can handle it. This task may be as important as ours. The rebellion must be in top shape when the time comes to fight Dalafar. I now put you in charge of making that happen."

"I understand," Kojmeer answered. "I will do my best. I do believe that you would do a better job at it, but I understand you are needed elsewhere. I will make sure the rebellion continues its training and make sure all the necessary supplies are acquired. The rebellion will be ready when you return."

"Thank you, my brother. I knew I could count on you." Ravanak knew his younger brother would always have his back. They were close. They had never been separated since the day they were born. When Ravanak first told of his plans to start a rebellion, Kojmeer was the first to stand by his side. Kojmeer had been by his side ever since.

"Meeting adjourned," Ravanak announced, ending one of the longest meetings that the rebellion had ever had. It was probably also the most important. Ravanak smiled. After all these years, three children had come and brought him the biggest lead he'd ever had, and to add to that, a dwarf clan had joined them. The children were really something special. Perhaps with their help, the rebellion would one day defeat Dalafar and restore peace to the land.

Journey to Rekadon

"Time to get going," Ravanak called into their room the next morning. Ravanak had made sure that they went to sleep early the night before. He had told them the journey would be long and hard. They had already had a taste of traveling on a mountain when they went to the cave of legends. They knew it would be tough.

Once they were ready, they took packs that Ravanak had prepared for them from the table and went outside to wait for everyone else. Michael looked at what was inside his pack. It contained food, a full water skin, and other essential supplies for the long journey. Michael had his sword hanging by his side. Julie and Steven carried their weapons on their backs. He knew they were different people now then they had been when they first came to the rebellion. They were all trained in the art of fighting. Their weapons were now a part of them.

The others arrived one by one. Avram was first. Barki and Rumin came a few minutes after him. Jabertormitch took a longer while. Michael thought that he was more excited than any of them to go to Rekadon. It was his home. Michael knew he would love going back to his home. But his home was destroyed. It was the reason he was here.

Ravanak came last, with Kojmeer at his side. Ravanak was talking to Kojmeer about last-minute things they needed to deal with concerning the rebellion. The two brothers hugged good-bye. Ravanak joined them with fresh tears in his eyes. "Ready?" Ravanak and his brother had never been apart before.

"Ready," was the reply. They were ready. They had never been more ready. The eagerness for the journey to start could be felt in the air. The rebellion had been around for years, trying to find ways to stop Dalafar. The time had finally come. They were going out to actively go against the tyrant. Michael knew he was excited to do it. He would stop Dalafar for all those who suffered under his reign. He knew what he was fighting for.

"Let's be off then," Ravanak said. "Jabertormitch, take the lead." Jabertormitch stepped in front, and Ravanak went behind him. The rest followed. They were going to travel on foot. Dwarves didn't ride horses. Rumin and Barki were on Avram's shoulder.

Animal sounds were all around them as they traveled in the woods. The bulky trees blocked sight of the makers of those sounds. There was still nothing to be afraid of. No animal would ever be able to hurt the group of skilled fighters. The animals knew that and never attacked.

They slept at night in an enclosed, protected area and took shifts as watchman just to be safe. There was no real enemy in the woods. The only thing that gave some of them a small scare was the occasional howling of wolves. There weren't many animal sounds back in Periphia. The only harmful animals that they would come across were snakes and scorpions, but that was only if they went deep into the desert. Michael had come across scorpions once when he was with Marki. The scorpions had attacked Marki but ran off at the last second.

It was a few days before they were out of the woods. The mountains towered over them. Rekadon was deep in the mountains. They would have to travel in the mountains for a while before reaching the dwarf city. They camped at the foot of the mountains.

"So far, so good," Barki said.

"You've seen nothing yet," Jabertormitch said. "We haven't gotten to the hard part. We also have to go through enemy territory." He laughed at the thought of creatures other than dwarves heading onto the tough mountain terrain.

"We'll be able to do it," Ravanak said confidently.

"Don't be so sure, centaur," Jabertormitch answered.

"Why not? I've trained the rebellion to defeat any threat. I'm sure their leaders can handle a few dwarves."

"You and your rebellion probably wouldn't have been able to defeat my army if you tried."

"Is that so?"

"Of course."

"Would you like to test it?"

"Time and place."

The argument was getting intense. Tension was building between the two. Michael could tell that most of the creatures didn't get along with one another. Ravanak and Jabertormitch's argument proved that they fought over who was the superior race. It reminded him of when Ravanak had told him of the elves. He'd said they thought themselves to be too graceful for the world. That could be both the faults of the elves and also Ravanak's stereotyping.

"Settle down," Avram said to calm the two. The two turned their backs to each other. "I know we all come from different races, but in order to succeed—to destroy the evil that rules our land—we must work together. Unite and act as one. Learn to accept each other's differences as advantages." The two grunted. After that there was a long period of silence. Almost all the rest of the night was spent in silence.

The next day was as Michael expected. The mountain traveling was tough. The trails were rocky, narrow, and steep. They traveled for days with still no sign of anything but the mountaintops. He reminded himself to look at the positives, as his mother had always taught him. He did enjoy seeing the sun rise beyond the mountain in the morning and set behind the trees of the Living Woods in the evening.

"We're getting close," Jabertormitch explained quietly after another few days. "We are now in enemy territory. We can only hope that they do not have scouts out." They were being more careful here. No fires, no talking above a whisper, and trying to stay hidden as they walked. Just another few days, and they would make it.

Night fell. It suddenly became scary out. Since they were in enemy territory, it no longer felt safe. The mountains no longer looked like they were protecting them from the outside threats, but rather they now looked like giants, reaching out to get them.

Barki came into their tent the next morning. "Shh!" she said before they could open their mouths. "Get ready and get your weapons. Jabertormitch thinks enemy dwarves are surrounding us. Hurry up and come out."

Barki left their tent and went back to Ravanak. "I can't find Rumin," he said. "I'll need you to go up and scout to see if they are there."

"No need for any scout, Ravanak," Jabertormitch said in a deep, angered voice. "They are there. I can feel it."

"We need to be sure," Ravanak responded. Jabertormitch turned to face Ravanak. Apparently he didn't like being doubted by a centaur. Ravanak saw the anger in Jabertormitch's face. "I would also like to know their numbers," he added to calm Jabertormitch down. But Jabertormitch was far from calm. He wasn't angry at Ravanak. He was angry at the smell of the dwarves surrounding them. He grunted, and Ravanak nodded at Barki. Barki took off.

She ran as fast as her little legs could take her. The trees were like massive towers that loomed over her. She dodged them left and right as she made her way through the grass up the hill. No animal, bird, or snake dared to touch her as she ran. They sensed no fear. She wasn't afraid of the enemy, and she was definitely not afraid of any animal, no matter how big. She would not fail this mission. She needed to get to the enemy and back before the attack started. It would give them the advantage in the battle that they needed. If she failed, they might all be doomed. She concentrated on the task at hand.

A rustling noise came from the bush ahead of her. She didn't stop running but merely drew her swords in preparation to take down whatever came out of the bush. Rumin squealed as she almost sliced his head off.

"Sorry," she panted. "I didn't know it was you. What are you doing here?"

"Shh," He placed his finger to his lips. "Quiet. The enemy is upon us."

"What are you doing here?" she repeated in a whisper.

"I woke up early and couldn't go back to sleep," he explained. "I felt something was wrong and went to take a walk to look around. And you wouldn't believe what I found." His voice was getting louder.

"Shh," Barki reminded him.

He lowered his voice again. "I found a camp of dwarves surrounding us. They were sharpening their weapons and preparing for battle. I was just on my way back to warn the others."

"Ravanak just sent me to scout them out. You go back, and I'll join you later." Rumin nodded, and they both ran off in opposite directions.

The enemy camp wasn't far from where she'd met Rumin. What Rumin had said was true: There were dwarves suiting up in armor and sharpening their weapons. The dwarves all looked dirty, and the laughter of victory filled the camp. The dwarves were unorganized. They did not align or review strategies. They must have thought it would be a slaughter, not a battle. Barki smiled when she thought that they would have a surprise. It would be no slaughter.

Her smile turned back into a frown when she remembered her mission. She continued to walk among the enemy. They didn't pay her any attention. She was too small for them to notice. Her only obstacle was avoiding the occasional muddy boot that threatened to squash her. She watched their grubby hands on their axes, maces, and swords as they held them high above their heads. They yelled out dwarfish chants. Or maybe they were just yelling noises; she couldn't really tell.

Now was her chance to get back. She needed to get back before the dwarves started their charge, which would be soon. She started running again. She pulled out her two rapiers while she ran so that she would be ready for the battle.

The rebellion encampment came into view. Rumin was there. She saw their stances. They were standing side by side in a circle with their backs facing each other and their front to the enemy. They left no room between any of them for the enemy to get in the middle of the circle. They were protecting each other's backs. Their weapons were drawn.

Barki joined the circle on the opposite side of Rumin, next to Ravanak with his double swords and Avram with his thin, long sword. Rumin, with his rapiers drawn like Barki's, was between Jabertormitch with his typical dwarf battle-ax and Julie with her golden bow. Michael with his sword and Steven with his mace were across from each other.

"There are about seventy dwarves," Barki said in a cautious tone.

"We can take 'em," Jabertormitch said, the anger still evident in his voice. His own kind was fighting for Dalafar and against him. This thought disgusted him.

Then the silence came. It was there before every battle. They could hear each other breathing. The sound of battle cries could be heard in the distance. Michael felt the sweat forming on his brow. He heard his heart beating as loud as the boots of the dwarves hitting against the hard ground as they ran. Michael tightly clutched the golden hilt of the sword he had received from Mr. Mim. The green blade shimmered like the sweat on his face. The first of the dwarves came running out of the trees.

Clang! Michael's sword clashed with the ax of a dwarf. The battle had begun. Michael thrust his sword into the belly of the dwarf in front of him and watched him fall to the ground. It was his first kill.

More dwarves were coming his way. From the corner of his eye, he could see Julie retreating to the center of the circle, shooting arrows and killing dwarves when they came into view. She hit her target with almost every arrow.

Michael spun to his side to protect himself from a dwarf on his right. He watched one of Ravanak's swords cut the dwarf's head off. A dwarf behind Ravanak was killed with Ravanak's second sword. Ravanak fought with grace. It was like a dance of death to him. Michael was amazed at the way he fought, but before he could watch him any longer, a dwarf charged at Michael. Michael was almost caught by surprise, but he lifted his sword just in time to strike the dwarf in the groin and slice him up to his head. The dwarf fell, and blood stained the green grass as it oozed from the dead body.

Two more dwarves came at Michael. Michael ducked out of the way, causing the dwarves to crash into each other. Before they could recover, Michael killed one and turned to the other, who was already on his feet. The dwarf battled with Michael until Michael was able to knock the ax from the dwarf's hand and strike him down.

Michael went for another dwarf, but the dwarf fell before he could get there. Rumin and Barki were fast and hard to see as they made their cuts to the dwarves' legs, causing the dwarves to fall before they could do anything. That was when the timen would make their final blow. The dwarves started to watch where they stepped in fear of their invisible killers.

Avram was having some trouble killing as many dwarves as the others. Michael saw Steven join him. Avram's sword was no match for the dwarves' armor as he struck them again and again. But he blocked each blow that came at him. He persisted and defended himself while killing a few dwarves on the way. Steven, on the other hand, used his mace to crush the dwarves. He and Avram made a good team. The new duo stopped the dwarves from attacking Avram. Now they were just trying to keep their distance from Steven. Michael watched Steven crush through the armor of two dwarves with one swing of his mace. The two lifeless dwarves fell on top of each other. That was not the brother he used to know.

Jabertormitch's anger gave him an advantage in the battle. Most dwarves cried out in surprise when they saw another dwarf's ax killing them. They started to understand, but it was too late. Jabertormitch had already cut down more than he could count on his fingers.

There was blood on the ground everywhere Michael stepped. Dwarves crowded the ground. The movements of the rebellion were just too fast for the enemy. Michael found himself going after dwarves now instead of waiting for them to come to him. The enemy's numbers decreased until the point when the enemy started to flee. None of the dwarves were successful in their attempts to run. Only a handful of dwarves remained. Michael saw one dwarf getting closer to Julie than he liked. He ran to her, but she hit the dwarf in the neck with the edge of her bow. The dwarf fell, and Jabertormitch killed him with his ax.

Michael used his instinct as he slashed at the remaining dwarves. Mr. Mim had taught him that when fighting, he had to use instinct over skill. He knew that if he thought about it too much, he would not be able to kill. This was the first time he had taken a life, and he knew that he would never be able to forget this moment. After this battle, killing would no longer be murder. He knew Steven and Julie felt the same way.

It was done. There were no dwarves left standing. The sound of the metal against metal was no more. Their clothes were dirty and their weapons bloody. Michael was gasping for breath. He lowered his sword. It was more red than green now. Michael took a look around at the others. The anger still didn't leave Jabertormitch's face.

He locked eyes with Julie. He could see the pain in her eyes. They were now killers. There was no turning back. There would be more battles in their journey, and they would kill more beings without a second thought. It was now a part of them that would never go away. The battle had changed them forever.

Michael was about to turn to look at Steven when Julie raised her bow. She aimed at Steven. Steven froze, and his face was full of shock. Before he could move, Julie let the arrow go. The arrow hissed past Steven's right ear and hit a dwarf behind him. The dwarf dropped his ax and fell with a screech of a dying animal. Steven still didn't move, but his shoulders relaxed. His sister wasn't trying to kill him.

"Thanks," was all he could manage. He put his head down. How could he even think his sister would do something to hurt him? Julie smiled to reassure him.

Jabertormitch and Ravanak walked up to the dwarf on the ground. He wasn't dead. The dwarf was struggling to get up and reach for his ax, Julie's arrow still in his chest. Ravanak kicked the ax aside. Jabertormitch grabbed the dwarf by his sides and held him up.

"Traitor," Jabertormitch spat in the dwarf's face.

The dwarf snickered. "Ha! You think I'm the traitor. Look around. How did all these dwarves, our brethren, die? By my hand? Or by yours?" The dwarf kept the grin on his face.

"I wouldn't be so impolite if I were in your place," Ravanak threatened. He held up his sword. The dwarf kept snickering. "Who sent you?" the dwarf didn't answer and kept his gaze on Jabertormitch, who was dumbstruck.

"Nobody sent me to kill my brothers," the dwarf said. "Who sent you to kill yours?" Jabertormitch dropped the dwarf, and his body hit the floor with a thud.

"That's enough," Ravanak said as he ran his sword through the heart of the dwarf. The dwarf's lifeless face still held a smile.

"Jabertormitch." Ravanak tried to calm him, but Jabertormitch didn't answer. "Jabertormitch, don't listen to what he said. He was only trying to provoke you. Don't let it get to you. He was working with Dalafar. In my book, anyone who works with Dalafar is a traitor, not the other way around."

"Well then," Jabertormitch said. He let out the anger he had bottled up during the battle as he yelled, "I guess I don't hold by *your* book. A dwarf is a dwarf. It doesn't matter who they side with. Dwarves are brothers. We may have been from different clans and we may have arguments with different clans, but we don't fight or kill. It's not our way. We are all people of the earth and mountains."

"Dwarf clans always fight," Ravanak said.

"That is true. We always fight in words, but not in battle. The only dwarf battles are caused over the biggest of arguments between clans. There hasn't been a battle like that in over a century, and I may have started the next one." He put his head in his hands.

Avram put a hand on Jabertormitch's shoulder. "You didn't start the war." Avram spoke calmly. "Dalafar did. By joining him, they started the war with you. Dwarves were neutral in the battle until now. By choosing a side that was against you, they started the battle with you. They are to blame. And they would've killed you if they could; the same as you killed them. They didn't care to kill one of their brothers. They are the heartless ones. You were serving your clan by ridding these mountains of its enemies. You should be honored."

Jabertormitch looked up. "Wise words, satyr. I respect you for that and grant you my deepest gratitude for helping me see the truth." Jabertormitch's anger left him. Avram smiled. "I am more in unity with all of you than I am with those dwarves. And you are more loyal to my clan than they are."

Avram stepped away from Jabertormitch and almost fell.

"You're hurt," Barki said, indicating his leg. There was a large gash across Avram's left leg. Most of it was covered in blood. The fur on his leg was stained red.

"It's nothing," Avram said. "It's only a small wound. Nothing to worry about. We must move on." He winced as he walked. They could see his pain even though he tried his best to hide it.

"That is not nothing to worry about," Jabertormitch said. He examined the wound a little more. "That is definitely something to worry about."

"Yes," Ravanak said. "Let me patch it up." he gestured toward Jabertormitch, who was already heading to the tent where he kept his pack. He came out with roll of cloth and handed it to Ravanak. Ravanak wrapped the cloth tightly around Avram's wound. When he was done wrapping it, he tied it once and then tied it again. "How's that?"

"It eases the pain," Avram said. "Now I am ready to go. Let's move on." He started to walk. He had a heavy limp.

"There is no way you can walk on that leg," Rumin said. "If he walks on that leg, he may lose it forever. I think we have no choice but to wait here until it heals. We can continue our journey after Avram is healed." Some of the others nodded.

"No!" Avram said. "We must go on. I can handle it." He started walking again, but he could hardly put any pressure on his leg. "See?"

"No, I don't see," Jabertormitch said.

"Very well." Avram gave in. "I will stay behind. You go ahead, and I will catch up when I can."

"Nobody gets left behind," Ravanak said. "And I agree that we can't wait. Therefore that leaves us with one option. You must ride on my back while we travel to Rekadon."

"No, I won't do it. I can't do it. I will wait here while you go on."

"Nonsense!" Jabertormitch said. They continued their argument. Rumin urged that they all should wait for Avram to heal. Avram kept denying all the others' opinions and said he would wait while the others went on. Barki stood on the side quietly.

Michael didn't understand why Avram was refusing Ravanak's offer. Steven had the same confused look. They turned to Julie, who sighed when she saw their expressions. "Centaurs are not horses." She was whispering, but she wouldn't have been heard anyway over the argument. "How would you like it if I rode on your back? That's what it's like to ride on a centaur's back. It's not polite, and it's not proper. It's just not done, and Avram won't do it even though Ravanak offered."

"Don't worry about it," Ravanak said. "It's for the best of all of us. I will not go on if you stay here, and if you want us to continue and not let your sacrifice go in vain, then you will ride on my back, because otherwise we will go nowhere. You decide."

Avram looked around. Nobody was on his side. He had no choice. He couldn't let them stop because of him. He nodded and agreed with Ravanak. He always wanted to do the right thing for others and cared of their well-being more than his own. It was the main reason he had joined the rebellion. He wanted to help the world by saving the country from Dalafar. He wanted to fight and give his life for the right cause. It had always been his dream to do so. He would not let his care for one centaur's honor be the downfall of his beliefs of caring for the whole world.

"It would've taken us just a few more days," Jabertormitch said, "if not for this battle and Avram's injury, but now it will probably take about a week before we reach Rekadon. We will have to travel slower. We might as well get started."

Nobody argued with that. They would have to try to get there as fast as possible now that they'd lost a lot of time.

Avram frowned. It was his fault that they would have to travel more slowly. He scolded himself for his injury. He'd tried to help, but he only made things worse. There was no consolation for this. He put his head down in shame as he climbed onto Ravanak's back. Ravanak didn't seem to mind at all that a satyr rode on his back as they continued to travel in the mountains.

New Rekadon

They reached the gates of Rekadon in another week, just as Jabertormitch had predicted. The surrounding mountains isolated Rekadon. The narrow pathway that they were traveling on was the only way in or out of Rekadon. Obviously they were not scared of any attacks on their city. Invaders would have a hard time getting in, but if they did, there would be no retreat. All that could be seen from outside were the tall stone gates of the city. One dwarf stood in front of the gate.

The dwarf saw them coming. "General Jabertormitch!" he said excitedly. "I mean, right this way." His tone changed to more serious and solemn. The dwarf couldn't keep a straight face. No matter how much he tried to conceal it, the worried expression still showed under his orange beard. The dwarf knocked in a certain sequence on different stones of the gate. The gate opened.

They walked through the gates, and immediately dwarves holding axes surrounded them. Michael wasn't even able to take in what the city looked like before they were being bound with ropes.

"What's the meaning of this?" Jabertormitch bellowed. "I am the general of the army of Ish Ketanim. I am going to see my chief. How dare you treat me this way?"

The surrounding circle made way for the lead dwarf to walk between them. The lead dwarf looked equally as strong as Jabertormitch, and his black hair covered most of his face.

"Hello, Jabertormitch," the dwarf said in a sinister tone. "Nice of you to come back and bring the rebellion leaders right into our hands."

"What!" Ravanak said turning to Jabertormitch. "This was all a trap?" Ravanak was full of fury. He had trusted Jabertormitch, and now the despicable dwarf had betrayed them. Jabertormitch had seemed to be on their side the whole time. The fact that he would betray them couldn't penetrate Michael's brain.

"I told you," Rumin cut in.

"No, I swear," Jabertormitch tried to defend himself. "I didn't know. This isn't even my clan. Look at their armor. Their insignia are two crossed battle-axes. You know that my clan's insignia is the mountain lion. This is the neighboring clan that I was telling you about. We share the city. This is the clan that follows Dalafar."

"You also betrayed your own clan?" Rumin said. "I think it's clear that you are really working with this clan and with Dalafar."

"I would never deal with these filth," Jabertormitch said.

"Oh, stop being modest, Jabertormitch," the lead dwarf said. "You did your job. No need to deny it any longer."

"Be quiet, Karzenthack," Jabertormitch said angrily.

"Fine. If you don't want to take the credit, then you will be beheaded with the rest of them. Send them to the prison pit." Before another word was said, they were being blindfolded.

Michael felt himself being dragged, his feet probably getting blisters from the floor, by a dwarf. He was dragged for about an hour before he was thrown. He was falling until he hit the hard wet ground. He tried to get up, but he couldn't break loose from the ropes that bound his hands. He turned over on his stomach and felt a jolt of pain run up his back. A spider crawled up his arm. He tried to shake it off, but it was no use.

"Is everyone all right?" Ravanak's voice came.

"That depends," Jabertormitch kidded, "on what you mean by all right."

"Jabertormitch," Ravanak said. "I'm sorry for accusing you."

"It's all right," Jabertormitch said. "I wouldn't have believed you either. I was lucky you believed me from the start." Then he started mumbling to himself. "Now how do we get out of here? I don't understand what happened. They must've found out what my chief was planning, but how? I'm sure the rest of my clan fled to the secret hideout that my chief had set up in case something like this was ever to happen. The only thing that I don't understand was that the dwarf at the gate was from my clan. If we can only get out of this pit…"

"I can help with that." A voice came from above the pit. Michael heard something hit the floor near him. He heard the sound of a knife cutting thick rope. "Good to see you are all right, General Jabertormitch," the voice said.

"Rokesfeld, I should've known," Jabertormitch said to the voice. Michael felt himself being lifted and the ropes being cut from his hands. He was free. He removed the blindfold. It took a few seconds before his eyes adjusted. Jabertormitch was standing near the orange-bearded dwarf that was at the gate earlier. The dwarf was a little shorter than Jabertormitch but just as strong. Most of his teeth were yellow. He was missing two fingers on his right hand. Ravanak was cutting loose the rest of them.

"Katensthiv left me to stay behind and wait for your return," the dwarf said. "I pretended to ally myself with the enemy. But now we must go and join the others. Hurry."

"Right," Jabertormitch said. "This is my trusted advisor, Rokesfeld," he introduced.

"Hurry, General," Rokesfeld said. "There is no time for introductions. Climb up." Jabertormitch took hold of the rope that was hanging down from the top of the pit. He began to climb. "Now the rest of you." When they were all out of the pit, Rokesfeld urged them on. "Let's go."

"Right," Jabertormitch said. "Follow me. I know the way. We are close. Just be quiet." They followed Jabertormitch to the edge of the city, right past the jail pit. There was nothing around them but other jail pits. Michael guessed that they were against the back mountain that surrounded the city and Jabertormitch was leading them right to the mountain. There was nowhere to go but back into the city. They reached a dead end by the mountain.

"*Aven zuz*," Jabertormitch called out to the mountain. A large piece of the mountain started to go inward. Then it went to the left. There was now an opening in the mountain. It was like a doorway to a tunnel.

"You're not the only one who can do magic," Jabertormitch said. Rokesfeld smiled.

"What do you mean?" Michael asked.

"Dwarves also have an element of magic. Dwarves are the people of earth. We have certain power over rocks and earth. We know certain spells that we are able to conjure."

"I get it," Julie said. "The first dwarves were found in the mountains. Dwarves have lived there ever since. They are one with the mountains."

"Exactly," Rokesfeld said. "Let's go. The chief made this hideout a few months ago. He anticipated something like this would happen. My orders were to stay behind and bring Jabertormitch here when he returned."

"You did well, Rokesfeld," Jabertormitch said. "This isn't the first time Rokesfeld has saved my life. I owe him everything."

"You owe me nothing, General. It's my duty and loyalty to you and to our people."

Footsteps could be heard in the distance. "I'll go quiet those prisoners." The voice came from around a nearby rock formation. "They are making too much noise. I'll show them the meaning of the word silence."

"You are so cruel," a second voice said. "I love it." The footsteps were getting closer.

"Hurry," Jabertormitch said. He and Rokesfeld stood at the doorway while they herded the others into the passage. The passage curved to the right. There were dim lanterns along the pathway. It looked like it went on forever.

The two dwarves turned the corner. "Go," Jabertormitch said to Rokesfeld.

"The prisoners! They escaped! Sound the alarm! The prisoners! They escaped!"

"Go," Jabertormitch repeated.

"No," Rokesfeld said in a strong, courageous voice. "You go. I will hold them off. I will follow you, I promise."

Jabertormitch's glance went to Rokesfeld's two missing fingers. "The last time you said that…"

"I promise," Rokesfeld stood his ground. Jabertormitch realized that there was nothing that he could do to change Rokesfeld's mind.

"Good-bye, my friend," Jabertormitch said as tears streamed down his face. Rokesfeld reply was drawing his ax. Jabertormitch ran into the passage.

"*Sagur,*" Rokesfeld said, and the opening covered up.

Jabertormitch's chin was still dripping with tears as they walked on and on. They walked in silence. The pathway started taking all kinds of turns. Michael couldn't tell how far into the mountain they were. It was damp. The walls were wet, and the floor was slippery. Twice Michael had to save Steven from falling. The lanterns on the walls made it somewhat hot. How could they stay lit forever?

Michael was about to speak his question aloud when Jabertormitch said, "They are light rocks."

The tunnel seemed endless. Michael could tell by the look on Julie's face that she was starting to get claustrophobic. She didn't usually have a problem with it, but they had been in this tunnel for a very long time. A light, not coming from the light rocks, could finally be seen from the distance. It was the light of the sun. He heard Julie, Steven, and a few of the others, including himself, sigh with relief.

They started walking faster with determination. Again Michael had to save Steven from tripping. They stumbled out of the cave. Their eyes were almost blinded by the light. They had been without the sun's light for...well...nobody could tell. It could've been days that they had been traveling in there, or maybe mere hours. It sure felt like days. Michael felt his empty stomach. He heard Steven's stomach growl.

"Welcome to New Rekadon," Jabertormitch said. "Good to be back with my own people. I'll show you where the chief is staying." Houses and shops lined the stone pathways of the city. The city, like Rekadon, was completely surrounded and hidden by mountains. In the center of the city was a large building.

Dwarves started to crowd around them. More dwarves came when they realized who was there. "General Jabertormitch," they said, "you're back."

"Clear the way, clear the way." A dwarf shorter than most and not as muscular as the others came in the crowd. He looked like a messenger dwarf with the bag around his shoulder. The crowd dispersed. "I am to escort you to our chief. Follow me."

The dwarves seemed friendly, but their faces told Michael that their smiles were just trying to mask their depression. It was hard times for everyone. The dwarves had finally taken the hit from Dalafar's hand. It had given them a reason to fight Dalafar, and it made them want to join the rebellion to defeat Dalafar. The more that wanted to fight Dalafar, the easier it would be to defeat him.

Next to the large building in the center of the city was another large building. This building looked like a temple of some sort. There was a large statue at the front of the temple. Before Michael had a chance to ask what the temple was, they reached the golden doors of the building next to the temple.

"In here," the dwarf said. He opened the doors. Inside was a large hall. Rocks that gave off light hung from the ceiling. Dwarves in armor, standing in a line in the hall, put fists to their chests and bowed their heads in salute to their general as they passed.

"They are waiting upstairs," he said, pointing to the staircase. "The meeting will take place there." The dwarf left the building. Jabertormitch took the lead as they walked up the stairs and through the doors of the large chamber.

Jabertormitch and the messenger dwarf fell to the floor when they came into the room. The others mimicked their action. Michael knew the chief was in this room. He was a ruler, and they had to bow in respect for him. His mother had taught him to respect others.

"Rise, my sons," Michael heard a voice say. Michael got up and looked around. The voice came from a dwarf sitting at the head of a long table. There were dwarves sitting all around the table. Torches lined the walls of the room. The dwarf who spoke looked like the chief. He wore a crown of diamonds. It was beautifully carved. His body seemed too large and muscular for his short height. He had a black beard that almost touched his feet. He smiled and laughed a loud, booming laugh.

"General Jabertormitch, Sir Ravanak," he said. "How joyous it is to see you once again." He looked around. "Where is Lieutenant Rokesfeld?" Jabertormitch remained silent and looked at the floor. The chief got the message and took a minute of silence for the brave lieutenant. "Now that you are finally here, we can start the meeting."

"Chief Katensthiv," Ravanak said. "I would like you to meet the leaders of the rebellion." Katensthiv realized the others were there.

"Perfect," Katensthiv said. "They are always welcome, just like you, Ravanak. Let's get started."

"Get started with what? What's the problem?" Ravanak asked.

"As you know," Katensthiv said, "our brethren clan—"

"They are no longer our brethren," Jabertormitch said in a disgusted tone.

"Jabertormitch, that is no way to talk about them," Katensthiv said. "Even though we are no longer at peace and we may have to come to fight, it does not mean that we are both not dwarves."

"Sorry," Jabertormitch muttered.

"My chief war advisor, Shlatenthzat, will give you the details of what has happened."

"As you saw," Shlatenthzat said, "our brethren clan has taken over Rekadon. Chief Katensthiv foresaw this event and in advance had set up New Rekadon as a backup plan in case we needed to retreat. That time came, and here we are."

Michael knew Ravanak was going to follow up on the conversation and see what they wanted, but had he forgotten so quickly the reason they had come? They had come because of the clues on the map.

"Ravanak," Michael whispered, "what about the stones?"

"I'm getting to that," Ravanak said. Then he spoke louder. "Let me tell you the reason we came. We have reason to believe that a magical force that Dalafar is looking for may be in Rekadon."

"That's ridiculous," one dwarf said. "There is no magic here. If you're looking for magic, then go to the elves, although they probably won't be as kind and hospitable to you as we are."

"Zakenesht," Katensthiv said, regarding the elder dwarf. He had a long white beard, and his face was full of wrinkles. Each wrinkle looked like it contained wisdom. He wore a simple robe. His head was inclined downward. Michael thought that he must be a humble man.

"In my old house in Rekadon," Zakenesht said, "I had many ancient scrolls. Some were relevant to magic. Perhaps one of those scrolls can help you with what you're looking for. I didn't have time to bring them here, to New Rekadon."

"Is it possible to get to them?" Ravanak asked.

"I'm afraid not," Shlatenthzat said.

"Then what must we do?" Avram spoke up. He walked forward. He was still limping, but he wouldn't admit to his pain. He was more stubborn than any of them.

"That brings us to what we want," Katensthiv said. "We want to recapture the city. Once we do that, you will be granted full access to the ancient scrolls."

"If we have surprise on our hands, we can win," Rumin said. "They won't know what hit them, and we'll crush them."

"Surprise never fails." Another dwarf spoke up.

"So you will help us?" Katensthiv asked hopefully.

"What choice do we have?" Ravanak replied.

"How should we plan the surprise attack?" Barki said.

"I have an idea," Steven said.

"A mere child," Shlatenthzat said.

"Shlatenthzat, you know everyone has a say in my court," Katensthiv said.

"Sorry," Shlatenthzat said.

"Speak up," Katensthiv said. Katensthiv was very kind. He treated everyone with equal respect even though he was the chief. He was the opposite of Dalafar. His example showed Michael how a ruler should truly rule. They should be good to the people, not a cruel tyrant. Dalafar treated everyone like garbage. He didn't care for any of the people. Michael could tell that Katensthiv cared a lot for his clan.

Michael saw that Steven was nervous. Everyone turned to him. A drop of sweat rolled down his face. He opened his mouth to speak, but no words came out. Julie hit him lightly on the back. "We can trick them," he spat out. "The plan will take everyone in the city to participate."

"How's that?" Katensthiv said.

"We must leave New Rekadon. Everyone will have to travel. We will travel in sight of their scouts. All the citizens will be in front, and half the army will be in the back."

"I see where this is going," Shlatenthzat said, "but let me expand. This will lure their army out. We will have three armies. One will be with the people. The other will be behind, ready to surround the enemy. The third will enter the city, which is unprotected, and reclaim it. Once we win, we can send the citizens back to Rekadon."

"It's brilliant!" Katensthiv said. Rumin smiled.

"Good job." Michael patted Steven on the back.

"Yeah," Julie agreed. Steven smiled. He enjoyed the praises he got from his brother and sister. He always wanted them to be proud of him.

"Let's start preparing," Katensthiv said. "There is no time to lose. The longer we wait, the more risk there will be of the plan failing. Meeting adjourned. Thank you, everyone."

They bowed as they left. Michael knew it would take at least a week to prepare. He told himself that he would train in combat during the time that the dwarves needed to prepare.

"Where are the training grounds?" he asked Jabertormitch.

"You are so devoted," Jabertormitch answered. "I want to show you three something before you train. I think it might interest you. Take one day for yourselves. There'll be plenty of time to train for the battle." He paused. "Besides, I saw your skills in our previous battle. You three are great fighters for amateurs," he added.

"What is it?" Steven asked curiously.

"Where are you taking them?" Ravanak asked Jabertormitch.

"I thought that I'd show them the temple," he said innocently.

"Actually," Ravanak said, "I think that wouldn't be a bad idea."

"The temple!" Steven exclaimed.

"It does look interesting," Julie said.

"I'm sure you will find it interesting," Ravanak said. "The rest of us will help the dwarves prepare for travel."

Religion

The temple was a massive building. It was the largest building in New Rekadon. The temple was built from stones, but its walls were decorated with gold, silver, and diamonds. There were two flights of stairs to the door. At the foot of the stairs was a statue that was almost three times Michael's size. The temple's beauty showed how much the dwarves revered the gods.

"This temple was built for the dwarf god, Adema," Jabertormitch said. Michael looked up at the statue. The statue was of humanoid form. He wore a helmet and had a hairy face that ended with a beard that reached his waist. His right arm was up high, holding an ax above his head. He stood on what looked like a large boulder.

"I thought there was only one god," Steven said.

"Is that what you were taught?" Jabertormitch laughed. "Let me explain. There are different religions throughout Charldena. One has, as you believe in, a monotheistic god. Another is a nature or spiritual magical force that lives within everyone and everything that controls the nature of the world, but no ultimate omniscient being exists. The elves believe in that. The third is many polytheistic gods. Our belief is many gods. You'll see more of that in the temple."

They walked up the marble stairs. The doors were made of gold and decorated with diamonds.

"The temple is a sacred place to all dwarves," Jabertormitch explained. "No dwarf would even think of pilfering or filching anything from the temple. Even if there were a war, we wouldn't destroy or even touch the temple of another clan. The dwarf who would ever dare touch the temple would be condemned to immediate death."

Jabertormitch pushed the doors in. They were in a big hall with a beautiful fountain in the middle. A red carpet went from the front door and around the fountain on both sides to a door across the hall. The carpet went to other doors along the left and right walls. The big door at the end was made of gold, while the smaller doors on the side were made of silver. Atop the fountain was a chandelier large enough to brighten the entire hall.

"The door at the end is where the sanctuary to Adema is," Jabertormitch said. "The others are of other gods. Even though this temple is dedicated to Adema, we still have respect for the other gods. Let me show you each one and explain what they stand for. First I'll explain to you the story of the gods. There were an allpowerful god and goddess. These two had ten children."

"Gods can have children?" Julie asked.

"Course they can. They have creature-like physical qualities like the rest of us. Anyway, the children plotted against their parents to overturn them. They succeeded."

"Aren't gods immortal?" Steven asked.

"That's true, but the children sealed away their parents in an inescapable prison. Before the parents were sealed, they cursed their children by creating a world with creatures and charged their children with the duty of running it.

"The children took this as a contest. Their parents created all the animals of the world. The children grew arrogant because they had defeated their parents. They believed that they could create better creatures for the world. If they had to watch over the world, then they would at least have some fun with it. These minor gods were the ones who created all the intelligent creatures."

"Each one of these gods is in a room?" Michael asked.

"You got it now. Let's get started." There were five rooms on each side. "We'll start with the god of humans." Jabertormitch led them to the third door on the right.

They were in a square room empty other than a statue against the back wall. The marble floor was cold on their feet. Candelabras on the walls lit up the room. The statue was of a man. He wore only trousers. He had a short beard and hair that reached the back of his neck. His right hand was outstretched, holding a sphere.

"This is Anashim," Jabertormitch said. "He is the creator of humans. It's the basic form of most of the other creations because he was the first in the contest."

"What's that sphere?" Michael asked.

"Each god also has a characteristic that he was cursed with to help this world to exist. That represents the cycle of life. Anashim is also the god of the cycle of life. Do you know of this concept?"

The three nodded. They had learned that from their mother. She had given the example of a lion eating a deer. When the lion died, it decomposed and turned into minerals to help the grass grow. Then the deer ate the grass. The lion ate the deer, and it continued. It was how the world worked.

"I know you believe in only one god," Jabertormitch said, "but if you wish, then you may pray to him. After all, he is your god."

Michael didn't think that was a good idea. His mother had said not to believe in other gods. Besides, he believed that he had to work for himself and not rely on a god for everything. Steven and Julie didn't make a move either.

"No?" Jabertormitch said. "Fine, let's go to the next one." They left the room.

"Where to next?" Julie asked.

"I'll let you decide what to do next."

"That one," Steven said, pointing to the second door on the left.

"Interesting choice. You might not like this god."

They went into the room. It was the same as the other but had a different statue. It was a stone statue like before. It had a human form but was covered with feathers. It had two wings coming from its back. Its head was of a hawk. The statue was standing on a cloud with its clawed hands facing up.

"I can guess what he is the god of," Julie said with fear in her face. Michael had a blank expression. The memories came back: the avengers blasting through the door, their sinister smiles spreading across their faces as they laughed. He remembered the courage that his mother always used to try to have when the avengers came. He knew that she did it for them. Now that was his job. He put his arms around Julie and Steven's shoulders when they moved closer to him.

"Yes, the avengers." Jabertormitch saw that they shivered at the sound of the word. "Sorry. He wanted to create a creature better than Anashim's by giving his creature the power of flight. Rakia, this god here, is also the god of the sky, wind, and air. As you can see, he is standing on a cloud. I can tell you guys don't like it here, so let's get to the next room."

They quickly left the room. "Bad memories, I assume," Jabertormitch said when they got outside. They just nodded. "We all have them. The avengers don't bother the dwarves in the mountains, but I've heard stories of them. Let me take you to a room that you'll like." He took them to the first on the right.

This statue was a man's body together with a horse's body. It looked just like a centaur. His hands were held up high, holding a sphere with dents in it.

"Now this is a good god," Steven said.

"I agree to that," Julie said, "but what's he holding?"

"This is Sus," Jabertormitch explained, "the god who created centaurs, as you can see. He wanted to create Anashim's creature with more speed and strength by combining it with a horse. He is also the god of the moon, which is what he's holding. The moon guides the tide of the ocean; therefore he coincides with the god of the ocean. They work together. He also works together with the god of the sun because the moon is also used to tell time just like the sun. Day, night, and seasons are all determined by the sun and moon. Let me show you his two partners."

They left the room and went into the room across from them. There was a statue of a women's top half of a body and a fish's bottom half. Michael could easily make out each scale. These statues were expertly carved. The dwarves had real talent with stones, and they probably took extra care with their temples, so each statue turned out perfectly. She was riding a wave.

"Who's she?" Michael asked with awe. He could see her beauty. It amazed him that a creature could be this beautiful.

"Her name is Maim," Jabertormitch said. "She is the goddess of water. She is in charge of the oceans, lake, rivers, rain, and all water in the world."

"What creature did she create?" Steven asked. He would love to meet such a beautiful creature that this goddess probably created.

"Nobody knows much about her," Jabertormitch answered. "Some say the creatures died out. Some say she thought of herself too highly to enter such a silly competition."

"Women don't compete in such childish competitions of men," Julie said proudly.

"There were other goddesses who did participate," Jabertormitch said. "First I'll show you the sun god, and then we'll get to some more goddesses." Julie frowned in disbelief.

They went to the fourth room on the left. This statue had a scaly body. His clawed hands were held high, holding what looked like the sun. Wings spread from his back. He had talons down his back to the end of his long tail. He stood on an erupting volcano.

"This is Esh. He was an exceptionally powerful god. He wanted to create a creature unlike the humanoid form of the gods and the other creatures. He wanted to create a beast-like creature. He created the dragons and granted them his power of fire. Later the dragons adapted other powers, such as acid and lighting breath. He gifted the dragons with scales almost as tough as diamonds to shield them. It's said that he personally created the Gazh Isles as a home for the dragons. He cared for his creation more than any of the other gods.

"He's also the god of the sun. That includes fire and light. That's what makes him so powerful. He is in control of some of the most important aspects of the world. He was the eldest son, and therefore he was gifted with the most power."

The statue looked fearsome. It looked as if he could come alive any second and attack. It reminded Michael of Darkon. He could see where the dragons got their power.

They left this room and headed to the second door on the right. There was a statue of a woman. She caressed a baby goat in her hands.

"She is Ayil. She did participate in the contest."

"I'm sure she had a good reason for it." Julie tried to justify her theory of women being superior to men. She didn't think women would participate in silly competitions.

"Either way," Jabertormitch continued. "She created the satyr. She is also the god of fertility. Legend has it that she came across a mother goat that couldn't give birth. She gave her the power to give birth, but the mother died in childbirth. Ayil felt awful about what she did and raised the baby goat herself. Then she decided to give something back to the goats by creating Anashim's creature of a human with part goat."

"I told you she had a good reason," Julie beamed. "She was only trying to do the right thing." Jabertormitch just grunted.

They left that room. "We're past halfway done. We better hurry and finish up before the day comes to an end. Don't worry Julie. The next one will prove your theory wrong."

Jabertormitch walked across the hall and took them to the third room on the left. In this room was another goddess. She had long, beautiful hair. Her face seemed so pure and innocent. She had long, pointed ears. She wore a long robe that went from her neck to her feet.

Michael could tell from Steven's face that Steven had just fallen in love. He couldn't blame him. This goddess was just too beautiful to explain. Any man would fall for her. Even though she was only a statue, her beauty was evident. Michael thought that if he had not already fallen in love with Sheri, then he would have the same look now that he saw in Steven's eyes.

"I see you like this one," Jabertormitch said to the boys in a teasing voice.

"She's all right, I guess," Julie said in an annoyed tone. She felt as if this statue was just showing off her beauty and had competed for no good reason other than to show off more. She made a disgusted sound.

"Or was a magnificent goddess. She was beyond the others. Her beauty shone with a blinding light. Her body glowed. She wanted to create Anashim's creature with better features. She gave them her ears. She gave them beauty and gracefulness. She granted them the power of magic. I'm not sure exactly what it is because other creatures can also perform magic. In addition, she granted them with immortality."

"Elves can't die?" Steven asked.

"Right," Jabertormitch asked.

"Then where are they?" Julie asked rationally. "They can't all fit in Tudanosti Forest if they were living from the beginning of time."

"They have disappeared," Jabertormitch answered. "The elves of old have disappeared from the face of the planet. Nobody, not even the existing elves, knows where they could've gone."

Steven frowned. Michael knew that he probably wanted to meet an elf, but if most of them were gone, it wouldn't be that easy.

"Or is also the goddess of beauty and everything that is good in the world like good fortune, wealth, health, and more."

Michael could tell that Steven wasn't ready to leave just yet. He was still staring at the statute.

"I would like to meet an elf in person if they look anything like this," Steven said.

Michael thought it was possible. They might have to travel all around the world to find the stones. It could lead them to Tudanosti Forest. They also needed the elves' help when it came down to finally defeating Dalafar and his forces in a war. They could definitely use the elves' ability to do magic when they were going to fight Dalafar. Dalafar was sure to have spell-casters of his own, and they would need some to counteract Dalafar. Steven knew he would be excited when the time came that their journeys took them to Tudanosti Forest.

"They aren't that great," Jabertormitch said in a grumpy vice. "Now, if you talk about the dwarf women, they are something to look at. Their strong features and hairy beards are qualities to look for in a woman." He sighed. The others smiled. That was hardly what they would say a beautiful woman looks like. They could hardly tell the difference between dwarf men and women.

"Do you have a..." Michael trailed off. What he wanted to ask was obvious.

"There is someone," Jabertormitch said, "but I can't marry or have kids. I'm too involved with wars and the rebellion now. I wouldn't want to put anyone I love in danger. Maybe after this is all over. I mean, if I am still living..." he laughed. Michael didn't think that was funny. There was an awkward silence.

"Let's move on," Jabertormitch said. They left the room. Steven looked back and took one last glimpse before the door closed behind them. The smile fell from his face. "Let me show you the opposite god of Or," Jabertormitch said. He led them to the fifth door on the left.

Julie was taken aback when they went in the room. This statue was of a male. He had a disfigured face and body. He was hideous. It was revolting to look at him. Half of his teeth were missing in that evil grin. He wore ripped and tattered clothes. He had a mess of hair. His skin had more wrinkles than Zakenesht. He held out his hands in front of him in a position like he was about to grab you.

"This is Smale, the god of evil and darkness. He is the god of everything bad in the world, which is the complete opposite of Or. He created trolls, goblins, and Minotaur. All his creations are disfigured in some way. It made him really angry that he couldn't create a perfect creature like Or. He kept trying but failed again and again.

"Legend has it that he created the Urakian Mountains to hide his abominations. He wanted to ruin everyone else's creatures as well. Therefore he created an evil inclination that lies in everyone's head telling them to perform evil acts. The other gods wanted to punish him by placing him in charge of death and the dead souls. He got angrier after his sentence and further strengthened the evil inclination inside all creatures.

"The world turned to chaos. Everyone was evil. When Or saw her beautiful creatures using their special powers for evil, she created a counter to the evil inclination. The good inclination was placed in all creatures. It created balance between good and evil in the world. It makes up our conscious."

"Can we please get out of this room?" Julie whined. She had closed her eyes, but she could still feel Smale's bloodshot eyes beating down on her. Michael thought he heard a growl coming from the statue, but it was just his imagination. Michael agreed with Julie. He didn't like the looks of this statue. Steven just found the sight upsetting, especially after the sight of Or.

"Let's go," Michael said. Jabertormitch nodded and led them across the hall.

This statue was smaller than the rest. It was shorter than Michael. He was like a miniature version of Anashim.

"This is Yofe. He created the timen. He wanted to mimic Anashim's creation, but being that he is smaller and has less power, he ended up with timen. Yofe is also the god of the arts. He is the god of pictures, landscapes, poems, writings, jewels, music, science,

154 | The Scroll of Kanavar: Legend of the Twelve Stones

and more." Yofe was holding his hands out straight with his palms facing up. It was like he was trying to give something. Michael almost reached out to take that something.

Steven yawned. "It's getting late," Julie said.

"I think it's time for supper," Michael added when his growling stomach reminded him that they hadn't eaten for over a day. Their last meal had been before they had even gone into Rekadon.

"We're almost done," Jabertormitch said. They left the room and went to the one on their left. There was a large statue in this room. It was bigger than the rest. The figure of a large man held a large hammer in his right hand, which he was holding over his head, ready to strike. His mouth was wide open. He wore only shorts. His bare chest was muscular.

"Milchama is the god of war, strength, and power. He wanted to create the strongest creatures, so he made the largest creatures. The giants were granted three powers, one for each type. He gave them the powers of fire, ice, and earth."

Michael walked forward and touched the statue's thigh. He couldn't reach any higher.

"We got one left." Jabertormitch indicated for them to leave. They followed him into the room at the end with the large golden doors. "Now for the god that this temple was dedicated in honor of," Jabertormitch introduced, "Adema, god of the earth and the dwarves."

The statue was larger than the rest, only because it was the main statue in the temple. In any other temple it would be smaller than most of the other statues. The only statue that would be smaller than it would be Yofe. But in this temple, it was even bigger than Milchama. It was the same statue as the one outside.

"Adema is my god and the god of the other dwarves. We give him the utmost respect. He granted us with the power of earth from which he created us." Jabertormitch went up to the statue and went down to the floor on his knees. He started bowing his body. The three just watched. They kept silent out of respect for Jabertormitch. Jabertormitch said a small prayer before getting up and walking back to them.

"That just about wraps it up," he said. "Let's be heading back. We don't want to miss supper."

"You can say that again," Steven agreed. Michael and Julie just laughed. Same old Steven. Steven laughed when he heard their stomachs growling.

Jabertormitch smiled at their laughter. Times were rough, and it was enjoyable to hear laughter now and again. It wasn't healthy to always be serious. You could always count on children for laughter.

They headed out of the temple and down the many stairs. Jabertormitch put his index finger to his lips, kissed it, and threw the kiss at the statue of Adema when they passed.

"It was a day of relaxation," Jabertormitch said as they walked back to the others. Katensthiv had prepared a feast for them in honor of their arrival. "I hope you three enjoyed it. I knew you needed this day to relax after all that has happened."

"Yes, thank you," Michael said.

"We did need it," Julie added.

"Let's hurry and get back, so we don't miss the food," Steven said in an urging tone. Michael and Julie laughed again.

They walked past a few more buildings and houses to where the town center was. Dwarves were all around. Michael saw Zakenesht, Katensthiv, the rebellion, and other dwarves gathered around a table full of food.

"How was your day?" Ravanak asked when they got back. They nodded in reply. "You didn't brainwash them, did you, Jabertormitch?" Ravanak laughed.

"They don't believe in the gods," Jabertormitch sighed. "It doesn't matter. It was good for them to know about other cultures."

"I agree with you on that," Ravanak said. "Have some food," he added. "We have a lot of work ahead of us."

Michael suddenly lost his appetite. He realized what Ravanak meant. They only had a few days before the war would come. Michael knew he would have to kill again. The picture of blood that came into his mind made his stomach turn. He knew he would definitely not be able to eat anything tonight.

Expect the Unexpected

"Rise and shine, sleepyheads," Ravanak called into their room the next morning. "You three had a nice break yesterday, but today you have to train. We have a war coming up. Get ready and I'll meet you outside."

Michael sat up on his bed. He let out a loud yawn as he stretched his arms. He rubbed his eyes and got out of bed. It was a long time since he'd had a sleep like that. But he was still hungry. The others had all eaten last night, but he couldn't bring himself to drink a cup of water.

A few minutes later, they were all outside their temporary home. Ravanak was there, waiting. "Come and let's eat before we start the day." He took them a few houses down to his house. The guesthouses were all similar. They were all made of the same stone. In the front room was a table and in the back was a bedroom. On the table was an assortment of food for breakfast.

Without a word the children sat down and began to munch on the food. Steven grabbed an apple and a piece of bread at the same time, while Julie gently took a piece of fruit. Michael took a piece of bread and put a jelly spread on it.

"I can see you three are busy," Ravanak said in a humorous tone. "I'll wait for you outside." Ravanak picked up a piece of bread and walked to the door. "Come out when you're done."

It took a little more time than it should have for them to finish. Michael used his sleeve to wipe his mouth before getting up. When the others were done, they went outside. Ravanak wasn't there.

"Where'd he go?" Julie asked.

"Let's wait a few minutes," Michael said. "Maybe he'll come back."

Dwarves were running about, preparing for the journey. Michael saw one door open and a dwarf running in and out, each time bringing something out of the house and packing it in a case in his lawn. Across the road was a dwarf woman—at least Michael thought it was a woman—along with her kids, emptying the house of all their possessions.

Ravanak came back a few minutes later. "I had some business to do," he explained. "There's a lot of work to be done before the war." They nodded. They knew he was helping the dwarves prepare for the upcoming war. It was a complicated plan that had to be executed perfectly. "You three have improved your battle skills immensely since you first joined us, but I don't think you're ready for a full-fledged war. I'll show you to the training grounds."

They followed him past many houses until they reached a place that consisted of a lot of open fields. There were targets lined up and archers shooting at them from across a distance. There was also a place where dwarves were engaging in head-on combat with their weapons. There weren't many archers, but there were many dwarves battling with swords, axes, and maces. Dwarves had a lot of upper-body strength. They concentrated more on heavy weaponry than bows and arrows.

"Feel free to train as you please," Ravanak said before leaving them.

"I'm going to head over to the shooting range," Julie said. She didn't think that she would learn much from the dwarf archers. Archery wasn't the dwarves' specialty. Elves were known to be expert archers. She wished that she could learn from an elf.

Michael and Steven went to the other part of the training ground, which included the head-on combat. Steven admired the dwarves' strength and how they easily held and used their heavy weapons. He couldn't wait to learn all that he could from them to use his mace better. Maybe he would even be able to upgrade to a higher-level mace. The dwarves were the right race to train him.

Steven went looking for someone to teach him. He watched the dwarves duel. One dwarf caught his attention. He was bigger and more muscular than most. He was fighting three other dwarves at once. He deflected all of their blows with ease. Steven moved closer. The dwarf saw Steven. He lowered his ax, and the other dwarves did the same. He motioned for the others to leave. When they had gone out of earshot, Steven walked up to the dwarf.

"Can you please train me?" Steven asked respectfully.

"I *can*," the dwarf replied. Steven could tell from the tone of his voice that something was wrong.

"I mean may you please train me?" Steven corrected himself.

"I'm much too busy," the dwarf replied in a grumpy voice.

"But I wish to learn the true essence of heavy weaponry in order to master my mace." Steven was pleading now. "I see the way you use your ax, and I wish to learn from you all that I can, so that I can be as good as you with my mace."

"You are interested in heavy weapons?" the dwarf asked, surprised.

"Yes. I fight with a mace."

"Not many of your kind understand how to use a heavy weapon. If you really wish to learn, then I will teach you."

Steven grinned. "Thank you. And by the way, my name is Steven."

"I am Vishvanovitch, commander of the army of Ish Ketanim."

Steven bowed his head. Vishvanovitch bowed back. Steven realized that Vishvanovitch was a respectful dwarf. He kept eye contact with Steven. Steven realized that Vishvanovitch's beard was shorter than most other dwarves.

"In order to use a heavy weapon," Vishvanovitch started the first lesson, "you need to have strength. Not only outer and physical strength, although you need that too, but also inner strength and willpower." Vishvanovitch took a deep breath and lifted his large ax, using the strength of his chest and the strength within him.

"You also can't have a gentle nature. You have to be aggressive and be able to strike hard. You need to put full power into you strikes to crush the enemy. This is the way of the heavy weapon." Vishvanovitch hit his ax hard on the ground. Steven looked at him with interest but took a step back when the ax hit the ground.

"Let me see your strike," Vishvanovitch said. "Come at me." Steven took his mace from its holder on his back. He ran at Vishvanovitch with his strongest strike. He wasn't afraid to use all his power. He screamed self-consciously as he ran.

Vishvanovitch raised his ax and blocked the blow without even flinching. Steven fell back from the feedback of his blow. He was sitting on the floor in a daze. It didn't make sense that his blow could have been blocked that easily.

Vishvanovitch saw his obvious confusion. "Let me give you a tip to raise your aggression when you fight. Try to anger yourself. Try to be furious. Then use your anger to strike. I know this will be hard, but think of the moment in your life that made you the angriest. That blow would be much more devastating and effective on an opponent." As Vishvanovitch was saying this, the memory of his mother, dead on the floor, boiled inside of him. His anger rose.

Steven leaped off the ground in anger and charged at Vishvanovitch with all his might. Again Vishvanovitch took out his ax to defend himself against the blow. This time he was pushed back a few steps from the impact. Vishvanovitch smiled as his heels dug into the ground.

"You see how your blow strengthened," Vishvanovitch said. "We will work on this. I'll also teach you a few other techniques to master the heavy weapons."

It was time, and they were ready. The three had been training very hard for the past two weeks. Julie had further perfected her speed and aim. Michael had trained in combat with dwarves to increases his battle strength and skill. Steven had learned how to use his weapon better. They were to leave the city at noon with the villagers and the first third of the army. They restlessly waited for the time to come. The hours went by slower than ever before. This was how it was before every battle.

Vishvanovitch came up to them at the front of their house. He was holding a large mace in his hand. Steven got up out of respect for his master. He smiled when he saw the mace.

"Steven," Vishvanovitch said, "you trained hard and well and mastered the ways of the heavy weapons. I have taught you all there is to know. I think you have graduated from your mace to a new and better one. It's time for you to take on a larger task and master this new mace and make it a part of yourself. There is only one mace that I know of that is bigger and stronger than the one I'm holding, and that is the one that belongs to the king of Flamborsia. His grandfather came to my grandfather and asked my grandfather to make it for him. It was passed down in the family ever since. Only a true master can make such a mace. My grandfather was the last true master of the mace. Treat this one well. I know you deserve it."

A tear went down Steven's face. It was like he was graduating. He felt ready for the new mace and honorably took it from Vishvanovitch's hands. He lifted it above his head. The mace was heavy, but Steven would learn to use it like he had perfected his old one. "Thank you," was all he could manage, along with a bow of his head. Vishvanovitch did the same and walked away.

Soon after that Ravanak showed up. "It's almost time to get going. Let's get with the rest of the group." Ravanak, Jabertormitch, and Avram were joining them with the first group. Barki and Rumin were going with the third group.

Most of the dwarves were waiting at the end of the city to leave. The mothers had packages on their backs and children in their arms. The men wore armor and carried weapons, standing behind the women and children to protect them from harm. There must have been thousands of dwarves. Michael had never seen this many of one type of creature gathered in one spot. If they were to gather all the creatures like this, then the rebellion would for sure be able to defeat Dalafar.

"It's time to go," Katensthiv announced from the front. He had a loud voice that befitted a leader. "Do not be frightened. We will catch our enemy by surprise and retake the land that is ours: our home, Rekadon!"

The crowd cheered as they marched out of New Rekadon. Katensthiv held his ax above his head as they walked.

Michael took a glance at Avram's leg as they were walking. He still had a small limp. Michael was afraid for Avram. How would he be able to fight with that injury? He hoped that Avram would be all right, and he knew Avram would reject any idea of sitting out. Avram never cared for himself. He always fought for the greater good. A small injury wouldn't stop him.

The march was silent. There was not a peep, even from a child. Only the sound of the feet walking across the rocky floor could be heard. Anxiety filled the air. The women looked down as they walked. The men's heads turned every way, on the lookout for a threat. The villagers grew frightened as they passed Rekadon. They walked in sight of the scouts. Michael could see one of the scouts run into the city. He smiled. Their plan was working.

His smile turned to a frown when he realized what it meant by their plan was working. Now they had to have a war. The dread came over him. But there was nothing he could do. Certain things, even if they didn't feel right, had to be done. He hated to kill, and it went against everything that he had ever believed in, but there was no other choice.

They kept walking past the city. They were to wait until they saw the enemy army, and then they would turn and fight. They wanted to make it seem that they were surprised when the enemy came to attack them.

Soon after, the sound of the army could be heard in the distance. The armor hit the rocky ground. They were closing in. it was almost time. The sound got louder as seconds passed. The civilian dwarves in the front kept going, while the rest of them in the back stopped and turned to face the enemy. Michael didn't understand how the enemy army was able to get ready so quickly. It usually took longer to prepare for battle. It was like they were ready.

The enemy army was charging at them with full speed. The screams of battle cries were heard throughout the army. And finally the armies clashed. Battle-axes hit battle-axes. The war began. Dwarves were already hitting the floor. The armies started to mesh into each other. It became hard to differentiate between ally and foe. Only the symbol on the armor showed whom they were fighting.

The enemies' numbers seemed lower than Michael expected. Michael could see the enemy losing the battle as he slashed his way through dwarves. The dwarves' armor was thick. He usually went for the neck to cut their throats, where the weakest part of the armor was. If he would strike straightforward, he would hit a human's stomach. But for the dwarves, he would hit their necks, so it all worked out. He thought that it was easier for him to kill the dwarves than the other dwarves because he had a height advantage.

He blocked a blow from a dwarf on his right while spinning to strike a dwarf behind him. He smashed his sword into the belly of a dwarf to his left. A few other dwarves were in his way as he tried to reach Avram. He began to cut through them. Michael was still concerned for Avram. Avram's leg had never recovered. His limp was getting worse the more he used it. Michael could tell that Avram was struggling to fight.

Michael wasn't able to reach Avram due to another blockade of dwarves that got in his way. He turned his attention away from Avram, hoping that he'll be all right. He saw Steven using his new mace with a new dexterity. It made him smile. Then he saw Julie behind their dwarf allies, shooting her bow. She was aiming for dwarves that were closing in on Avram. At least she was able to help him.

The armies were evening out. The enemy soon took control. It was time for the backup army to join in. Jabertormitch took out a war horn and started to blow it. The sound echoed throughout the mountains. Michael knew what it meant. It was the signal for the other two armies. The second army would come help them, while the third would enter the unprotected city.

The second third of their army came rushing into the battle. The tides were turned. The enemy was outnumbered. Michael thought that the enemy was probably caught by surprise. They didn't stand a chance now. But it did feel a little too easy. He thought the enemy army would be larger in numbers. His thoughts were cut short. *No.* He couldn't believe what he was seeing. A large enemy dwarf army followed their own second wave of troops.

He had thought the war was over. He was already exhausted. Turned out that the war was just beginning. Somehow the enemy had predicted their strategy and had reinforcements ready. Or the enemy knew of their plan. In that case the city probably had some more troops in the city waiting for Rumin, Barki, and the rest of the dwarves. He wished that he could warn them.

Michael watched as their numbers thinned. The enemy was taking over. The new reinforcements took everyone by surprise. Michael saw his allied dwarves falling on all sides. He protected one by killing a dwarf, but another one was killed behind him. Michael had a hard time protecting himself, let alone others. It didn't look like they could win. He started to give up hope.

Michael straightened up. They could still win, and even if he went down, then he would go down with honor, fighting for what was right. He charged into a section of the enemy dwarves. He spun around as he cut through two dwarves, deflecting the blow of a third. All of his allies had the same determination. They kept on fighting. They had willpower. Enemy dwarves kept on coming at him. He hit one on his left and turned to his right to kill another. He jabbed the hilt of his sword into the nose of a dwarf behind him. The dwarf fell in agony, and Michael gave the fatal blow.

He hoped that their attempt to win this battle wasn't in vain. Their numbers were diminishing. He kept fighting. They had to win. They couldn't give up hope. The only way they could win was a miracle, but miracles did happen.

Barki and Rumin led the dwarves into Rekadon through the secret tunnel. The city streets were deserted. It didn't feel right. Even though the army should be gone, there should still be other civilian dwarves here. They were expecting to encounter citizens. Barki had a bad feeling in the pit of her stomach. She motioned to the others to be quiet. They skulked through the streets, looking for any sign of life. Rumin looked calm, but then again, he always wore a calm face. Nothing ever bothered him.

"Let's check out the houses," Barki suggested. The others nodded.

Before they had a chance to move, enemy dwarves surrounded them and attacked. The enemy outnumbered them. Why were they still here? They should have been fighting in the war. None of the army should have been left in the village. Did they somehow know of the plan? Barki drew her two rapiers. She saw Rumin do the same. The dwarves pulled out their battle-axes. The brawl began.

Barki used her height as an advantage. The dwarves weren't looking at her. She went by them, unnoticed, until it was too late for the enemy and they found themselves falling to the floor. She couldn't see Rumin. He was lost within the mob of dwarves. She had to make sure that she only took down the enemy.

She soon realized that the enemy dwarves were crushing them. There was no possibility for them to win. She could only hope that the others were having better luck on their side of the battle. The enemy was closing in. She found herself surrounded. Rumin was still nowhere in sight. She was too small to handle all the dwarves that were surrounding her. She dropped her weapons to the floor. It was over. This was the end. She had fought with valor, and that was what counted.

A burst of flames from above consumed the enemy dwarves around her. She looked up. She had never been so happy before to see that big green bulk flying over her. The dragon smiled at her. His giant teeth munched on some more dwarves.

Darkon shot another blast of fire at the enemy. The tides turned.

"Go and help the others," Barki screamed up to Darkon. They were fine and could handle themselves. The others probably needed more help.

He flew off in a hurry. She just hoped that they weren't too late. Somehow the enemy had known of their plan. Darkon was their only chance now.

Michael was getting really worried. They couldn't hold off the dwarves much longer. He just wished that they could hold off the enemy so that the other dwarves could get far enough to get away. They may have been defeated, but at least they could try to stall long enough for the citizens to escape.

Michael saw a group of dwarves moving in on Avram. He knew that he couldn't make it in time to help Avram. Avram was fighting hard, but he couldn't take on more than two dwarves at a time. His leg was a real disadvantage. He could hardly move with that limp. Michael thought that this was the end for Avram. Michael tried to push through dwarves to reach Avram, but more kept coming at him. Michael had to defend himself first.

Michael felt a chill run down his back. The hot sun was no longer beating down on him. It was darker. Something was blocking the sun. He forced a dwarf back and took a second to look up.

Darkon let out the loudest roar Michael had ever heard. He was shooting flaming pillars in the midst of the enemy. It caused the enemy to scatter. Michael smiled. Their miracle had come.

Another burst of flames shot out. The enemy was getting scared. Some even retreated. They realized that they couldn't fight against a dragon. Michael saw Darkon's attention turn to Avram. The dwarves' axes were inches away from slicing right through him. Avram tried to defend himself as best as he could. The dwarves got closer with every strike.

Darkon flew straight for him to help him. He couldn't risk shooting fire wherever any of the allies were. Instead he used his claws to kill the enemy. He was almost in reach of Avram. He swooped down and picked up one dwarf, who almost sliced Avram in two. The dwarf squealed as Darkon dropped him to the ground. Another one of the dwarves ran away, abandoning the attempt to kill Avram. Darkon took a third dwarf in his mouth.

But there was one dwarf who came from behind Avram and picked up his ax to strike. Michael could hear himself screaming as he sliced through a dwarf in front of him. Darkon was almost there. His claws were in reach of the dwarf. The ax came down.

Death and Damage

The war was easily won, thanks to Darkon. Michael knew there would be celebrations in the streets of the city. But before the celebrations he knew there would be depression throughout the people. There were many casualties. The buildings in the city were badly damaged. Many dwarf families were left homeless. The only building that was left fully intact and untouched was the temple. There would have to be a lot of repair before the celebrations.

Michael was on his way to the infirmary and passed many crying dwarves. There were all sorts of dwarves in the streets with miserable faces. Children without their fathers, women without their husbands, and others grieving over lost family members and shattered homes roamed the streets. Their beards were soaked with tears. It was a tragic sight.

When he neared the infirmary, the crowd of dwarves grew. They were all waiting to see what would become of their injured family and friends. Soon it was hard to walk without bumping into dwarves or squeezing between them. It was sad that there were so many dwarves waiting near the infirmary. He made his way through all the dwarves into the infirmary.

The infirmary wasn't ready for the patients that came in that week. It was only one room with not more than twenty beds for the sick, and there were only a few nurses able to run around and tend the sick and injured. Hundreds of injured soldiers needed attention. All the houses surrounding the infirmary were full to capacity with the injured. Michael was sure that they would have been able to save more soldiers if there were more help.

Avram was in one of the beds in the infirmary. Ravanak was standing over Avram's bed with his head down. Barki sat on a night table on the left of the bed. Neither Rumin nor Jabertormitch were there. By the looks on Ravanak's and Barki's faces, it didn't look like Avram was doing too well. They didn't look up when Michael neared them.

Steven and Julie were still in bed. Michael didn't want to wake them. He knew this day would only bring pain and sadness, and he didn't want it to be longer than it had to be for them. Michael hadn't seen this much destruction and death since the raid in Periphia. It brought back bad memories. He didn't want Julie and Steven to be reminded of those memories.

Michael took another step closer to the bed. This time Ravanak looked up. His face told Michael all he needed to know. Ravanak's eyes were watery. Barki's face was solemn. He could feel the message that they were sending him. There was no need for them to speak. He knew the truth. He rubbed his eyes as tears started to fall. More and more people that he had grown close to were dying. He knew the future would only bring more deaths. Maybe joining the rebellion was not the best thing for him and his siblings. He wouldn't be able to bear it if anything bad happened to them.

He was about to tell Ravanak that he was done with the rebellion when he remembered his mother. She had wanted this for them. There must be a good reason. He would stick to it. But top on his list would be to protect his sister and brother.

Michael walked over to the bed and stood next to Ravanak. He took Avram's hand in his and held it tight. It was furry. Michael could see the fatal wound on the left side of Avram's neck. No blood was coming out. There was no pulse in his body.

"He was brave and honorable," Ravanak said as he put his hand on Michael's shoulder.

"I know." Michael nodded. Avram was the most self-sacrificing person he knew. Avram had been injured this whole time but had refused to sit back from helping to save Charldena. He would have given up everything, and in fact he had given up everything. He didn't care for himself at all. He always put everyone else before him. If only everyone had the dedication of Avram, their progress would grow, and they would be able to defeat Dalafar in no time.

"The funeral will be tomorrow," Ravanak said. "The dwarves are giving him the great honor of being buried in their graveyard for his valiant efforts. This will be the first outsider to ever be buried in a dwarf graveyard." With that Ravanak left the infirmary.

Barki sat there in silence. She hadn't moved the whole time. She was as still as Avram.

Michael decided that it was time for him to go wake up the others. It was already almost midday. But he wouldn't bring them here. They didn't need to see all the tragedies. He would let them know what had happened in a gentle way. He didn't want to upset them.

The streets became more crowded. More dwarves were waking up to the tragic day that awaited them. It would take time to recover from all the losses. At least when they recovered there would be a great celebration in honor of their victory. Great victories always came with great sacrifices. Although Michael had to admit that without Darkon it wouldn't have been a victory. They had really gotten lucky. They would have to do much better the next time if they were ever to defeat Dalafar.

When Michael arrived back at the house, Julie was sitting at the end of her bed and Steven was still lying down with his eyes closed. Michael suspected that he was awake. Steven always liked to lie in bed a little before he actually got up. The hour was late, and he was surely awake by now.

"Where'd you go?" Julie asked. When Steven heard that Michael was back, he sat up straight. Michael didn't answer. He couldn't let the words out. He just put his head down and let tears pour down his cheeks in response. He hoped that they would make the same inference that he had made when Ravanak had done the same to him. It was the easiest way to show them.

Julie seemed to get it when she also put her head down and tears fell from the end of her chin onto the bed. Steven didn't seem to get it right away, but he fell back down and pretended to sleep again. Steven never liked to face the truth when it wasn't good. Michael knew that he was crying, but his sobs were muffled by the pillow that Steven buried his face in.

"The funeral will be tomorrow," Michael said. That was all he wanted to say. He wasn't in the mood to talk today. He left the house. He had to take a walk to clear his mind. He joined other dwarves who were aimlessly roaming the streets, moping. Life would go on soon. He knew that it had to. All the dwarves would soon be hustling and bustling about their daily routines in a few weeks after everything was rebuilt. The memories would always be there, but life always went on after death.

The rain poured down hard. The funeral still wasn't canceled. Michael knew there would be countless funerals this day. No amount of rain would stop that. The dwarves crowded into the cemetery. They all wanted to honor the brave satyr who gave his life to fight for them.

Michael found this fascinating. Soon after he had left his home back in Periphia, he had realized that different creatures didn't get along well with each other. This showed that they were able to overcome their differences to help one another. Perhaps Avram's example would be a big step into peace for the world. Leave it to Avram to help the rebellion's cause even after death.

Jabertormitch gave the eulogy. He stood next to the coffin at the entrance of the cemetery next to Ravanak, Barki, Rumin, Katensthiv, Michael, Julie, and Steven. He was loud, so all the dwarves could hear him.

"Here, in this coffin," Jabertormitch started, "lies the first outsider who will be buried in a dwarf graveyard. Why, some of you might ask. It's a simple reason. Because this creature gave it all; he gave his life for you to be standing here. He fought to his death for us to live on and survive. He fought for the greater good.

"It was all he wanted in life. He wanted to serve a greater cause. He cared not for himself. He always looked after others. His legacy will live on in all of us forever in hope that we will someday fulfill his only desire in life. In hope that we will win this war and defeat the evil that dominates us. And we will do it.

"We will do it for all those, like this satyr, who gave up everything that they had for this cause. That's why it will be accomplished. We have the willpower. We have something that Dalafar doesn't. We have honor and hope. Here's to a creature that never gave up on these beliefs and instilled these beliefs in all of us.

"Avram, even though he was no dwarf, was my very good friend, and I am honored to have the privilege to speak for him. He was the greatest satyr I know. His actions will be remembered for all eternity. When our children tell the tale of how the rebellion defeated Dalafar and restored peace to all Kanavar and even all of Charldena, this battle will be remembered. Avram will be mentioned as a war hero."

There were tears in everyone's eyes. That was the most touching speech Michael had ever heard. Even the dwarves who had never even seen Avram before were crying. Michael never knew that Jabertormitch could be so deep. He knew that he would remember Avram forever, and if the time ever came, he would definitely tell his children of Avram.

Four dwarves came over, two on each side, and lifted the coffin. The crowd of dwarves split into two groups to make way for the coffin. The four dwarves walked the coffin into the cemetery until they reached the spot designated for Avram. They lowered the coffin down into the pit.

"*Lehastir*," Katensthiv said. Dirt came from around the pit and fell into the pit, burying the coffin underneath. Avram now laid in his resting place among the dwarves. There was a moment of silence. Their silence wasn't only for Avram, but also for all the other dwarves who had perished in the war for the sake of peace.

The silence lasted for a few minutes before dwarves started to leave. The cemetery emptied out within the hour. The dwarves would return many more times on that day. There would be more burials in the same cemetery.

After all the brave dwarves were resting beneath the ground, the rebuilding began. In fact for the next week everyone pitched in to help rebuild. Even young children and mothers helped. Everyone worked together to rebuild their city, Rekadon. Children helped their fathers by running back and forth with tools and messages. The women helped their husbands by cooking the meals that fuled their energy to work.

Everyone was working together to rebuild the city. There was no arguing or fighting. They were one unit. There was much progress. The city was getting rebuilt faster than any of them had imagined. The city was being built by the determination of the dwarves. Michael watched as stone after stone, rock after rock were placed down on the buildings and houses. Michael could see that dwarves were hard workers. They worked very well with stones and rocks and were able to build very fast. It wasn't long before Rekadon returned to its glory.

The Elder's Scrolls

When the day came that the rebuilding was finally done, that very night was the celebrations and festivities. All the dwarves gathered outside in the streets under the night sky filled with shining stars to celebrate their miraculous victory over the enemy. Lamps were lit all around to lighten up the night. Music was played throughout the city. Everywhere you turned were dwarves singing, jumping, and dancing, all with happy faces. They had their city back.

The most festive area was the center of the city. Dwarves gathered in circles and began to dance. Michael, Steven, and Julie joined the dancing dwarves. Drummers and trumpeters were on the side of the circle, playing famous dwarfish folk songs that were played at all dwarf festivals. A large feast was set up nearby. Dwarves were eating and drinking. Laughter filled the table.

Steven left the dancing for the food as soon as he saw the spread. Michael and Julie came to eat soon after. Michael didn't recognize half the food, but he ate it anyway. Most of it tasted good, although some did not, and then there were other things that he stayed clear of.

Jabertormitch, Vishvanovitch, and Katensthiv sat at the head of the table. Ravanak was near them. They were all smiling. One dwarf pulled Jabertormitch into the dancing circle. Jabertormitch started to dance and was the best one out there. The circle crowded around him and watched his dance moves. There were clapping and whistling.

Kids ran in the streets dressed up in masquerade costumes, trying to scare the adults. They were playing all types of games. Some games Michael knew, and some he didn't. Some dwarves were putting on puppet shows for the younglings. They cheered and laughed at the amusing puppets.

The festival lasted the whole night. Even most of the children stayed up for the night. Nobody wanted to sleep when such a celebration was going on. The only ones sleeping were some drunken dwarves with their heads in their arms at the table.

It wasn't until sunrise that the last of the dwarves went home to sleep. The city slept till noon that day. At noon life returned to the way it had been before the war. All the dwarves came out to return to their daily jobs. Even the rebellion returned to their mission of locating the twelve stones.

Their mission brought them to the house of Zakenesht, the elder dwarf. Zakenesht was the only dwarf who had been quiet the previous night. He had been outside, but he did not sing dance or even laugh. He knew that the victory was only a door to many wars and battles in the future. To him it was more of a defeat than a victory. He dreaded what was to come in the world.

"Let me show you where I keep the ancient scrolls," Zakenesht said. His face had more creases than usual. They followed him into the back room of his humble house.

The room was empty except for one chest against the back wall. "Feel free to browse the scrolls as you wish," Zakenesht said before leaving the room. They walked closer to the chest. The rock floor was cold on their feet,

Ravanak bent over the chest. He wiped dust from the top of the chest. Steven sneezed. Julie gave him a look when he wiped his nose with his shirt.

"It hasn't been touched in years," Ravanak said as he opened the chest. The hinges made a creaking sound.

"We better get a move on and start looking through these scrolls," Jabertormitch said. The chest was piled high with probably over a hundred scrolls. Any one of them could be what they needed, or maybe none of them was.

Ravanak, Jabertormitch, Michael, Julie, and Steven all picked some scrolls and started to read. Rumin and Barki just sat and watched. They were too small to even hold the scrolls; forget about reading them. Steven looked at the few scrolls that he held. They were interesting but had nothing to do with the twelve stones.

THERE IS STILL TO THIS DAY
A MEMBER OF BRIN'S DYNASTY
THAT STILL LIVES
THE DYNASTY SHALL RULE FOREVER

IF YOU ARE TO SURPASS
THE BLOCKADE IN THE
ANCIENT SEA AND
DEFEAT THE CREATURES BEYOND
THEY WILL AGREE TO HELP
YOU AND YOU WILL NEVER GET
INJURED IN ALL YOUR DAYS

THE MAGIC IN THE FAMOUS
DYNASTY IS UNDENIABLE
THEY HAVE A GREAT MAGIC
WITHIN ALL OF THEM

Michael saw Ravanak taking his fourth scroll to read, while he hadn't even started his first. He was daydreaming about what had happened to them and how much had changed in the past few months. He concentrated on the scroll in his hand. He unrolled it and started to read.

THE VERY POWERFUL SORCERER HAD
A NAME THIS NAME WAS A FAMOUS NAME
THIS NAME WAS BRIN HE MADE THE TWELVE
STONES AND THE GUARDIANS TO PROTECT THEM
ONE GUARDIAN OF ICE IN ITS DOMAIN
AND ELEVEN OTHERS IN THEIR DOMAINS
GUARDIANS MUST BE DESTROYED IN ORDER
TO CAPTURE THE TWELVE STONES

"I think I found it," Michael said excitedly. The first one that he picked up was the right one. It was like fate. Everyone dropped their scrolls and crowded around him.

"This is it," Ravanak said. "'One guardian of ice in its domain,'" Ravanak repeated the most important line. "We need to find where the ice domain is in order to get to the stone."

"That's easy," Barki said. "The only place that I know of that is covered in ice and snow is Icicle Island."

"We have to go there?" Jabertormitch asked.

"Apparently," Rumin answered. It looked like he was in a bad mood. He stormed out of the room.

"What's his problem?" Jabertormitch asked.

"He gets like that," Barki answered.

"Icicle Island it is," Ravanak said. "We have to leave as soon as possible. Let's get some supplies ready, and we'll be off in a few days."

"Where is it?" Julie asked.

"Icicle Island," Ravanak answered, "is near the southwest corner of Kanavar. We can get a ship in Lanhoin and sail to it."

"How are we supposed to get a ship?" Julie questioned. She wanted to make sure the plan would work. Ravanak made it sound so easy. Typical Julie, always making sure everything ran smoothly. She could never just go with the flow and plan it out as they went along. There had to be a thought-out plan.

"We have supporters of the rebellion in Lanhoin," Ravanak explained. "We can get a ship from them."

"There are supporters of the rebellion?" Steven asked.

"Of course," Ravanak said. "The rebellion has many supporters throughout Kanavar. We wouldn't be able to survive otherwise. Where would we get all the weapons and supplies without supporters? Our main supporter in Lanhoin is the Leed family. You'll meet them when we get to Lanhoin."

Julie frowned. Ravanak made it sound so easy, which bothered her, but she had no other arguments to throw at him. "We better start getting ready," was all she could say.

Zakenesht was waiting for them on a couch in the first room of the house. "Did you find what you needed?" he asked.

"Yes we did," Ravanak said. "Thank you."

"Do you need to keep the scroll?"

"No, thank you. We left it in the chest. We found out what we have to do. Thank you so much for helping us."

"My pleasure. If you ever need anything else, you know where to find me. Have a good day."

"You too."

They left the house and went their separate ways to gather the things that they needed for the upcoming trip.

"Let's get something to eat," Michael suggested to Julie and Steven. A smile came across Steven's face. Michael caught a smirk from Julie.

"I knew you guys would like that idea." Michael laughed. "Let's see what they have in the market." They walked a few blocks until they reached the market. The market was where all the shops in the city were. Dwarves swarmed the market, buying the things that they needed to fill their new houses. The market looked as it was before the war.

"Ravanak gave me some money," Michael said. "Let's get some food."

Steven ran over to one shop. "Over here," he called back to them. He ran into a bakery. Michael knew why Steven had chosen the bakery. The aroma filled the whole area. It drew anyone who was near into the store. The fresh smell of the newly baked cakes and bread reached all the noses that passed by.

There were bread, cookies, and cakes lined up on shelves behind the counter. An old dwarf lady stood behind the counter. She had a long white beard and wrinkly skin. They all looked the same to Michael. Steven was paying more attention to the colorful cookies.

"How may I help you children?" the dwarf said. She had a nice and sweet voice, which was unusual for most dwarves.

"We'd like to buy some bread," Julie said. Steven sighed. Julie didn't want them to have cakes or cookies now. They had a limited amount of money, and they should spend it on real food like bread. Eating dessert for lunch wouldn't be too healthy. Steven didn't care if it was healthy or not. That was why Julie needed to look out for him.

"Here you go." The old dwarf handed them three pieces of bread when Michael handed her the money. Steven was already munching on his bread. Michael took a bite. It was warm and tasted good. It felt good going down his throat. He took another bite as they left the shop. It was delightful. The bread was fluffy.

One bite was filling enough. But they all kept eating. It was great bread. By the time they left the town center, all three of them had finished their bread.

"That was really good," Steven said.

"I'll agree to that," Julie said.

Their walk back to their house was very noisy. There were many dwarves on the roads. The city was back to normal. It looked as if war had never struck the city or its people. Michael was happy for the dwarves. They were able to continue their lives. He hoped the war would encourage them to fight with the rebellion in the future. Dwarves were strong and would help in battles that were to come.

When they got back to their house, they realized that they didn't really have any preparing to do for the journey. They didn't own many things. All they had were the packs they had received from Ravanak when they'd first started their journey to Rekadon and a few extra pieces of clothing that they got from the dwarves.

"Now what?" Steven asked.

"I don't know," was all Michael could answer. There were still a few hours left to the day. They would sleep early that night, but he didn't know what to do until then.

"We can just walk around," Julie suggested, "and have a look at the city. It would be nice to see the rebuilt city after we worked so hard to get it this way." The boys nodded. They had nothing else to do.

They walked back out of the house into the roads of Rekadon. Dwarves greeted them as they passed. They even got some "thank you" greetings from a few dwarves who were more than glad to be back in their homes.

Lanhoin

After a few days of preparation, the group was ready to leave for Lanhoin. They were standing at the gates of Rekadon with Katensthiv, Zakenesht, Vishvanovitch, and a few other government officials.

"Good-bye my friends," Katensthiv said.

"Good luck," Zakenesht said. "You'll probably need it."

"Steven," Vishvanovitch said. "Someday you may perfect your new mace. Come back when you can, and we will train more. Until then, good-bye." Steven bowed his head to his master. They hugged each other.

"Thank you all for helping us," Ravanak said. "We hope to see you again in the future, in a better future." Ravanak walked aside with Katensthiv. Michael tried to hear what they were saying. "You know what this war meant, Katensthiv."

"Yes. I very much do," Katensthiv answered.

"There must be a traitor in your courts. You have to be more careful whom you share your information with. We don't want anything like that to happen again."

"I will be careful. But you as well have to consider what happened. It doesn't necessarily imply there is a traitor among my people. Your group was in the meeting as well, Ravanak."

Ravanak frowned. "I trust all of them with my life."

"And I trust all of my people with mine. That is our problem, Ravanak. Just be cautious."

They walked back to the others. Ravanak knew the traitor was not among the rebellion. It was impossible. He had made sure to check each one's background before letting them join. The traitor must have been a dwarf. He only hoped that Katensthiv would heed his warning. With those thoughts in his head, he set out with the rebellion for Lanhoin.

They traveled in a similar path to the one that they came on. It wasn't an exciting journey. The traveling was easier this time because there was more downhill than uphill. But it was still tough traveling on the mountains. One trip on a rock, and that was the end. Everyone was a little more relaxed on this trip than the last. Things weren't so intense between everyone. They had all grown closer after the last couple of weeks.

But the days were still long and hard. They traveled for long hours without rest. Many times they even went into the night. They were going at a fast pace. They wanted to get there as fast as possible. They needed to get there before Dalafar. Maybe Dalafar already knew where to go and was already on his way. They couldn't risk letting him get his hands on any of the stones. Too much was at stake to fail just because they didn't travel fast enough.

The traveling eased up when they reached the end of the Urakian Mountains. There was no more danger. They were traveling on open land. But they still traveled at their fast pace. They decided before they left that they wouldn't pass through Harvusera. There was no time. Ravanak made that decision. Michael knew how hard it was for Ravanak to do that. Ravanak must have missed his brother and want nothing more than to return to him, but he put the mission first.

They traveled straight to Lanhoin. They had enough supplies to last until they reached the city. The dwarves had been generous enough.

After two weeks of the open land traveling, the city of Lanhoin could be seen on the horizon. But they saw something that they didn't expect to see. Lanhoin was different from the last time Ravanak had been there, and not for the better.

"What happened!?" he screamed. He was getting very frustrated with the dwarf in front of him.

"We lost...sire," the dwarf stammered. He was scared to death. *Of course he was.* Anyone in his place would be.

"I can see that. My question is, how? Did you not know of their plan? You did. Then how can you lose when you know your enemy's strategy? Did you not act against it? From my sources I know that you did. Then how can you lose?"

"Um...there was a...a..."

"Get on with it!"

"A...a..."

"Spit it out before I force you to!"

"A dragon."

"A what?"

"A dragon—"

"I heard what you said. But how can this be? A dragon? This is impossible!" His anger was growing. The dwarf was shaking where he stood. He stood there for no longer when Dalafar mercilessly struck him down. He motioned for some of his servants to remove the body from his throne room.

"Call in the next one," Dalafar said. A guard moved from Dalafar's side and left the throne chamber. He came back in a minute, dragging in another dwarf. This dwarf was not as scared as the first. Dalafar would have to change that. The dwarf had a scar on his right cheek. Dry blood was all over his face. His hair was a mess, and his clothes were torn.

"What news do you have?" Dalafar's angry tone scared the dwarf. Dalafar smirked.

"Our sources tell," the dwarf said, "that the rebellion has located the whereabouts of a stone." Dalafar's smile caused the dwarf to sigh with relief. "They are on their way to the location now," the dwarf continued. "They are headed to Lanhoin to get a ship. They are going to Icicle Island. I've heard all of this straight from your source, my liege."

"Finally some good news," Dalafar said. "Be gone with you, you scum." His bad mood had turned to a good one.

"Prepare my things," Dalafar said to a guard. "I'm heading off to Keedor."

The usually open gate for the outside traders to come into Lanhoin was closed. Soldiers of Dalafar's army stood at the gate.

"This is bad," Ravanak said.

"What's wrong?" Julie asked.

"Lanhoin has always been free of trouble," Ravanak answered. "There has never been any interference from Dalafar in this city. The satyrs have always been peaceful. Their trade is a big part of Kanavar's economy, so Dalafar never got involved with them. He let them be, until now. We had many supporters among them. Now that the army is here, it will be hard for us to get in, and our supporters might not be able to help us without getting into trouble. This is bad news."

"So what do we do?" Michael asked.

"We have to get disguises and a plan in order to get in," Jabertormitch said.

"I have an idea," Barki said. "Obviously Rumin and I can stay hidden with one of you. So we won't be a problem. The problem will be a centaur, a dwarf, and three humans coming into a city of satyr merchants. Humans aren't that bad because they come and go all the time for trade. So Michael, Julie, and Steven can say they're here on business for their uncle in Keedor. The only way I can think of you two getting in is by getting arrested because of a fight."

"A fight?" Ravanak said, confused.

"I'm liking the sound of this." Jabertormitch grinned.

"Yes, a fight," Barki continued.

"I see where this is going," Rumin cut in. "Jabertormitch will be chasing Ravanak. It's not uncommon for dwarves and centaurs to fight, so you won't need a legitimate reason. When you reach the gate, start screaming at each other. Then make it like you're going to start a fight. The guards will break it up and put you in jail inside the city. Barki and I will stay with you unseen. We will help you break out of the prison."

"Where should we be?" Michael asked.

"You guys wait near the prison," Ravanak said, showing his agreement to the plan, "but out of sight of the guards."

"What if we don't see you?" Julie asked.

"Don't worry, we'll find you," Jabertormitch said.

"Sounds like a plan," Steven said. "Let's go." He ran off. Michael and Julie followed.

The guards at the gate stood up straight when they saw the three humans coming.

"What's your business here?" one guard asked.

Michael was a little nervous. The spears in their hands made him hesitate before answering.

"We have come to make a business trade offer to a satyr for our uncle's business," Michael said.

"You three? Here to make a business offer?" The second guard laughed. "You are just kids."

"Our uncle is really busy. He's working hard in the business. He couldn't leave. After our parents died—" Julie and Steven started to cry, "our uncle took us in. It was hard enough for him to support himself, but now he also had us. Soon he would no longer be able to. The only way his business will remain in existence is if we make this deal for him."

"Please let us in," Steven pleaded.

"You can go in," the first guard said. He seemed to be of higher rank. Michael wiped the sweat from his brow. Their story had worked. He gave a silent compliment to Julie and Steven for the fake crying.

"Open the gates," the second guard screamed. The gates opened slowly. Guards were standing inside the city as well. There were more guards here than in Keedor. They had gotten themselves into a tough situation.

"Get back here!" Jabertormitch screamed. "You filthy half-breed!"

"You'll never catch me alive!" Ravanak yelled back. Ravanak was galloping toward the gate to Lanhoin. Jabertormitch was running after him—screaming and cursing. When he got to the gates, Ravanak came to a halt and turned around. "Let's settle this once and for all, dwarf," he said to Jabertormitch.

"You're asking for a fight?" Jabertormitch sounded surprised.

"Isn't that what you wanted? Are you scared now?"

"Ha! Scared of what? You? Never! I'll take you on anywhere anytime. Bring it, half-breed."

"You asked for it." Ravanak charged at Jabertormitch. Jabertormitch dodged out of the way, just in time. "Who's the one running now?" Ravanak mocked.

The guards at the gate faced each other and exchanged worried faces. "Should we do something?" one asked the other.

"Yeah. Let's stop them," the other said. They walked over to Ravanak and Jabertormitch.

"Hey!" one guard screamed.

"Stop!" the other one said. The guards held out their spears.

"Never!" Jabertormitch said in a furious voice.

"There's one thing we can agree on," Ravanak said as he got ready to charge at Jabertormitch again.

"Let's arrest them," one guard said. The other guard nodded and blew a small horn.

The gate opened, and a few other guards came running out. "Arrest them," one guard said. The rest of them ran for Ravanak and Jabertormitch. Some drew their swords and others held their spears as they tried to contain the rogue centaur and the wild dwarf. Ravanak and Jabertormitch put up a small fight before willingly giving in to the guards. The guard used strong ropes to bind the two.

The city was nothing like Keedor, but it was still magnificent. The buildings weren't as large, but instead of humans walking about, satyrs swarmed the roads. It looked like they were all working hard. Avram hadn't been kidding about being trained in the art of being a merchant at a very young age. Some satyrs had their young with them. Some looked like they were less than ten years old. The satyrs were all traders and merchants. It didn't look like there was much other business going on in the city.

Lanhoin was a port city. The docks were full of large merchant ships belonging to the wealthy satyrs. Satyrs crowded the docks. There were ships on the horizon that had just left the docks, and others were coming in with loads of goods. The three humans looked around. They didn't see any other humans. The city was crowded, and it was hard to find anything.

"Let's look for the prison," Julie said.

"Oh, right," Michael answered. He had forgotten for a second about what they had to do. The city was amazing. He had never seen a city as busy and hardworking as this. The satyrs all looked determined to do their jobs. The satyrs looked like friendly folk, but Michael could see in their faces that a portion of their kindness and joy had been recently taken away. He assumed it was because Dalafar's army had taken over the city. The soldiers, no doubt, treated the satyrs badly.

"That looks like the prison," Steven said, pointing to a run-down-looking building that looked as if it was going to collapse. It was completely surrounded by a fence with barbed wire. There were some guards around the building.

"What took you three so long?" a voice came from behind them. Julie jumped, which made Steven laugh. "Shh!" Jabertormitch said. He put a finger to his mouth. "It's just us." Steven laughed again.

"How did you guys escape?" Michael asked.

"It was easy," Barki said. "There was a sleeping guard, and the keys were on the desk. Rumin and I just climbed up the desk and got the keys. And these two put up a good fight."

"Yes. It was enjoyable to watch," Rumin said.

"Very funny. But it could've gone without 'half-breed.'" Ravanak looked at Jabertormitch.

"Sorry." Jabertormitch laughed.

"Let's get to the Leeds," Ravanak said. "Follow me."

Ravanak led them down a maze of streets. It was amazing how well he knew the streets of the city. It was like he lived here. Michael thought that he must come here often. Whoever this supporter was must really help the rebellion.

They walked along the docks. Parallel to the docks was a series of supply stores and houses of the rich merchants. They walked a couple of blocks before Ravanak stopped.

"There." Ravanak pointed to one large ship. Carved along the side of the ship was

The General

"That's their ship," Ravanak continued. There were a number of satyrs working aboard the ship. Some were mopping the floors, and others were doing usual ship stuff. Michael didn't know what that meant. The sails were down. There were no goods on board. The ship didn't look as if it was ready to leave or coming from anywhere.

Ravanak led them up the dock until they reached the ship. Ravanak jumped aboard, and they followed.

"Ravanak?" the oldest-looking satyr asked. "Is that you?" He smiled. "Of course it is! What in the blazes are you doing here? Is my son with you?" The other satyrs were all young. This one looked like he was old enough to be their father.

"Let's talk inside," Ravanak said. The satyr nodded. He beckoned them forward. A satyr opened the door to the captain's quarters for them. It was a small room. There was a bed against the back wall. In front of the bed was a desk with a few chairs.

"Here, sit down." The satyr indicated chairs for them as he sat down himself. "What can I help you with?" the satyr asked Ravanak.

"First with the introductions," Ravanak said, indicating the others. "This is Itzak Leed, our main provider for the rebellion. He is our best supporter. He supplies us with weapons and other essentials. We would be nothing without him." Then he turned to Itzak. "You know Rumin and Barki already. This here is Jabertormitch, Michael, Julie, and Steven. They have recently joined the rebellion. I'm sure you have been in contact lately with my brother, Kojmeer. I had to leave on an important mission and left him in charge."

"Yes I have, but where is my son?" Itzak asked again. Michael didn't understand. Who was his son? Then he hit himself on the head for being so stupid. He must be Avram's father. This would be hard. How would Ravanak tell him the news?

Ravanak looked down to the floor. "I'm sorry," he started, "but your son has given his life as many veterans before him for his country and for the rights of others."

Itzak went cold. He couldn't even open his mouth. He almost fell off his chair. Tears started to stream down Itzak's eyes. He looked from one person to another for help. He didn't want to believe it was true. No one said a word.

"Now before you say anything, just hear me out. He died with honor. He died in battle. He fought with every last one of his breaths. He wouldn't give up. We tried to stop him because he was injured, but he persisted. All he ever wanted in his life was to help others and fight for what he believed in. He was a role model for us all. The dwarves have given him the highest honor by burying him in their graveyard. He died how he wanted to die. I thought I should let you know.

"All we need to do is continue his legacy. We must continue our cause, his cause in defeating Dalafar." That was all Ravanak could do to console Itzak. He'd just found out he had lost a son. It wouldn't be easy for him to just push it aside. "We'll leave you alone for a few minutes." Ravanak got up, and the others followed him out, back onto the deck.

"My dad's still in there?" a satyr asked.

"Yes, Shal," Ravanak answered.

"I'll go in then." Shal headed into the captain's quarters.

"That's also Itzak's son?" Julie asked.

"Yes," Ravanak answered.

"But he's so much older than Avram," Julie said surprised.

"Itzak has many children," Ravanak explained. "Shal is the oldest. Avram is the second to the youngest."

"All these satyrs here on the ship are his children?" Jabertormitch asked.

"Yes," Ravanak answered. "He has six children. Well, now it's five children. Shal is the oldest. He's the one who just went to see his father. Then there's Mosh," Ravanak continued while pointing at each one. "Next comes Jacov. That's Divad. The youngest is Jesof." All of Itzak's sons were working around the ship. They were hard workers. They reminded Michael of Avram.

Itzak and Shal came up together. "You may stay at our house for a while," was all Itzak said. There was nothing else to discuss at the moment. They would have to give time for the family to recuperate from their loss before they would ask them for anything. The whole way to the Leeds' house, they were silent.

"Before we can ask them for anything," Ravanak explained to the others when they neared the house, "they have to mourn for a week. They lost a family member. It's very important to the satyrs to respect the family member's soul by mourning a week for them. We'll have to wait until then. We must not disturb them while they mourn."

Michael looked up at the Leeds' house. It was a mansion. He thought that it was probably three times the size of his old house in Periphia. *They must be one of the rich merchants,* he thought. *Well, it's good they are supporting us.*

The week went by slowly. Everyone in the Leed house was depressed. Michael didn't enjoy the week. It reminded him of Avram's death and all the deaths of the ones that he loved. Itzak's wife, Sara, stayed in her room and didn't come out for the week. Michael could hear her crying every night as he passed her room.

At least the house was nice. It was a fancy house that suited a rich merchant. Chandeliers hung from the ceilings. Fine leather furniture filled the rooms. The chairs were comfortable, and the beds were even better. Michael's best sleep was in this house. The dining room table was twice as big as the one back in Periphia. The kitchen had more closets than things to put in them. There was a large collection of books in Itzak's study. Michael thought that the satyr probably hadn't even read any of them. The books were probably for show.

When the week was up, joy returned to the household. The Leeds were more jolly and hospitable. It made the warm house even warmer. Michael started to enjoy the stay. But he knew that since things were back to normal, they would be leaving soon.

The night of the eighth day, they all sat around the dining room table for dinner.

"Eat up," Sara said with the first smile she had on since Michael saw her. She had a nice smile. It caused Michael to feel warm inside. It was the same smile that Margot had.

There was plenty of food for all of them, but Michael thought there would be a feast. If the Leeds were rich, then there should have been more food. Half of the table was empty. It was more food than Michael had ever eaten at home, but it was hardly a meal for any rich man.

"What happened?" Ravanak asked Itzak.

"Somehow I believe that Dalafar found out that I'm supporting you and sending supplies to the rebellion. Pirates started attacking my ships left and right. I believe Dalafar hired them to stop me. I'm not making as much money as I used to. People stopped trading with me because of the rumored pirates that are attacking my ships. It's hard times."

"I'm sorry to hear that, but nevertheless, I need to ask a big favor from you. The rebellion still needs your help. This favor can be one of the most important things you can do for us. You remember that I told you I am on an important mission?"

"Of course. Even though I don't have as much money as I used to, I haven't failed to continue supporting you. Anything for the rebellion. It would be what Avram wanted most. Let's talk inside."

Itzak led the rebellion members into his study. Of his family he only let Shal come in with them. He didn't want his family to get involved any more in the rebellion. It would put them in too much risk. Michael understood.

Michael sat down on a couch-chair. The fireplace in the corner was lit. Every time that Michael came into the study, he looked at the bookcases. He never really read books. There weren't any books at home to read. He knew that Julie would probably love to read all these books. She would be able to live in the study. She always used to rave about reading. She always wished she could read a book.

"What is it?" Itzak asked. There was a small time of silence. The fire was crackling. Itzak waited for Ravanak to answer.

"We need a ship," Ravanak said flatly, after contemplating how to tell Itzak their plans.

"The only one I got left after all those pirate attacks is my own ship, *The General.* What do you need the ship for?"

Ravanak knew this and knew that it would take a lot for Itzak to give his most prized possession away. In any other circumstance, Ravanak wouldn't ask this of Itzak, but they needed a ship.

"We need to sail to Icicle Island. It's not too far off."

"I was planning on giving my ship to my son—"

"I will take them," Shal cut in.

"What?" Itzak seemed surprised. He turned to his son.

"I will take them to Icicle Island. They have no experience with ships. They wouldn't be able to go themselves. And I might as well earn the ship. I want to get the feel of it, that it's mine."

"But it will be dangerous. There could be pirates, and—"

"They are rebellion fighters. They've fought wars. I'm sure they can handle pirates."

"Very well," Itzak finally agreed. He was still uneasy about it, but it had been the same way when Avram had insisted on joining the rebellion. Then he turned to Ravanak. "My son will take you there. I think a week's time will be enough to prepare."

"Itzak, you always come through for me, my friend." Ravanak gave him a smile.

"I hope that I'll never fail you. I know the rebellion could use all the help it can get. And I hope to be alive to see the overthrow of Dalafar."

"We want to help," Mosh insisted. His brothers stood behind him on the docks. Their father was walking off the ship, *The General.* Shal and the rebellion were aboard the ship. Itzak had already said good-bye to his ship and Shal. He didn't want to have to say good-bye to the others. He wouldn't let all of them put themselves in danger.

"And besides, Shal can't handle the ship by himself; he needs a crew," Jacov added.

"Well, ah…" Itzak was lost for words. He had no argument to that. It was true. He was just hoping that Shal would teach Ravanak and the others how to handle the ship. He had to agree with Mosh on this one. It would be easier for them to go, and it would establish Shal's command as a captain over them.

"So we can go?" Mosh asked.

"Fine, you can go, but Jesof stays here. He's too young." Itzak took Jesof's hand in his. Jesof let out a sob. He really wanted to go. Every little kid wanted an adventure. Itzak didn't blame him, but there was no way he would leave his house empty. He needed at least one of his sons to stay home, or he would lose it. "The rest of you, be careful and come back safely."

"We will, Dad," Mosh promised. "Don't worry about it." He, Jacov, and Divad boarded the ship and started to untie the lines from the dock. Itzak smiled. They were already working even before Shal gave the orders.

"And one more thing," Itzak called to them from the docks as the boat started to drift away. "I don't want any of you going on Icicle Island. It's only for Ravanak and his group to go. You guys stay and wait on the ship. Got it?"

"Yeah, Dad," Shal called back as they waved good-bye. Sara showed up just in time to wave good-bye to her sons. She took Jesof's other hand. The boy almost ran off the docks to catch the ship.

Trouble in the Seas

"Hoist the colors, men," Shal called out. Michael watched the Leed brothers put up *The General's* insignia, two crossed swords with a silver dragon on a green background. "Get the halyard and set the sails, and we're ready to go," Shal continued.

Jacov and Mosh went and unfurled the sails. The winds were blowing in the right direction, and the conditions were perfect for their journey. The sea was calm. No clouds appeared to be coming from any direction.

"Close reach with the wind and bow the sails," Shal said. "It's straight for Icicle Island." They would sail fast and reach Icicle Island before expected if the conditions kept up.

"Mosh, take the helm," Shal said. Mosh went up to the stern of the ship and took the wheel. Mosh turned the wheel very slightly when the wind changed direction a bit. Jacov and Divad were working on the sails. Michael wasn't really sure what they were doing, but it looked like they knew what they were doing. He didn't want to interfere. He would probably only make things worse. Shal was instructing Jacov and Divad on what to do with the sails.

"What are you guys doing?" Michael asked Shal.

Shal didn't turn his attention away from the sails. "Trim the sails. That's perfect." Then he turned to Michael.

"Sorry, what was that?" Shal was engrossed in his work.

"What are you guys doing," Michael repeated.

"We're just getting the sail in the right position so we'll move the fastest. The wind is going in the perfect position for us to sail at an angle where we can move the fastest. I told Jacov and Divad to trim the sails so that the sails can catch the exact amount of wind needed for this ship to go the fastest it can. The sails have to be constantly watched, and if you want to go the fastest, then they also have to be constantly changed based on the wind and direction you want to go. Sailing is complicated. It takes years to learn how to do it precisely. I'm sure by the end of this trip you'll understand some of the basics." Shal turned back to Jacov and Divad. "Jacov, take the jib, and Divad, take the mast."

"Is there anything I can do?" Michael asked. He was eager to help and learn. It would be cool to know how to work a ship. He always liked to learn useful skills. That was the main reason he had wanted to work for Mr. Mim and learn how to make a weapon.

"All right," Shal laughed. "Get your brother, get the mops from the cargo hold below deck, and mop the decks."

Michael sighed as Shal laughed. That wasn't exactly what he'd had in mind. But he guessed that every little thing helped.

Steven was next to Mosh at the helm. Michael went up to them. "Steven."

"Yeah," Steven answered.

"Shal said we should mop the decks."

"Why?" Steven whined. That was the reaction that Michael was expecting. He knew Steven wouldn't like to mop the decks. The last time he did any work that didn't have to do with training was when they traveled with the army.

"Well, somebody has to do it."

"But why us?"

"Well, I sort of asked how we could help."

Steven punched Michael on the arm. "Why did you get us into this mess? I'm going to get you back for this."

Michael laughed, even though he wasn't too thrilled about mopping the decks either. He shrugged. "Fine."

Steven stamped his feet as he followed Michael. Michael knew that Steven would much rather be at the helm.

"Come on," Michael said. He took Steven below deck to the cargo hold. The cargo hold was full of different supplies and barrels of food. Michael hoped it was fresh. "Get a mop and bucket," Michael told Steven as he took one of each himself. They went back up.

"Let's get to it," Michael said as he dipped his mop in the bucket filled with soapy water. Steven sighed again as he dipped his mop in the bucket. They both walked to opposite ends of the deck and started scrubbing the deck.

"Make sure you clean up well." Shal laughed. Steven grunted and Michael just smiled.

They were mopping the whole day. Although Michael didn't complain as much, they both felt it was tedious work. All the Leeds had cool jobs around the ship that actually helped sail the ship. Ravanak was with Shal the whole day, looking at maps and things of that sort. They were discussing the important matters of the trip. Jabertormitch was just walking around, helping out where he was needed. Rumin and Barki were sitting on a pole near the helm. There wasn't much to do around the ship. Everything was going smoothly. That was why they were stuck on mop duty. Julie just watched them and reassured them that it was better that there was nothing to do. It just meant that there were no problems.

Before they knew it, the sun was setting on the horizon. Divad was going around and lighting lanterns around the ship.

"Whoever wants to hit the hay," Shal announced, "can do so. We don't need much work done for the night." He went over to his brothers. "Mosh, you take the first shift. The rest of you can get some sleep for now."

Michael and Steven headed down to their small cabin. There was a wooden bunk bed. "I get the bottom," Steven called. The beds had thin sheets and covers. The bed themselves weren't so comfortable, but Michael had slept on worse. There wasn't any room to really move in the cabin.

Getting to sleep was even worse. Michael could feel every bump of every wave that the ship went over. He was getting seasick and thought that he would never get to sleep. Eventually his fatigue overtook him and he fell asleep.

It was too soon when he woke up again from a giant bump and a loud sound. He heard pounding above him. Another large bump came. He almost fell off his bed.

"Steven," Michael whispered. Steven didn't budge. "Steven," he said, a little louder.

This time Steven looked up at him. "What?" He was a little annoyed.

"You hear that?" Michael asked. Steven was silent for a minute as he listened.

"It's raining," Steven said.

"Yeah, that could be trouble," Michael said. "Let's go check it out. Maybe they need help up there."

"All right," Steven said. "I'll be up in a minute." Michael didn't know if Steven would get up, but he left the room anyway to see what was going on.

When he got aloft, he felt the rain pounding down on his head. It was pouring hard. There was lightning and thunder. The winds were blowing hard. He almost fell over. The deck was slippery. The sky was darker than ever. It was the largest storm he had ever seen. Periphia hardly got any rain. He had never dreamed that such a storm could exist.

"Hey!" Shal called. "We could use some help. Thanks for coming."

Michael could see that the Leed brothers were having a rough time. Ravanak was there too. They were trying to keep the boat under control. Shal was at the helm now instead of the usual helmsmen, Mosh. He shouted orders as he tried to keep the boat straight so they wouldn't alter course. But it was difficult to tell where they were.

"Trim the sails!" Shal shouted. Mosh was controlling the sails. Jacov was holding on to the jib sheet, and Divad was holding on to the mast.

"Let's hold out!" Shal yelled out. The waves were high and reached the deck. Michael tasted saltwater on his lips. The seawater was mixing with the rainwater and flooding the deck. The boat was being pushed around like a rag doll. The sails were flogging in the wind. "Trim!"

A line securing some crates ripped.

"Make fast! Port!" Shal screamed. Ravanak trotted over to the left side of the boat where the crates were and secured the lashing. Michael went over to help him. They got it down. One crate fell overboard. Michael hoped that nothing important was in that crate.

Soon the others came. It was impossible to sleep through this storm. Nobody was able to tell what time of day it was because the storm clouds covered the whole sky. Michael had never known that it could rain for this long. They took turns taking naps, getting food from the galley, and going to the head when they needed to.

Fatigue was overwhelming them. Sooner or later they wouldn't be able to handle it anymore. To their delight the storm finally started to calm down. There was no more lightning and thunder. It wasn't pouring as hard. The storm clouds were drifting away. When the clouds were finally gone, they could see the sky again. It was night, but it was still unclear how much time passed. It was definitely not the same night when the storm started. The moon and stars were clear. Michael saw Ravanak, with a map in hand, talking to Shal. He walked over to them.

"So where are we?" Ravanak asked.

"By the judging of the stars," Shal said, "I would guess that we are farther north than where we were before. The storm pushed us at least four days north from our destination. We lost a lot of time. Let's try to make it back."

"Mosh, take the helm," Shal said. "Everyone else to your usual stations. Let the sails out a little. Turn this ship around." The stern was facing south. They had to turn fully around to get to their destination. That would put them in irons, straight into the wind. It would make them move very slowly. There was no more smooth sailing.

"Head up and head to wind!" Shal said. "Move the sails to midline. At this rate we'll be at Icicle Island in a week." Jacov was at the jib, turning the boat as Mosh handled the helm.

"That's too long," Ravanak said to Shal. It was supposed to take less than a week when they started.

"Fine," Shal answered. "Let me try something else. Close hauled to starboard! Maybe now we'll get there faster."

"I sure hope so," Ravanak said. "Not just for our sake, but for the sake of Charldena."

They were making good progress after two days. The wind had changed a little to their advantage. "Close reach," Shal said as the wind changed. The Leeds knew what to do at this order. Michael still didn't get most of the orders that Shal said. They were sailing terms on how to move the sails, but Michael didn't know what each term meant.

On the second night after the storm, Shal announced that they should be by Icicle Island in just three more days. Ravanak was happy about that. They finally had some good luck. Michael was excited because they were closer to finally getting off the ship, but there was also that small of fear of what the guardian of ice could be. Everyone headed off to bed after the first of the stars came out.

Michael had started to get used to the sleeping, but it was still hard. He would never fully get used to sleeping on a ship unless he practically lived on it, like the Leeds. Steven seemed to be doing a better job. Michael was always a lighter sleeper than Steven. Steven was asleep right when he hit the bed. Michael took about an hour to fall asleep.

This time it was Steven who woke Michael in the middle of the night. "I think I hear something," Steven said. Michael listened. He heard nothing.

"I don't hear anything," Michael said. He thought that Steven must have been dreaming because he didn't usually wake up from noises from outside. Michael was mad that now he had to try to fall back asleep. "You were probably having a nightmare. Go back to sleep."

"I'm going to check it out," Steven said as he started getting dressed. Michael sighed. He tried to fall back asleep, but it was no use. Steven left the cabin. Michael heard a thud after the cabin door closed behind him.

"Steven," he called out in a hushed tone. There was no answer. He got dressed and opened the cabin door. Was Steven trying to trick him or something? Before he could even think, he was knocked on the head. He collapsed to the floor, and everything became black.

Michael woke up on a wet wooden floor. He saw all the others asleep beside him. They were all in a small jail cell that he knew was on a ship because of the bumps that he recognized so well. He thought that was the reason he had woken up before all of the others. On the other side of the bars were stairs going up.

Before he moved some of the others started to wake up. Shal went over to the bars and tried to shake them. He looked very frustrated. He was muttering to himself. Michael could tell that it wasn't the right time to ask questions. Shal banged his head against the bars.

Michael heard footsteps. Someone was coming down the stairs. It was a man wearing a nice hat. That was the only nice thing about him. He had a short gray beard that matched his gray eyes. His face was somewhat wrinkly and dirty. He had gray hair, but it didn't show much because of his pirate hat. Over his dirty and messy gray sleeveless shirt he wore a knee-length blue coat with golden buttons. The once elegant blue coat was filthy and looked like it belonged in antique shop. He had black boots. A sword was sheathed in a black sheath on the left side of a green sash that he wore around his waist of his tattered brown trousers. Michael saw his yellow teeth when he gave an evil grin. He had one golden tooth. The man was obviously a pirate. Michael had never seen one before, but there was no doubt this man was a pirate. It was just as Michael had imagined a pirate would look. The pirate laughed an evil laugh.

"Shoded," Shal said in disgust.

"Leed," the pirate spat back in equal disgust. "And that's *Captain* Shoded to you." He laughed again. "Nice of you to join my crew. I hope you enjoy your stay."

"We're not planning on staying."

"Aye, that may be so, but you be the ones who are on my ship in my brig. I'm the one who decides who's stayin' and who's leavin'. And I say you're stayin'. At least until I figure out what I wanna do with ya."

"And what's that?"

"Well, I got a few possibilities. I could sell ya for ransom. I can drop ya off on some deserted island. Or I can just slit your throats. Maybe I'll even give you a choice." He laughed evilly. Shal was silent. The pirate laughed again. "I'll let you rot down here for a few days first." He continued to laugh as he went back up the stairs.

"Who's that?" Steven asked. Michael still didn't have the guts to ask, but Steven was always able to ask questions.

Shal's head was down. His face was red with embarrassment. "That was Deror Shoded," Mosh said. "He's the fiercest pirate in all the seas. He has been trying to get our ships for years now. We've been rivals."

"Once he has captured you," Shal said, "you never see the light again."

"Then we'll just have to break that tradition," Jabertormitch said. "We're gonna bust out o' here. We just have to figure a way out."

"I think that's easy," Barki said.

"That's right," Ravanak said. "I almost forgot about the last time we broke out of prison."

"One problem," Jabertormitch said. "Where are the keys?"

Rumin was already out of the cell.

"Where are you going?" Barki asked.

"To find the keys," Rumin answered. "You coming?" Barki didn't even answer. She went through the bars, and the two of them headed up the stairs.

"Now what?" Jabertormitch said.

"We wait," Ravanak answered, "and hope they find the keys."

"I doubt it," Shal said. "In the meantime we should figure out another way to get out of here." His brothers nodded. They didn't seem to think that these pirates could be stopped. They all had the same hopeless expression. Michael didn't like the way they thought, but they knew the most about these pirates. They probably knew that the pirates couldn't easily be fooled.

They had to find another way out. The Leeds were probably right. Michael walked over to the bars. He held them firmly and shook. The door of the cell was not secured properly on the hinges. The metal was rusty, and with proper leverage it would break.

"Look," Michael told the others, pointing to the hinges. "The door can easily be broken off the hinges with the right leverage."

"There," Shal said, pointing to a broken thick pole in the corner.

"That would work," Ravanak said.

"Told you we'd escape," Jabertormitch said with pride.

"Just because we escape the brig," Shal said seriously, "doesn't mean that we will escape the ship alive." Jabertormitch was silent. Shal was putting a negative mood on everything. It was like he had already given up. Jabertormitch was never one to give up.

"Well," Ravanak broke in, "let's get out of here." Ravanak lifted the back of the pole with Shal. Michael and Jabertormitch took the front. They put the pole in between one of the square openings between the bars and lifted. As they expected, the door came off its hinges.

"It worked!" Steven said. They moved the door aside and got out of the cell.

"We need our weapons," Shal said.

"Where do you think they are?" Ravanak asked.

"I believe they are in the room aloft at the bow," Shal said. Nobody argued or questioned him. He knew the most about Shoded.

"Let's go then." Jabertormitch rushed up the stairs. The others followed him cautiously. How would they do this without getting caught? It worried Michael. They were at the stern. How could they pass the whole deck with nobody noticing them? It was impossible.

Before they opened the door, Michael could hear fighting outside. He heard swords clashing and the yells of pirates. A loud sound made him jump. The boat shook. Cannons were being fired. Michael had heard about cannons. Only pirates knew how to make cannons and use firepower. He also heard rain hitting the deck. He was scared of the cannons, but at least this would all be good cover for them.

Jabertormitch opened the door, and they all ran outside. Pirates were fighting pirates. Shoded was by the helm, fighting another pirate who had a bandana on his head and an eye patch covering his left eye.

"Your time has come, Shoded," the other pirate said. Michael marveled at their skills with a sword. They had no professional training, but they were better than he was.

"You know you'll never be able to defeat me," Shoded answered as he threw a blow at the other pirate. The pirate blocked it and threw one back. It was like they were in a rehearsed dance. "Not even when I'm fifty."

"You shouldn't expect to live that long." The other pirate laughed.

"You'll never see yourself living another day." Now it was Shoded who was laughing. They continued fighting.

The ship shook as the cannons shot at it. Michael turned. He saw a ship on the starboard side that was about the same size as the one they were on. It must be the other pirate ship. Shoded's crew was shooting back. Pirates swarmed the decks, locked in duels. Michael even saw two pirates fighting in the crow's nest. Pirates were swinging back and forth on ropes between the two ships.

Julie nudged Michael. "Let's go," she said. He almost lost himself in the battle. He turned away from the pirates and followed the others. None of the pirates paid them any attention. They were too engrossed in the battle.

Just as Shal had thought, the weapons were in the room at the bow, and so were Barki and Rumin. "We couldn't find the key," Barki said.

"It's all right," Ravanak said. "As long as we escaped. Let's go." They picked up their weapons. Michael felt more comfortable with King Lucent's sword at his side.

Shal pointed astern. "*The General* is tied by a line to this ship. Let's get to it and get out of here before either of these pirates sees us." They went behind the helm where the line was tied. Shal went first and grabbed the line. He put his hands and feet around the line and started to climb back to *The General.* The others mimicked his actions.

Divad cut the line with his knife when they were all aboard.

"Hoist the colors. Set the sails." Shal had already started to announce orders. He was eager to get away from the pirates. "Come about." Mosh used the wheel to flip the ship around. "Running to port." The sails were all the way out. The wind was on their side. They were moving fast. Soon the pirate ships were on the horizon behind them. "Now we're finally on our way to Icicle Island," Shal said. "It shouldn't be more than a few days away."

The Frost Giant's Daughter

E veryone was happy as the days went by. They were nearing Icicle Island. The wind was with them. There were no storm clouds or pirate ships in sight. Everyone on deck of *The General* had a smile. There were no complaints. There was even a small humming in the air from some of them. They ate well. They slept well. It was a good way to start off before they would have to face the guardian. Even Steven mopped the decks without complaint.

But none of them even thought of the guardian, the stone, or Dalafar. They thought only about the good time that they were having. Their minds were clouded with jolliness. Michael heard a beautiful sound in the back of his mind. It was the cause of his happiness. He didn't care who was making it or where it was coming from as long as it didn't stop.

Icicle Island soon appeared on the horizon in front of them. They cheered when they saw the beautiful island. It was completely covered in a sheet of sparkling white snow. There was one mountain in the center of the island. The mountain seemed beautiful and peaceful. The island was beckoning them. Snowflakes fell from the sky. Michael caught some in his mouth. They were sweet.

They reached the island at dawn the next day. None of them paid any attention to the beautiful sight of the rising sun behind them. They only cared about the beautiful island in front of them. It didn't seem like there could be any danger at all on that island. Michael knew that defeating this guardian would be easy. They would have the stone in no time.

When the ship reached the island, no orders needed to be given. The Leed boys put down the anchor, and all of them got off the ship. They left their ship unprotected. There was no danger around. They walked through the snow without a problem. The snow felt soft under their feet. The cold didn't bother them. They never stopped to take a break or to eat. They were all determined to reach the mountain.

They didn't stop when they reached the foot of the mountain. They started to climb right up. There were no difficulties for them. It was easy to get up. Michael found the climb much easier than when they had climbed the Urakian Mountains. That felt like so long ago and so unimportant at this time. None of them said a word about the avalanche of snow that had barely missed them.

A strange man was standing at the top of the mountain. He had a wrinkled old face that looked like it had gone through the most horrible torture one could think of. He had untidy gray hair. He wore tattered and dirty clothing. He was shaking. He couldn't walk straight. Michael didn't like the man.

"Go back," the man said in a terrified voice. "It's a trap. Don't be fooled. You have no idea what you're getting yourselves into. Please. I beg of you. Go back."

They walked right past the man, completely ignoring him. The man collapsed in the snow behind them. They still didn't stop.

The man seemed dangerous. He was trying to stop them. Michael knew that they couldn't be fooled by him.

At the center of the mountain was a hole. They all leaped down into the hole without even considering what might be at the bottom or the consequences of hitting the ground. They got lucky and landed on soft cushions. Without the cushions, they would've fallen to their deaths, but none of them even thought of that. They didn't even wonder why the cushions were there. It didn't matter. They needed to get to the center of the mountain.

They were now in an empty cavern. There were two tunnels, each leading a different way. One tunnel was pitch-black. They didn't even consider heading down that tunnel. The other tunnel had a bright light, and there were diamonds along the walls. That was the way to go.

They walked down this tunnel without consulting each other. They started to hear singing. The voice was so natural and beautiful that it pulled them farther into the tunnel. The song was getting better by the second. They were being drawn in. Michael realized that it was the song that had been in the back of his mind back on the ship. All he wanted was to get closer to the song.

The tunnel opened up into a large empty cavern. In the center of the cavern was a woman. The woman was the most beautiful woman that Michael had ever seen. Her song drew him in. Her beauty caused him to lust for her. It was unbearable to stand there without moving toward her. Yet he stayed in his place in fear of making a wrong move that the woman wouldn't like.

Her perfect figure made it impossible for any of them to take their eyes off her. Her flawless pale skin matched her fair hair. Her blue eyes sparkled like stars. She wore a white fur. She looked like a goddess. Michael thought that a statue of her belonged in the temple that Jabertormitch had showed them.

Michael felt himself being drawn to her. Her amazing voice fit to her unique body. There were no words to describe her exceptional beauty. The only way to truly know what she was like was to see her in person. He wanted to go to her and be with her forever. He never wanted to leave this place.

But there was one thing stopping from throwing himself at her. Something didn't feel morally right about choosing this one to be his girl. The song in his mind faltered. He remembered the girl who he really loved. Sheri was his love. Then he remembered why he had left her. He had to follow the Master Wizard's map that led to the rebellion and the legend of the twelve stones. He remembered why he was in the cavern. He needed the stone. A wave of realization swept over him. This was all a trick. This must be the guardian. He had to snap the others out of it.

He grabbed a knife from Divad's belt. Divad didn't seem to even notice. He was just staring at the woman. So were all the others. The woman continued her song. She wasn't watching Michael. Michael picked up his hand and threw the knife. With great accuracy, the knife pierced the woman's heart.

The song stopped. The other came back to their senses.

"What…" Ravanak said. It took them a moment to realize what was going on.

"Nobody tricks Jabertormitch and gets away with it," Jabertormitch said furiously.

The woman laughed. "Who threw this knife?" she asked as she pulled the knife from her heart. "That wasn't very nice. You stopped my beautiful song. Nobody stops my song. How were you able to resist?" She studied Michael. Her mouth fell open. "I see." She regained her calmness. "You'll pay for that." She saw their confused faces. "Oh, and about the knife that you threw at me." She laughed. "I have no heart. I'm coldhearted. I care for no one.

My heart has been frozen long ago. You can't kill me." Then she stood up straight. She put on an angry face. "And how dare you interrupt me!" she yelled at the top of her lungs. "I was almost done. I wanted to finish my song. I wanted to feast." She calmed down a little. Michael could tell that she was having major mood swings. "Oh well. I guess I'll just have to do this the hard way." She raised her arms in the air. Then she lowered them. Stalactites started to pour down from the ceiling.

Michael jumped out of the way, only to have to dodge another. They were coming down fast. They were all running around the cave to dodge what they possibly could. Rumin and Barki were with Ravanak. One stalactite scraped Michael's left arm, and another just missed his right. They were sharp. A direct hit would badly injure or even kill any of them.

The woman put up her hands again. The stalactites stopped falling.

"I'm so sorry. I forgot to introduce myself. I am the frost giant's daughter." This was when Michael saw the truth about the woman. He saw evil and hatred in her eyes. She was vicious. "I lure people to my lair with my song. No one can resist it. Once trapped inside the song, there is no way out. But somehow someone here escaped its power." She turned her head to Michael. "Tell me, child. How did you do it? But of course you don't know. I know because I am all knowing." She waited for an answer. Michael didn't say a word. "Well, no matter. I will still destroy you all."

Steven built up his courage. "You can't take on all of us," he said. He ran up to her with his mace. She was caught off guard. Steven got a direct hit. She went flying into the wall and was covered by a pile of icicles. Steven stood panting in the center of the cavern.

"Is that it?" Julie asked.

"I doubt it," Ravanak said.

The ice crystals flew off her as the frost giant's daughter stood up in anger. "Who do you think you are?" She shot icicles at Steven. Steven put up his mace to block the attack. He saved himself but still flew back from the impact.

"That's it! You are all dead!" She put her arms out. Icicles from the walls came and surrounded her body. She wore the icicles like a suit of armor. She shot icicles at them from her hands.

Michael nimbly jumped out of the way when icicles came flying at him. He saw Julie string an arrow and shoot. The frost giant's daughter didn't even flinch as the arrow bounced off of her icicle armor. There was no penetrating the ice.

"How do we defeat her?" Julie yelled. It seemed impossible. They wouldn't be able to doge her forever.

The frost giant's daughter yawned. "It's time to end this." She turned her head to the ceiling. "My pet. Come, my pet. It is time to feast. Come, my frost dragon." Nothing happened. The frost giant's daughter stood there, looking up at the ceiling of the cavern. Then the ceiling burst open. A white dragon flew in. Its skin, horns, and scales were white with a hint of blue. The dragon let out a fierce roar. The frost giant's daughter gave a cruel laugh as she jumped onto the back of the dragon.

The dragon shot ice from its mouth. Michael dodged it just in time. He scanned the rest of the cavern to make sure everyone else was all right. They had all gotten out of that one. But how many more could they take?

Another blast of ice came at them. Barki ran in, closer to the dragon, as everyone else scrambled away. Michael heard Ravanak call her back. She didn't listen. The dragon didn't see her coming. She went to the back of the dragon and jumped to reach the dragon's hovering body. She took out her rapiers and sliced the end of the dragon's tail.

The dragon howled in rage. It shook back and forth, knocking Barki against the wall. It flew high in the air. It was flying in circles. The frost giant's daughter struggled to hold on. When she finally fell off, the dragon flew out of the cavern. The frost giant's daughter was on the floor. He icicle armor was unscathed.

The frost giant's daughter got up from the floor. "You think by defeating my beast, that you can defeat me. Well, then, think again." She put out her arms and continued to throw ice crystals at them. Barki got up just in time to avoid an ice crystal, but one hit Jabertormitch. He fell to the floor. Before he even had a chance to scream, his body was covered in ice, frozen.

Michael stopped running. He was shocked. Jabertormitch was frozen. He was stuck in ice. There may be no way to revive him. The tear that fell from Michael's eye froze and cracked when it fell to the ground. The frost giant's daughter laughed.

That was the last straw. He was going to end it before anyone else got hurt. It was time for her to die. He drew his sword. The green blade shimmered. He charged at her, avoiding ice crystals left and right. She laughed a mimicking laugh as she saw him coming. There was nothing he could do to stop her. As he neared her invincible icicle-armored body, he blurted, *"Shaber!"* Michael felt a surge of magic emerge from his sword. The smile fell from her face when she heard the words.

When the sword made contact with the armor, the armor shattered into pieces and fell to the floor. The frost giant's daughter's face was full of shock. She looked nervous. Michael even thought he saw a sign of fear in her eyes. She stopped throwing ice crystals and turned all her attention to Michael. She created a sword from ice and went for the attack. Michael deflected her blow.

He jumped out of the way and rolled to get behind her. She turned just in time to see his sword cut through her neck. Her sword fell to the floor. Her head followed. When it hit the floor, it melted into a puddle of water. The rest of her body joined the puddle soon after. Michael stepped in the puddle. That was all that was left of her. Michael stood over what had once been the frost giant's daughter, sword in hand, panting. He kicked the water. Unlike his sweat, the water didn't freeze.

Without anyone saying a word, Michael walked over to the frozen Jabertormitch. He put his hand on Jabertormitch. *"Shaber,"* he said. The ice shattered, and Jabertormitch was free. Jabertormitch took a deep breath of air. He lay on the floor for a few minutes. The others walked over.

"Thank you," Jabertormitch said. He kissed Michael's feet. "You saved me from that wretched woman."

The Real Icicle Island

Michael snapped out of the trance he was in and blushed. "You're welcome. I didn't even know what I was doing. It was like something came over me. It was similar to the time when I said those words that revealed the questions on the back of the map."

Ravanak came over to Michael, and they embraced each other. "You did it. You defeated the guardian of ice. You have magic in your blood. It always comes in handy when we most need it. Now let's find that stone."

"Let's look for the stone," Rumin said. "It has to be here."

"There's nothing here," Barki said. "The room is empty. The stone's not here."

"That's because," Shal finally stepped in, "this isn't Icicle Island. It's a small island just two days north of Icicle Island."

"Are you sure?" Ravanak asked.

"Yes. Mosh and I were doing some calculations. Ever since the song started, we'd lost our minds and didn't realize where we were going exactly. When we reached this island, it was two days earlier than when we should've reached Icicle Island. Also, Icicle Island is a lot bigger than this small island. Icicle Island consists of many mountains, while this island only has one."

"That would make sense," Ravanak said. "Why else would the frost giant's daughter lure people with her song? She is a decoy. She lures people away from Icicle Island. She's trying to protect it. The real guardian of ice is on Icicle Island, guarding the stone."

Now everything was clear. But everything had just become much more difficult. They hadn't even faced the guardian yet. The only reason they'd won this time was because Michael had used magic. If that didn't happen when they faced the real guardian, there would be no way to defeat it.

"Then what are we doing standing around?" Jabertormitch said. "Let's get to Icicle Island." Ravanak nodded.

"But how do we get out of here?" Julie asked, looking around. There was nowhere to go except the way that they had come. The problem was they'd come from another cavern from a hole in the ceiling. They wouldn't be able to get back up there. The song had clouded their judgment, and they hadn't brought any supplies that would help them escape.

"In the other cavern," Steven said, "there was another tunnel, the dark one. I'm sure it leads somewhere."

"First of all, who said it leads out?" Julie said skeptically. "And second of all, it doesn't have to lead somewhere. It could lead to a dead end."

"There's only one way to find out," Michael said.

"Michael's right," Ravanak said. "We have to try. It's our only option."

Julie frowned. Why was it that she was the only one always trying to be reasonable and logical and no one ever listened to her?

"Let's go," Jabertormitch said. He was the first to go back into the tunnel lit by diamond crystals.

As they walked through the tunnel, none of them dared touch the diamond crystals. They didn't know what curse lay in them. Knowing the frost giant's daughter, she wouldn't just put these here without reason. There was probably some terrible magic involved.

Michael remembered the man they had seen before they went down the hole. He had been shaken up. Michael remembered that he collapsed in the snow. He was probably dead by now. What had happened to him? Was it the frost giant's daughter who did that to him or the curse that was probably on the diamond crystals? It was probably the latter. If it were the former, the man wouldn't have escaped. He probably saw the diamond crystals and took some in his greed. Then the curse fell on him. Michael shivered at the memory of the man.

When they got back into the first cavern, they headed to the other side of the room, where the dark tunnel was. No wonder nobody ever went down this tunnel. It was spooky and scary. There was no light whatsoever. It would be impossible to see. The other tunnel looked much more inviting. That had obviously been done on purpose. That meant that the dark tunnel probably led somewhere good.

"How are we going to get through this?' Julie asked. No one answered. They all had the same question. It would be impossible to go through with no light, and there was no light available. The only light in the cavern came from the diamond crystals, but none of them would even dare to touch those.

"The only way to do it is the diamond crystals," Jabertormitch said. "I'll be the brave one and find out if it's safe." He reached for a diamond crystal.

"Wait," Michael said. He knew that they were cursed. The man who had collapsed in the snow was proof of that. But there were some crystals on the floor. Maybe those were safer than the ones on the walls. "Try those," he said, pointing to the ones on the floor. He had a feeling that those weren't cursed. His feelings were usually never wrong.

Jabertormitch shrugged and picked up one from the floor. As soon as he picked it up, he started to shake. He fell to the floor and continued to shake. The rest of them just watched, not knowing what to do. They all exchanged scared looks. They didn't know what was happening to him. Foam started to come from Jabertormitch's mouth. He started mumbling unintelligible sounds.

After a few minutes, Jabertormitch stopped shaking. He got up, laughing. "I was just messin' with ya," he said. Michael's jaw dropped.

"That's not funny," Julie said angrily.

"Yes, it was," Steven said. He went over to Jabertormitch, and they slapped each other's hands. "Nice one." He laughed again.

Julie frowned. "I was terrified."

"Now that we know they are safe, everyone take one from the floor," Ravanak said. Each of them took their own diamond crystal from the floor. Michael held it in his hand. The light shone from the crystal and illuminated the area around him. Jabertormitch took the lead. He held the diamond crystal shoulder-high in front of him and walked into the tunnel. The rest of them followed his example.

The tunnel was pitch-black except for the small area of light that surrounded them. They couldn't see what they had left behind them or what waited in front of them. The cave floor was moist and a little slippery. They had to walk cautiously to keep their balance. The sound of water could be heard up ahead.

"What's that sound?" Michael asked.

"This cave," Jabertormitch answered, "must have some sort of underground spring that leads to the ocean. It's nothing to worry about unless it's high tide. Then the cave will fill with water."

"It is high tide," Jacov said.

"That could be trouble," Jabertormitch said. "We'll have to hurry and get out of here before the tide comes in. Otherwise…" He didn't need to finish the sentence. Everyone knew what would happen; they would all drown. They started to move a little faster but still cautiously. The sound of the water grew louder as they walked on. Soon they could hear the rushing water. It sounded like a river. The smell of the ocean filled the tunnel. Michael saw Shal take in a deep breath of the ocean air.

The moist floor turned into a small puddle beneath their feet. The puddle got bigger as they walked on. Soon the water was knee-deep. It was getting harder to walk in the water. Michael's shoes were filled with water, and it made them heavy. His feet were getting cold.

"We have to get out of here," Jabertormitch said, "before the tunnel fills with water. Let's go fast."

They walked even faster now. They were almost running, splashing through the water. Michael rubbed his eyes every time some saltwater splashed in his face.

When the water reached their waists, they came to a fork in the tunnel.

"Now what?" Julie said loudly over the rushing water.

Jabertormitch didn't answer. He listened to each tunnel. "The water is coming from the right one."

Julie started heading toward the left, and Jabertormitch pulled her back.

"We go right," he said.

"Why would we go to the water?" she asked.

"The water is where the ocean is, which is the way out. That's where we need to go."

It made sense. But it was dangerous. They had to move fast and beat the tide. They had to swim against the current. It was hard and tiring. It seemed endless. There was no way they would be able to hold off and swim to the end. The water was too strong. Michael knew that Julie and Steven barely knew how to swim. There was no water in Periphia, and they had never learned how. He wasn't the best swimmer either.

The water was rushing in. Waves were coming over their heads. They were being forced under the water. It felt like they were moving backward more than forward. They would never make it out of there alive. The water was stronger than they were, and they couldn't go on any longer. Michael's arms and legs felt numb. He had no more energy. He almost let them go and succumbed to the water.

But then he saw it. From the corner of his eye he saw an opening in the tunnel wall on the right. It inclined upward, so the water passed the opening without flooding it. It was their only chance to survive. He had to reach the opening. This gave him a new hope of survival and the energy he needed to use his last might to swim to the opening. With every stroke of his arm, he pushed forward. The last of his energy was draining.

He reached it just in time. He didn't have an ounce of energy left in him. He sat on the floor of the new tunnel, panting. He held out his diamond crystal and saw that it led to a dead end. That was ok. He just needed to stay here until the tide went back down. He just hoped the others would be able to make it. He watched the rushing water that passed by with anticipation.

He saw Ravanak emerge from the water, followed by Jaber-tormitch. Ravanak had the two timen with him. Shal came with

Divad a few minutes later. Then Jacov and Mosh came. They all seemed as tired as he was. But he knew was worse off than any of them. The Leeds were probably expert swimmers, and Ravanak and Jabertormitch were stronger than he was. Michael was worried. Julie and Steven still hadn't come. He could only hope that they were all right and would come within the next few minutes. Otherwise they were doomed.

The seconds felt like hours. He didn't take his eyes off the entrance to the tunnel. He started to shake with anxiety. Then, right before he started to burst into tears, Steven came up from the water, holding Julie. The tears came anyway as he hugged them. He thought that he had lost them. He promised himself to not leave them out of his sight ever again. It was his responsibility to take care of them.

No one said a word as they sat there and waited for the water to calm down. After a few hours, or so they thought, the water stopped flooding in. It started to sink. When the water was waist-high again, Jabertormitch jumped back into the main tunnel. The others followed him. They trudged through the water. They weren't moving as fast, so it was easier to walk through the water this time. The end of the tunnel wasn't too far off. Michael could see the blinding light of the sun coming, giving light to the last few yards of the tunnel.

When they got out, Michael dropped the crystal and put up his hand to cover his eyes from the sun. The crystal shattered as it hit the floor. Michael heard the sound of other shattering crystals. They had been in the dark for so long. But Michael was more than happy to see the sun.

Jabertormitch smiled when they all regained their normal vision. Then Ravanak smiled. Soon they were all smiling. Even some laughter came. They had survived. They had all thought that they were goners. To be alive and out of there was a dream to them. They had had too many near-death experiences on the dreadful island.

Ravanak's smile soon turned to a frown. "The worst is yet to come." Everyone's smiles faded. They still had to get to Icicle Island and defeat the guardian of ice. That would probably be harder than this.

Michael groaned. It had taken them everything they had to defeat the frost giant's daughter. How would they possibly accomplish the impossible task that lay ahead of them?

"Back on the ship," Shal said. The tunnel led them right near to where they had anchored the ship. Michael thought he would never be as happy to get back on a ship. They all wanted to leave the horrid island. They all rushed onto the ship.

"Hoist the colors, set the sails, head south, running to port." Shal gave his orders.

The Leeds went to their usual stations. The Leeds felt at home on the ship.

"Shal," Mosh said.

"Yeah."

"That island is not on the map."

"So add it."

"What should we call it?"

Shal went over to starboard, where Ravanak and Michael were standing. "That island is an uncharted island. Since we found it, we can name it. What would you say we should name it?"

"How about Nightmare Island," Julie said. They all nodded. It was a suitable name. They would all have nightmare about their experiences on the island.

"Sounds good," Shal said.

"That song doesn't affect me," Dalafar said. "As long as I'm on this ship, it won't affect any of my crew either."

The good-for-nothing captain walked in. He wore elegant clothes. He had a red coat with gold buttons and blue pants. He had expensive black sailor boots. He had neat black hair. The man was clean-shaven. Dalafar liked people who looked professional.

"How long?" Dalafar asked.

"Another week or so," the captain answered. At least this idiot didn't have fear in his voice every time he talked with Dalafar, like the rest of his servants always had. But Dalafar would fix that. Everyone should be fearful of the ruler. That was how he ruled and maintained order: through fear.

"Well, then, pick up the pace, you scumbag."

"Yes, sir."

"So this is the real Icicle Island," Michael said. It looked more like Icicle Island should look. It was a few times the size of Nightmare Island. There were dozens of mountains on this island. The island, like Nightmare Island, was completely covered in snow. A blizzard was constantly going on. The snow kept piling in. The ground could've been yards under them. It was impossible to tell. Now the question was where were they supposed to go?

"Now what?" Julie asked.

"The guardian is probably on one of the mountains," Jabertormitch said.

"Yes, but which one?" Ravanak pondered. "We don't have time to search each one even if we split up." There were only seven of them, and two of them were timen. The Leeds had stayed on the ship, as they'd promised their father. They had only left it the last time because of the spell of the frost giant's daughter. Now the only things entrancing them were the massive white mountains.

"What about the middle mountain?" Steven suggested. "That's always the best bet."

"I'll agree to that," Jabertormitch said.

"Why not?" Ravanak shrugged and started to walk. It was much harder than on Nightmare Island. The snow was deep, and every step took effort. The wind was against them, and the snow blew in their faces. They could hardly see anything. At least they were prepared this time. They had brought supplies and food.

Michael couldn't feel his fingers or toes anymore. He felt like he had frostbite. He was colder than he had ever been in his life. It never snowed in Periphia. He was happy it didn't. He decided he hated snow. It felt like he was going to freeze. Only their determination kept them going. Even that was shrinking as time went by and it got harder to trudge through the snow.

It felt like they were walking for days as they passed mountain after mountain. Ravanak glanced at every mountain they passed to try to make out some sign of a guardian. There was no way of telling what was on top of any of the mountains. The snow blinded them.

They only stopped twice to eat and rest. Their stops were as short as possible. If they stayed in one spot too long, the snow would bury them. They had to keep moving.

When they neared the center of the island, Michael stopped in front of one of the mountains. He felt a connection, like some sort of surge of magic coming out of the mountain to him. It was his gut feeling that he always trusted.

"We have to keep moving," Ravanak yelled to him over the blizzard.

"This is the mountain," Michael said calmly and surely.

"Are you sure?" Ravanak asked. Michael just nodded. Without waiting to see what the others would do, he started to walk to the mountain. Having no choice, the others followed him. Michael had never been wrong before. His instincts never failed him before. They trusted him. He hoped that he wasn't letting them down.

The climb up the mountain was tough. The paths, if they existed, were narrow. Rocks were falling from under them as well from above them. The snow only made it harder. The ice made the climb dangerous. They had to be very careful where they stepped. It was the most difficult climbing that any of them even Jaber-tormitch had ever done. Jabertormitch was still the best climber and guided to the areas that were safer than others. The climb exhausted them of all their strength. That would be a problem when they had to fight the guardian of ice.

When they finally reached the top, they all dropped onto the soft snow. They lay there until a thin layer of snow covered them. Michael shook off the snow. When they got up, they saw that the mountaintop was empty. There was nothing up there.

Steven and Julie groaned at the same time. They had made that climb for nothing. They looked at Michael with annoyed faces, but he wasn't looking at them. Michael was walking to the center of the mountain. They unwillingly followed him.

Julie and Steven sighed with relief when they saw the hole in the middle of the mountain. For a minute they thought they would have to go back down and climb another mountain.

"How do we get down?" Julie asked.

"I thought this would be the case," Ravanak said, "so I brought a rope." He held out a long rope. "This should do." He went to the hole and dropped one end of the rope down. It reached the floor. "Perfect." He took out a peg. "This will hold the other end to the ground up here so we can climb down."

The Real Guardian of Ice

"Two tunnels again," Jabertormitch observed. The room was the same as on Nightmare Island. It was an empty cavern with a dark tunnel and a tunnel that shone like the sun from diamond crystals. Jabertormitch headed toward the light tunnel. Ravanak quickly pulled him back.

"What are you doing?" Jabertormitch said grumpily.

"We have to think this through," Ravanak said.

"Think what through? It's the same as on Nightmare Island. This tunnel leads to the guardian."

"I'm not so sure about that."

"Why not?"

"I'll have to agree with Ravanak," Julie said. "Everything since we got here has been the opposite of what was on Nightmare Island. On Nightmare Island, the traveling and climbing was easier, but here it was very difficult. We found the frost giant's daughter's lair very quickly and easily, but here it was slow and hard."

"Also," Steven added, "there was no cushion to fall on here like there was in Nightmare Island."

"I guess it sounds right," Jabertormitch said. "That means we have to go in the dark tunnel." Ravanak nodded.

They all were thinking the same thing. On Nightmare Island, they were drawn in. The diamond tunnel had helped do that. Over here they weren't wanted in. The dark tunnel clearly told them that.

"There are no crystals on the floor," Michael said. The only diamonds that they would be able to use to light the way were on the wall. But they might be cursed like the ones on Nightmare Island.

Jabertormitch laughed as he took a diamond crystal off the wall. "That's not a problem. Everything is opposite here. The diamond tunnel was put there to draw people away from the stone. The diamonds on the wall wouldn't be cursed. Whoever put it here wanted people to take diamonds so it would lead them away from the stone."

"Sounds logical," Ravanak said. He too took a diamond crystal from the wall. The others did the same. Nothing happened to them.

"Let's go," Jabertormitch said. He went into the tunnel first. It was the same as the last time except this tunnel had all turns. It was like a maze. They decided where to go based on Jabertormitch's knowledge of caves and tunnels and Michael's instinct. They only hoped that they were going the right way.

To Michael, it felt like the cave of legends all over again. It seemed like they were lost and going in circles. There was no way to tell where they were. There was darkness behind them and in front of them.

They came to a room that had five different ways to go. Jabertormitch went over to each tunnel opening. He listened and studied each one. After a few minutes, he decided which way to go.

"It's the last tunnel," Jabertormitch said.

"No, it's not," Michael said. "It's the second one."

"It's for sure not the second one," Jabertormitch said. "I've been living in mountains for years. I can tell that tunnel leads to a dead end."

"I have a big feeling that it's the second one."

"I'll have to disagree with you. I know for a fact that the only tunnels that lead to an open cavern are one and five. I believe five is the right tunnel."

Michael sighed. He realized that he wasn't going to get through to Jabertormitch. "Fine. We'll go to the fifth tunnel." He frowned. He knew it was the second one. He hoped that he was wrong. None of the others said a word. They didn't want to get involved in this fight.

They all followed Jabertormitch into the fifth tunnel. They were walking for a while and then saw an opening up ahead. Michael could see Jabertormitch grin in the dim light. Sure enough, they ended up in an open cavern. But there was one problem. The empty cavern was the same one that they had just been in with the five tunnels. They had just come out of the first one.

Without saying a word, Michael headed for the second tunnel. This time Jabertormitch reluctantly followed.

"The fifth and the first both lead to an open cavern," Rumin remarked to Jabertormitch mockingly. Jabertormitch just grunted. The second tunnel didn't lead to an open cavern like Jabertormitch had said. It led to a dead end, but the dead end was giant double doors of ice with carvings on them. There was no way to open the doors.

"How do we get in?" Julie asked.

"We can't open the door," Barki said. "None of us is strong enough to push it or break it."

Steven looked at Jabertormitch. Jabertormitch nodded. They both took out their heavy weapons and with all their might hit the door. Nothing happened. They stood there for a minute, panting to catch their breath.

Michael stood there, staring at the inscription. He was whispering something to himself. He didn't even realize what he was doing. "*Ani yachol lekanes,*" he said. The words flowed from his mouth like magic. When the sound waves hit the doors, the doors started to crumble down.

When Michael turned to Ravanak, Ravanak nodded. "You must have read the inscription."

"When did this magic thing start?" Julie said.

"And why don't I have it?" Steven said. He wished he had powers like his older brother.

"Now's not the time for this," Ravanak said. "We are about to face our greatest foe so far. We have to be ready." They turned to the cavern that was now in front of them and drew their weapons.

The room was empty. There was no guardian. There was, however, a boulder in the middle of the room. On the boulder was an icy blue topaz stone. Michael could feel the magic spurring out of it. He saw the others grimace. On the boulder was an inscription.

ICY BLUE TOPAZ
SPY ON OTHERS
THROUGH GLASS AND WATER

"Maybe the frost giant's daughter was the guardian," Julie said.

"And maybe I'm a graceful elf," Jabertormitch said sarcastically. Julie scowled.

"We might as well try to get the stone," Ravanak said.

As they neared the stone, the wall at the other of the cavern col-lapsed. Standing in its place was a giant. He didn't look like a nor-mal giant. He had whitish-bluish-purplish skin. He wore no shirt. He had black shorts. His muscles were bulging. He had icicles for hair. He held a giant ax in his right hand.

"What is that?" Julie said in amazement as well as fear.

"It looks like a frost giant," Ravanak said. "But I always thought they were extinct." The frost giant screamed out.

"He doesn't look extinct to me," Jabertormitch remarked.

The frost giant walked up to the stone, picked it up, and swal-lowed it whole.

They looked at him, surprised.

"That's disgusting," Julie said. Barki nodded her agreement.

The frost giant yelled out again. He opened his mouth and shot snow and ice at them. They scurried out of the way. He shot another icy breath. They were running around the cavern now to avoid the giant's deadly breath. Jabertormitch was moving faster than any of them. Michael thought that getting frozen once was enough for the dwarf.

The frost giant began to use his ax. Michael rolled around the giant and stuck his sword in the giant's heel. The giant bel-lowed. The pain went away as quickly as it had come. He was too large for small blows like that to harm him. The blade barely scratched him. The battle was a stalemate. The frost giant was using the same moves to try to kill them. They were nimbly avoiding his blows and at the same time giving futile blows of their own. The giant seamed to realize this as he stopped attack-ing them.

He stretched his hands out to the sky. "Dragon!"

Michael thought he knew what was coming. He was right. The roof crumbled down on them as the frost dragon flew into the cavern. The dragon let out a roar. His tail was still wounded from the last battle, but he looked well enough to fight. He blew ice out from his mouth. They had to dodge the frost giant and his ice breath and ax. They wouldn't be able to do that forever. They had to figure out a way to defeat the giant and his pet.

Michael heard noise from behind him. He turned to see Dalafar, in the flesh, with all his men. He had never seen Dalafar before, but he knew it was him. Anyone could feel the evil radiating from the fuman. He had two avengers, two dwarves, a Minotaur, and a goblin with him. Michael froze. How were they supposed to defend themselves against all three threats? He was still running, trying to dodge the ice.

Dalafar looked from his rebellious enemies to the frost giant to the frost dragon. He smiled. He took a dagger from his belt and threw it straight into the frost dragon's belly. The frost dragon bellowed. He turned to Dalafar. Dalafar just smiled. Michael realized that right now they had to work together with Dalafar in order to defeat the frost giant. They both wanted the stone. And that was the only way to get it. They would deal with each other later. He didn't like the idea—in fact he despised it—but he would do it anyway.

Dalafar grabbed the bow and arrow that the goblin was holding. He strung an arrow and pointed it at the frost dragon. "*Taharog*," Dalafar said as the arrow left the bow. As soon as the arrow touched the dragon, the dragon fell to the floor.

It was nothing but a carcass now. The life had left its body in a split second. Michael didn't know such magic existed. It was cruel and heartless. Only Dalafar could do something like that.

It must have been a powerful spell because it looked like Dalafar was drained of energy. He fell to the floor with his back against the cavern wall. His allies jumped into action when they saw him fall. They went in front of him and protected him from the attacks from the furious frost giant.

Their blows were no good against the frost giant either. Julie shot arrows at the frost giant. They bounced off him. Steven charged at him with his mace and got a direct hit on the giant's ankle. The giant screamed with pain and started to hop, holding his ankle. He turned away from Dalafar to Steven. The frost giant picked up his ax to strike Steven. Steven blocked the blow with his mace, but he was thrown back against the wall from the impact of the giant ax.

The frost giant opened his mouth and shot ice out in Steven's direction. Steven was too stunned from the last attack to move. Michael jumped in front of Steven with his sword out. The green blade was glowing. Michael hit the ice pieces away from Steven. He hit one back at the frost giant, directly between the eyes. The frost giant fell backward and hit the ground. The cavern shook when he hit the floor.

It was a big fall for someone as tall as him. He didn't get back up. He looked as dead as the dragon lying beside him. Dalafar opened his eyes. Michael went over to see if he was really dead. When he was standing over the frost giant's head, the frost giant's pale eyes popped opened, and he grabbed Michael.

Before the frost giant even had a chance to get up, Ravanak and Jabertormitch ran up to him and cut the hand that was holding Michael. The frost giant yelled from the immense pain. Michael jumped onto the giant's head and stuck his sword deep into the giant's head. The frost giant stopped screaming. Now he was a dead carcass just like his pet.

It was a tiring battle, but it was not over. Dalafar and his men stood behind them with their weapons drawn. Michael, Ravanak, and Jabertormitch turned to face them. They were already tired from their battle with the guardian. They were breathing heavily, while Dalafar and his men stood there full of energy.

Dalafar was about to make his charge against his weak and tired enemies when an arrow came and pierced the goblin in the heart. Then the two dwarves fell to the floor with cut feet. Julie smiled from the side of the cavern, and Barki grinned next to the fallen dwarves. Steven came from behind and knocked the Minotaur senseless with his mace. Now it was only Dalafar and the two avengers.

Getting Out

Dalafar looked at his fallen men. He scowled. His face turned red. It looked as if he would blow. He started to mumble and grunt to himself. He examined the group before him and measured his odds. He shook his head. He knew there was no way he could take down all of them. He had to flee in order to fight another day. He would get the stone. One day he would get all the stones.

"Get me out of here," he said to the avengers. His loud, booming voice made it sound like the frost giant was talking. His anger struck fear into the avengers like it did to all his subjects. He held out his hands, and the each avenger took one arm. They began to flap their wings in a struggle to carry their load. They rose above the floor. "Until next time." Dalafar grinned toward the group watching him get away. The avengers increased the speed and power of their flight as they flew out of the large hole in the roof where the frost dragon had entered.

"Now let's get the stone," Ravanak said.

"How exactly do we do that?" Julie asked. They all knew that the stone was in the frost giant's stomach, but how were they going to get it out? There was really only one way to do it. Julie looked around and knew they were all thinking the same thing. Steven gave her a mischievous look.

Ravanak took his sword and sliced open the giant's stomach. Guts were oozing out. The giant's lunch from yesterday poured out. Ravanak was soon standing in a puddle of...well...Ravanak reached into all the garbage in the dead body of the giant. Julie made a face of disgust. Steven stuck his tongue out at her. Ravanak's hand came out holding the icy blue topaz. The stone was totally clean, but the same could not be said for Ravanak's arm. He shook the garbage off of his arm.

"Here," Jabertormitch said. "Use this." He handed Ravanak a snowball. Ravanak took the snow and spread it on his arm, using it as water to clean off the garbage.

Ravanak held out the stone for all of them to see. Michael marveled at its magnificence. It shone blue like the sky without a trace of being in the stomach of a giant. "Icy blue topaz," Ravanak said loud and clear.

The floor of ice started to disappear. Steven jumped as the floor faded away beneath him. They weren't falling. They were still on solid ground. A picture started to form where they stood. The picture showed Dalafar and the two avengers waiting outside of the hole, weapons drawn, ready to ambush them when they came out.

"This is amazing," Barki remarked.

"Yes, it is," Ravanak answered. "And this is one of the weaker stones. They all have great powers. This one will grant its holder the power to see what is happening elsewhere via glass or water—in this case ice. That is why it's essential to gather all the stones and not only one. When one has all twelve stones together, the power is unimaginable, but still each one separately is powerful as well."

"So it looks like our friend Dalafar is waiting to ambush us," Jabertormitch said. "Ha! He will have a surprise."

"No," Ravanak said in a serious tone. "Dalafar is not naive. He knows the power of the stone. He knows that we know he is waiting for us; therefore he is not expecting to ambush us. He is expecting to fight us when we are ready. He must have another trick up his sleeve."

"So what do you say we do, centaur?" Jabertormitch said.

"We must find another way out."

"There's no other way out," Rumin said. "We can't fly out, so we must go back the way we came, where Dalafar is waiting. We will have to take our chances and try to defeat him. We have no other choice."

Michael looked up. Something was falling toward them. It was going to crash down straight into the cavern through the same hole where Dalafar had left. No, it wasn't falling. It was gliding, flying down; the dot got bigger and bigger as it approached. Soon the green color of its scales was visible.

"Darkon!" Michael said. The others looked up. Darkon landed with grace in front of them.

"Need a way out?" Darkon said in his usual telepathic deep voice. His sharp teeth would scare any of his foes, but Michael had come to love the dragon. His tail tapped the floor as he waited for them to answer.

"You always seem to show up at the right times," Ravanak said with a grin.

"I can somehow feel when I'm needed." Darkon let Michael, Steven, Julie, Jabertormitch, Barki, and Rumin climb on his back. He picked up Ravanak with his claws and flew off. "You guys need to lose some weight or I won't be able to save you anymore." He laughed in his dragon way. The others joined him.

"There were another two boys."

"And a note was left for them as well?"

"Yes. And one remarkably resembled one of the three children."

"Really? Now that's interesting. Did you get their names?"

"No. But I know where they are. They are working in an inn nearby."

"Fine. Keep an eye on them. Report to me if anything interesting happens."

"Yes, sire."

The man left. At least there was some good news after the failure he'd just had. No. It wasn't his failure. He never failed. It was the failure of his subordinates. It would not be tolerated again. The next stone would be his no matter what.

Darkon flew off after they thanked him for the lift. They were back on board *The General.*

Shal grinned when he saw that they had the stone. "So it was successful. Good to hear. I guess it's time to go back."

"We thank you and your family for all of your help," Ravanak said "Hopefully we will journey again in the future."

"We've still got the way back." Shal grinned and turned to his brothers. The anchor was up; the sails were set. There was only one thing left to do before they sailed off.

"Hoist the colors!"

Epilogue

The green light faded back into the scroll, and I returned to the real world. My mouth was dry. My mind was racing. My heart was pounding against my ribcage. Sweat fell from my forehead. Dad looked at me funny. "Just need a drink," I said as I ran into the kitchen to pour myself a glass of water. I gulped down the water quickly and poured another glass. I drank this one a little more slowly. I was dazed. If I told anyone what had just happened, they wouldn't believe me. I wasn't sure if I believed it myself. None of it made sense. It wasn't possible that this story took place on Earth, but I knew it was real. I could feel it. I had seen the story happen. I *felt* it happen. It was like I was a part of Kanavar, and I couldn't just leave it alone. But still the same questions kept running through my head. *Where is this place? When did this happen? How did this scroll get here? And most importantly what's the rest of the story?*

I searched in the box, looking for another scroll. There was nothing. The box was empty, and I couldn't find any secret compartments either. There had to be more scrolls—maybe hidden in the house.

I told my dad that I had lost my watch and went from room to room searching. I was trying to see if there was anything abnormal like glowing green lights. I even knocked on all the walls to try and find a hollow spot. Nothing in the bedrooms or bathrooms upstairs. I looked in the living room and kitchen but found nothing. I opened all the closets in the house. What was I thinking? The house was new now. I had helped put in all the new furniture. There couldn't have been any other scrolls here. There was only one place the other scrolls could be. We finished tearing down the wallpaper but still came up short. There were no other boxes or secret compartments. The other scrolls were not in the house.

I felt myself panicking. I needed to finish the story. The story had become a part of me, and I *had* to finish it. I didn't know where else to look, though. There were no clues that I could find. Frustrated, I took a deep breath and began to pace. If there were no clues in the house, maybe there was a clue in the story. I remembered it like it was my own memory. I started from the beginning, running the story through my head, scene by scene.

The answer hit me. How could I have missed it? The answer was in the story all along! Dad was now staring at me as I nearly shouted in triumph. "I think I got it," I told him. "I mean, I think Albert has it. I'm going to go get it."

I hid the box in the house and put the scroll in my pocket as I ran out the door. I felt bad about ignoring Albert's invite to join his soccer game. That thought caused me to stop in my tracks. This story was overcoming me. I didn't live in Kanavar. I lived *here*, in the real world with real people. They were more important than the story. The next scroll could wait until tomorrow. Dad would be proud of me. That was a mature decision.

When the game was over, I walked over to Albert. "I have something to show you," I said. He looked at me with curiosity. I took out the scroll.

"What's that?" Albert asked me.

"It's an ancient scroll. It's *magic*," I said. He had a look of disbelief. "I'll show you!" I opened the scroll and we began to read. The green light shot out and we were both pulled into the story.

**Stay tuned for the
next book in the
Scroll of Kanavar series
called
The Green Dragon and The Red Dragon
Here is a sample
of what happens next
to the rebellion group**

A New Journey

The village was desolate. There was no sign of life. Everyone was dead. Most of the buildings were destroyed. The smell of smoke filled the air. What once was Periphia was now a barren wasteland. Even the birds had deserted Periphia.

Marki felt so alone. There was no one around. His parents were both dead. He couldn't even find his little brother's body. The boy had probably burned into ashes with the rest of his house. Everyone he knew was dead. He felt as if he wanted to crawl under a piece of rubble and wait there to die. He no longer had a purpose to live. There was no more reason in this world for him. Everything he'd once known and loved was gone.

And it was all Dalafar's fault. Dalafar had sent his army and ruined everything. His life had been going great. He'd had a family, friends, and a job, and now he had nothing. If there was one reason that he still survived, he believed it to be to destroy Dalafar once and for all. The world had had enough of his tyranny. He knew that

Kanavar needed a period of peace after what it went through from Dalafar's reign. It was time to put an end to these dark ages.

He walked along the roads of what had once been Periphia. Perhaps there were more survivors. Maybe someone from his past did exist. He sank into a depression when he realized that there were no others. He recognized most of the bodies. But some had been burned so badly that they didn't look human. The shops and houses were destroyed. The soldiers had spared no one. What was the point of this raid? What had Dalafar gained? Was he that evil to kill a whole village with no purpose?

He got to his best friend, Michael's, house. It seemed as if the destruction had stopped there. Michael's house was mostly intact, and the house next door was untouched. The people were dead, but the houses weren't set ablaze or broken down. Marki's face brightened when he saw what was in the front lawn of the house. There was a tombstone. He bent down to read it.

HERE LIES MARGOT
A GREAT MOTHER

His heart stopped. Someone had put this here. He ran into the house. He saw the two dead bodies of Mr. and Mrs. Lormin. There was nothing else. No other dead bodies were around. He searched carefully to see if he could find Michael, Julie, or Steven. There was no trace of their bodies. Margot was obviously dead. Marki felt bad for her and the Lormins, but a smile still came to his face. This must mean that Michael, his sister, and his brother were all still alive. They must've buried their mother there. His best friend was still alive. There was hope yet. Something had survived from his old life.

He ran out of the house. He saw three pairs of footsteps in the mud. His smile widened. He ran across the entire village looking for a sign of them. He couldn't find them. They were already gone. If only he had a way to find them. He tried to follow the footsteps, but they disappeared as the village came to an end.

He sat in front of the blacksmith's shop. He placed his head in his arms as he thought. Where would they have gone? If only they had waited a little longer. Tears started to come down his face. He didn't know that he had more in his body. He had finally found survivors, but they were gone. He would never find them.

Marki looked at the sign behind him. Michael had worked at the blacksmith. He went into the blacksmith's shop. There were papers on the front desk. A sealed envelope was on top of the papers. Michael's name was on the front. Marki ripped open the envelope and read the note.

IF YOU ARE READING THIS THEN
YOUR MOTHER AND I ARE BOTH DEAD
YOU MUST GO AND SEE THE MASTER WIZARD
FOR THE SAKE OF CHARLDENA GO
DON'T WORRY, EVERYTHING WILL BE FINE
LISTEN TO EVERYTHING THE MASTER WIZARD SAYS
AND YOU WILL DO WHAT IS RIGHT AND
SAVE ALL OF CHARLDENA
PLEASE LISTEN AND GO
DO NOT LINGER
THE LONGER YOU WAIT THE MORE RISK THERE IS
GO

It was an urgent message. It was meant for Michael and probably his siblings. If Michael knew this, then he must've gone to the Master Wizard. But he didn't get the note.

Marki turned away from the desk. He had only been in the blacksmith shop a few times, but he realized right away that the green sword that used to hang on the wall was missing.

One thing was running through Marki's mind. He rushed over to the house of Mr. Mim, the blacksmith. He knew that Michael had been close to the blacksmith. Marki saw Mr. Mim's body under a large piece of wood. His arm was outstretched, and he was pointing at something. Marki turned his head, but there was nothing there.

Marki walked around the house. He saw a few dead soldiers with sword wounds. He tried to put two and two together. The green sword must have been used to kill those soldiers. Michael or Mr. Mim had used the sword. But either way Mr. Mim was pointing to something, which might have been the sword. Marki played the scene in his head. Mr. Mim had used the sword to kill the soldiers, but in the end he'd been defeated by the wooden plank that covered him. Then Michael had rushed in. He was unable to move the wood. Mr. Mim had urged him to take the sword and leave. If Marki was right, like he usually was, then Mr. Mim most probably told Michael to go to the Master Wizard. Marki's spirit returned. He was always good at puzzles. He was able to figure out what had happened based on things that were left behind.

He knew where Michael, Julie, and Steven must have gone. He had to get to the Master Wizard. Marki remembered his mother telling him stories of Kanavar before Dalafar became ruler. The king used to live in a castle in Keedor, and the Master Wizard was also in Keedor. He had to get to Keedor. It was a long journey, but he was determined.

Marki ran around the village to gather what supplies he might need. He went into the bakery. The food was still good. Marki went to the shop that he always worked in, the tailor's, and picked up some clothes and a bag to put everything in. He filled a few water skins. He made his last stop back in the blacksmith shop and took a few daggers and a sword.

Marki stood on a hill that overlooked the village. He took one last look at Periphia before turning west to travel to Keedor. He might have been leaving his home, but he was headed to the only living remains of it.

He began his journey. He saw traces of the cruel army as he walked. The army must not be too far ahead of him. He slowed his pace to make sure he wouldn't encounter them. The thought of Michael being captured by the army entered his mind, but he brushed it off. Michael was too smart for that.

He rationed out his food for the whole journey. It was a good thing he didn't eat a lot. He refilled his water skins with rain and the occasional springs that he encountered. He didn't like sleeping on the hard ground. Most of the time he tried to make a bed out of leaves.

It wasn't an exciting journey. The only thing that kept him going was the hope to see Michael again. The only strange thing that happened when he was traveling was that the sky turned pitch-black for a split second. He also had a constant feeling of someone following him. He always looked back to see if anyone was there. If there was someone, he never caught his follower.

He didn't bother stopping at Holechar when he reached it. He didn't even have any money, so there wasn't any use of stopping in the city. After a few more weeks, he finally reached the Hidukel River. It was about time. He was getting tired of the same old traveling. He wanted nothing more than to see the face of his best buddy. He reassured himself that it would be soon.

After he crossed the Hidukel and traveled for another week, Keedor appeared on the horizon. He started to run as he saw it grow before him. The walls were massive. He had never seen anything like it. He couldn't believe that such a thing could be built. It must have taken thousands of men to build the walls.

The guards at the gate were the first people that he had interacted with in the past two months since the raid.

"State your business," One guard said.

Marki stammered a little. "I need to visit someone." He despised the guards but at the same time stood in fear of them. He grouped all of Dalafar's soldiers in one section in his mind: monsters. He told the truth. There was no reason to lie to them.

"Who?"

"My friend."

"What kind of friend?" These guards had to know every little detail.

"My best friend moved here a couple of weeks ago, and I wanted to come see him." Marki thought that would be enough for the guards. The guard sighed as he opened the gates.

Marki stood in place as his head turned to all directions. The buildings were magnificent. Their splendor further humbled his home, Periphia. The roads of Keedor were crowded with all sorts of people. He bent his head all the way back as he looked at the tops of the buildings that looked as if they reached the sky. His head turned right and left as he tried to take it all in.

Booths lined the roads. There were people selling anything that you could think of buying. Marki thought this was all amazing. It was nothing like back home. He imagined living in a city like this. His life would be so much different.

He saw a beautiful woman standing outside a booth. She had black hair and black eyes. Her green cloak trailed on the floor as she paced back and forth. Her circular golden earrings dangled from her earlobes. When she saw him, she stopped pacing. Her eyes grew wide. She motioned for him to come as she went into the booth. Marki thought no harm would come, so he followed her. She looked like a pleasant woman.

She sat on one side of a small round table, and he took a seat on the other. "Hold out your palm," she said. Her voice was sweet. Marki did as he was told. She took his hand with her left hand and rubbed her right fingers across his palm. Her eyes widened again.

"You have great power within you," she said. "Great things can come of this power. If only you will learn how to use it well. There is one who is looking for an apprentice. Perhaps..." She trailed off in thought. "Yes," she continued after a few minutes of silence. "The Master Wizard can use someone like you."

Marki smiled. This was his lucky day. That was exactly where he needed to go. He didn't really believe her, but he wanted to go to the Master Wizard. Maybe she could tell him where to go. "Where is the Master Wizard?" he asked.

"So you are interested. Good. Good. He resides on Tower Lane in a small shack, or rather not so small," she laughed, "across from the large tower. You should go now. Hurry before he finds another." She shooed him off. He went out of the booth.

He started to walk but stopped when he realized that he didn't know where Tower Lane was. He had forgotten to ask. He scolded himself for being so stupid. Now he would have to go ask someone else. He stopped by a man selling fruit. "Excuse me, sir," he said as the man looked at him with a smile.

"You want to buy some fruit?" the man asked. Marki looked at the fruit. Most of it was rotten. It looked disgusting.

"Actually," Marki said, to the disappointment of the fruit seller, "I was wondering if you could tell me where Tower Lane is."

The man sighed. "What? All everybody wants to do is go to Tower Lane. What about my fruit?" Marki listened carefully as the man told him where to go. He thanked the man before heading off.

He walked down Tower Lane for almost an hour with no sign of a small shack or a large tower. He did see a large area surrounded by guards as workers scavenged things from the remains of the large building that had been there. The plot of land was bigger than any other building in all of Keedor. It had to be the castle of the late king.

Eventually he came to the large tower and small shack. The tower seemed deserted. It was very strange. Why would such a nice large building be deserted? Everyone who passed ignored the large building. He turned away from the tower and headed to the shack.

He stood in shock as he opened the door and saw what was really inside the shack. Twisting hallways and staircases led in all directions. Doors were everywhere. This was magic all right. He took a step, wondering where he should go and how he wouldn't get lost. If Michael were in there, he would never find him.

"May I help you?" a voice said. It seemed angry that he was in here.

Marki didn't know what else to do but answer. "I wish to see the Master Wizard."

"One cannot just come visit the Master Wizard. He is an important man and much too busy to be bothered by every little person who comes in seeking an audience with him."

"I need to see him," Marki persisted. He would do whatever it took to get to Michael.

"State your reason."

Marki didn't think that his reason to reunite with his best friend was good enough for the voice. Then he remembered what that lady had told him. She'd said that the Master Wizard was looking for an apprentice and that he qualified.

"I want to be the apprentice to the Master Wizard. I have come to learn under him."

There was silence for a few minutes. Marki stood there waiting for the answer of the mysterious voice.

"He will inspect you." The floor under started to move. It became a moving platform. The platform flew him down hallways and stairs. He couldn't tell which way it was going. It moved too fast for him to follow the directions that it turned. It stopped in front of a door.

613

Master Wizard

He was about to knock on the door when the door opened and said, "Powerful tryout." There was a young man sitting on a red chair in front of a red desk. Everything in the room was red. There was no other color. Even the young man was wearing a long red cloak. It hurt Marki to keep his eyes open. It was a shocking sight. It reminded him of the blood that was all over Periphia.

The man got up and walked over to Marki. "I am the Master Wizard." Marki felt inclined to bow his head, so he did. "Why are you here?" The Master Wizard sounded like he wanted Marki gone.

"I think my friend recently came here and…"

"Your friend! You came here and disrupted me from my work for me to find your friend."

"It's not like that. My friend was told to come here, and I really need to find him because our village was destroyed, and he, his brother, his sister, and I are the only survivors."

The Master Wizard smiled. His face brightened. He turned around for a minute.

"I see," the Master Wizard said when he turned back. "In that case I am truly sorry. Please accept my apology for yelling. I didn't realize the importance of the circumstance that you are in." His voice became sweet. It reminded Marki of his father.

"It's all right," Marki said. He knew the Master Wizard must be a busy man. It wasn't his fault that he would get angry and yell when he was disrupted. He was probably a really good guy.

The Master Wizard's eyes softened. "I believe I may be able to help you if you help me," he said.

"What do you need help with?" How could Marki possibly help the Master Wizard?

"You see, I am looking for an apprentice so I can teach him the ways of magic and he can take over after I am gone. If you help me find an apprentice, then I will help you find your friend."

It was a reasonable proposal. Marki would like to learn magic and be his apprentice. If he could be the apprentice, then he would get two wishes in one. He would get to find out where Michael was and get to be the apprentice of the Master Wizard. It would be awesome to know how to cast spells. If he had known magic when the raid had happened, he would have taught the soldiers a thing or two. "What about me?"

"I will have to test you. Stand still and I will see if you have the magic ability."

Marki stood in his place as the Master Wizard examined him. Marki could feel magic flowing through his body. His mind was being invaded, but he let the Master Wizard through. He had nothing to hide and he wanted to let the Master Wizard see every-thing. If the lady that he met earlier were telling the truth, then he would be able to become the apprentice.

"You are very powerful," the Master Wizard said at last. "You would make an excellent apprentice. The magic within you is growing. I can teach you how to use it. If you will accept the apprentice oath, then I will take you as my apprentice."

Marki beamed. Finding Michael was pushed to the back of his mind. Learning magic came to the front. He could start a new life for himself. Eventually he would become the Master Wizard, the most powerful being in the world. Then he would be able to put an end to Dalafar. "I will do it."

"Good. Now repeat after me. I, whatever your name is, hereby accept upon myself the burden of being the apprentice of the Master Wizard. I will listen to his teachings and learn all that I can from him about magic. And I swear to this. I also swear to fulfill my master's last dying wish."

"I, Marki, hereby accept upon myself the burden of being the apprentice of the Master Wizard. I will listen to his teachings and learn all that I can from him about magic. And I swear to this. I also swear to fulfill my master's last dying wish."

Marki went down on one knee and bowed his head. The Master Wizard placed both of his hands on Marki's head. A trickle of blood went from the Master's Wizard's pinky onto Marki's head.

"And wizards always keep their promises." The Master Wizard grinned.

Glossary of Mythical Creatures

<u>Avenger</u>: a man with hawk features such as a beak, feathers, claws, and wings who carries two golden swords and can leap into battle or make sandstorms to cover his movements for a surprise attack

<u>Basilisk</u>: a snakelike creature whose gaze and poisonous tail can instantly kill a person

<u>Centaur</u>: part horse and part human, with a horse's body and a human's head and torso; honorable and fierce

<u>Cerberus</u>: a giant three-headed guard dog with a snake tail and snakeheads coming out of its fur

<u>Chimera</u>: a monstrous creature with three heads: a lion and a goat head at front and a snakehead at the tail; it breathes fire

<u>Dragons</u>: flying serpent-like beasts that shoot fire or have other abilities

<u>Dwarf</u>: a short human with a strong chest and a long beard

<u>Elementals</u>: magical forces of nature

    <u>Air</u>: swift and agile; can create tornadoes

    <u>Water</u>: ferocious waves; can make whirlpools

    <u>Earth</u>: strong and tough; can make earthquakes

    <u>Fire</u>: fast; can burn people with its flames

    <u>Elemental</u>: the power of all four elementals

Elves: fair folk, immortal pointy-eared men and women who are stealthy and great archers and swordsmen

Fumans: born from a giant and a dwarf, like humans but a little bigger; they have more hair and they are stronger

Giants: giant people

> Cyclops: a one-eyed giant
>
> Fire Giant: a giant who produces and shoots fire
>
> Frost Giant: a giant who breathes ice that freezes people
>
> Mountain Giants: regular strong giants

Goblin: an evil, malicious disfigured elf

Gorgons: three sisters with serpents as hair; anyone who looks at them turns to stone because they are so ugly

Healers: people who live in water with blue skin and frog-like feet and hands; have the ability to heal wounds

Hydra: a serpent with numerous heads; every time a head is cut off, a new one appears, and it also has poisonous breath

Ladon: a hundred-headed dragon

Manticore: a lion body with a man's face and a scorpion tail that shoots poisonous spikes at its enemies

Minotaur: has the body of a man and the head of a bull

Pegasus: winged flying horse

Salamander: lizard-like creature whose skin is ice-cold; it can put out a fire, its spit can burn flesh, and it has the ability to poison food

Satyr: half-man, half-goat

Sphinx: a large creature with eagle wings, a lion's body, and a human head that brings bad fortune wherever it goes and challenges foes with riddles before killing them

Timen: tiny people up to the height of a human's ankle

Troll: hairy, large, ugly humanoid creatures

Unicorn: a horse with a horn

About The Author

A.K. Mage discovered his love for science fiction and writing in general at an early age. He honed his talent through writing courses in high school and during a stint in a special program for writers at Baruch College. Wishing to share his endless ideas with other fans of the science fiction and fantasy genres, Mage authored the book *The Scroll of Kanavar: Legend of the Twelve Stones* at the age of seventeen. He is currently continuing work on the series.

Mage resides in Brooklyn, New York.

www.ingramcontent.com/pod-product-compliance
Lightning Source LLC
Chambersburg PA
CBHW020051180626
46812CB00006B/2278

* 9 780615 814346 *